catalo

C000081117

Chapter 361

With a faint smile, Jin Zhanyi seemed unfazed by Zhou Yi's immediate rejection, as if he had foreseen it long before. The challenge from the Qilian Twin Devils and the battle between them held a distinct disparity.

It stood as their final chance to ascend to the venerable realm. Coupled with Jin Zhanyi's resolute approach to combat, the impending confrontation was undoubtedly a true fight for life and death.

In this battle, the occurrence of on-site casualties, even to the point of fatality, would not be surprising; it might even be deemed a natural outcome. If Zhou Yi had already manifested the Metal Flower and successfully Mastering the power of confinement, but failed to reach the "Three Flowers Gathering at the Apex" before the twenty-year deadline, he would undoubtedly consent to Jin Zhanyi's terms without hesitation.

At that point, he would find himself cornered and devoid of alternatives. If he were to fall short of achieving the Three Flowers Gathering at the Apex and advance to the esteemed rank of Venerable, his chances of safeguarding his life upon entering the dominion of the Deep Mountain Totem Clan would be precarious.

Given this predicament, a life-and-death confrontation against a peers of the same level would become his last irreplaceable opportunity. Striving to break his limits in the final moments and achieve the realm of the venerable required him to wager his life; how else could it be accomplished?

However, the twenty-year deadline was still some distance away, and Zhou Yi had no intention of taking unnecessary risks at this moment. Hence, without hesitation, he declined the invitation extended by Jin Zhanyi.

With a light sigh, Jin Zhanyi didn't offer any persuasion. Instead, he asked, "Brother Zhou, the technique you just displayed, is it the Thirty-Six Forms of Mountain-Crushing?"

The number of times he had executed the Thirty-Six Forms of Mountain-Crushing was already quite a few, but being able to readily call out the name of this technique, Jin Zhanyi was undoubtedly the most deserving first

In an instant, several thoughts flashed through his mind. He solemnly said, "Indeed, it's this Metal-element combat technique."

The Thirty-Six Forms of Mountain-Crushing is truly an outstanding Metal-element technique in the world. It encompasses not only combat techniques but also, if practiced continuously according to this technique, it can even replace the Metal-element innate qi technique," Jin Zhanyi explained calmly. "Because it's a special technique that integrates the circulation of true qi and martial forms. Its power is so immense that even within our Lingxiao Treasure Hall, it ranks among the top-notch secret manuals.

Zhou Yi's heart throbbed vigorously a few times. Although he had sensed faintly the complexity of this technique during his practice, he had never anticipated that Jin Zhanyi's assessment of it would be so exceedingly high.

"Brother Zhou, it seems you haven't yet mastered the twenty-fourth form," Jin Zhanyi remarked.

Zhou Yi instinctively nodded and replied, "Indeed, I've only practiced up to the twenty-third form."

"The twenty-third form..." Jin Zhanyi murmured thoughtfully before finally sighing, "Brother Zhou, as far as Jin knows, if you can successfully perform the twenty-fourth form, you should be able to condense the Metal Flower."

Zhou Yi's eyes immediately ignited with a blazing light, his heart overcome by exultant joy. In truth, he had a similar sensation—once he took the next step, he could indeed solidify the Metal Flower. This feeling had been particularly intense after successfully executing the twenty-third form that night. Yet, it was only after Jin Zhanyi's confirmation that his conviction truly solidified.

"Alas, what a pity, what a pity..." Jin Zhanyi shook his head abruptly, his expression filled with regret.

Zhou Yi, now greatly curious, asked, "Brother Jin, what's the matter?"

Jin Zhanyi offered an enigmatic smile and continued, "If I'm not mistaken, the manual in Brother Zhou's possession is likely not complete; it lacks the final three forms."

Zhou Yi's heart skipped a beat, his expression freezing for a moment.

As if oblivious to Zhou Yi's expression, Jin Zhanyi murmured to himself, "These final three forms are the true essence of the entire manual. It's said that if someone can successfully comprehend the first form, they can attain mastery in the martial way. And if they grasp all three forms, they can ascend to the legendary realm of the Supreme Divine Path."

Zhou Yi's throat twitched momentarily, and at this juncture, to claim that his heart remained unaffected would no longer be a true practitioner of the martial path...

"Brother Jin, are those missing three forms within your sect?" Zhou Yi inquired cautiously.

Jin Zhanyi revealed without hesitation, "Indeed, the complete Thirty-Six Forms of Mountain-Crushing is indeed housed within the martial repository of our Lingxiao Treasure Hall."

Zhou Yi's heart raced, but he knew that if the secret was so significant, it must be of great value. Even if he were to propose borrowing it, it wouldn't likely be an easy task.

Similarly, recalling Jin Zhanyi's proposal earlier, Zhou Yi had a vague sense of his intention.

Seeing Zhou Yi lost in thought, Jin Zhanyi smiled with assurance, "Brother Zhou, The Thirty-Six Forms of Mountain-Crushing were already the pinnacle of Metal-element techniques thousands of years ago. The versions passed down in common knowledge at most document up to the thirty-third form. As for those final three forms, aside from the original, no one else has been able to replicate them."

Zhou Yi asked in surprise, "Why is that?"

Jin Zhanyi's expression grew solemn as he explained, "Because all techniques that reach the Nine Heavens realm can only be understood through insight and not passed on through words. The Thirty-Six Forms of

Mountain-Crushing is an ancient scripture devoid of textual explanation. Those who wish to study it must rely on their own comprehension. How much they can comprehend is how much they can gain—there is no way to forcefully demand it."

He paused, his voice gradually carrying a touch of admiration. "Thousands of years ago, this manual was obtained by the founder of our sect. He poured his heart and soul into reinterpreting the first thirty-three forms in written form. "While this approach of comprehension might be slightly inferior to the original, they provided countless practitioners of the Metal element with the best opportunity and possibility to learn from a top-tier Metal-element manual.

As Jin Zhanyi spoke, he cast a meaningful glance at Zhou Yi and continued, "Those final three forms are truly exquisite, describing the profound truths of the heavens and earth, beyond the capability of human language to express. Hence, the founder of our sect ultimately abandoned his intention to rewrite them. Thus, this manual came to have thirty-three forms in its hand-copied version, missing the last three."

Zhou Yi listened as though entranced, for he had possessed the Thirty-Six Forms of Mountain-Crushing for quite some time, yet only now was he truly learning of its origins.

Taking a deep breath to calm the fervor within him, Zhou Yi inquired, "Brother Jin, are these last three forms illustrations images?"

"Indeed, those last three forms are all illustrations images, yet I have never laid eyes on them," Jin

Zhanyi admitted without concealment. "The content within these three illustrations images is undoubtedly beyond my current comprehension. In that case, why should I seek frustration?"

Zhou Yi nodded in agreement. While he knew that was the logical stance, a part of him still yearned to cast aside all caution and catch even a glimpse of those illustrations images.

Suddenly, Jin Zhanyi smiled and said, "Brother Zhou, the interpretations circulating outside are merely our Lingxiao Treasure Hall's founder's insights. However, compared to the original text, there are still some subtle differences."

Filled with astonishment, Zhou Yi exclaimed, "Your sect's founder was such a legendary figure throughout history. Could there be any errors in a manual written by someone of his caliber?"

Given the founder's stature, if he truly felt uncertain, he wouldn't have disseminated this manual. A founder of a sect would never engage in actions that would tarnish the sect's reputation.

Jin Zhanyi shook his head slightly and explained, "The founder's transcription is undoubtedly accurate, but Brother Zhou, you must understand that different individuals practicing the same manual may ultimately achieve completely disparate results. Above the Thirty-Six Forms of Mountain-Crushing, it originally relied solely on illustrations. Yet, our founder meticulously derived a combination of textual and illustrative annotations.

While this approach is undoubtedly error-free, for practitioners like you and me, it would be more appropriate to study the original manual.

Zhou Yi nodded slightly, his desire for the original manual becoming stronger than ever before.

He might have been fine if he hadn't known about it, but now that he did, even he couldn't control the overwhelming desire to take a glimpse. This yearning was so intense that it even led him to contemplate doing whatever it took.

He struggled to suppress this impulse, yet soon realized that all his efforts were in vain.

For Zhou Yi, the significance of the Thirty-Six Forms of Mountain-Crushing was paramount. It wasn't just about the key to condense the Metal Flower; it was also the first Innate manual he had encountered. In his years of growth, the technique had been an invaluable asset, aiding him in overcoming formidable foes like the Twin-Headed Spirit Beast and Sheru.

Therefore, upon hearing news about this technique, his intense longing was evident.

Letting out a long sigh, Zhou Yi raised his head and looked at Jin Zhanyi with a half-smile on his face.

Though he knew it was a lure, he found himself compelled to take the bait.

"Brother Jin, the Qilian Twin Devils dare to challenge you; they're truly audacious."

"Their courage is indeed commendable, but they possess the qualifications."

I heard they have reached the Three Flowers realm for a hundred years already. and I'm afraid I may not be their match."

"Brother Zhou, you're truly too modest. You have already mastered the true essence of the wind, capable of effortlessly breaking free from even aura-locked situations. Coupled with your expertise in Earth-Tunnelling Technique, While victory may be uncertain, you should at least be able to ensure your safety."

Zhou Yi clenched his teeth, his face twisted with determination. "Brother Jin, if that's the case, I have a somewhat unwilling request."

Jin Zhanyi beamed with an amiable expression, "Brother Zhou, we're like brothers. If there's something you need, just ask."

"I am not skilled, but I'd like to team up with you to face the Qilian Twin Devils. I hope you'll agree."

"It's a minor request, Brother Zhou. How could I refuse?" Jin Zhanyi nodded in satisfaction, then shifted the conversation, "Brother Zhou, I have access to the Lingxiao Treasure Hall's martial repository at any time. If you're interested in the archived texts, why don't we enter the repository together and discuss it?"

Zhou Yi stared at him in silence for a while, then finally exhaled, "Alright....."

Chapter 362

Amidst the garden, a riot of flowers competed for attention. In the scorching embrace of summer, sitting within the pavilion was a true respite. A pot of fragrant tea rested before, and friends were summoned, leisurely engaging in conversations, exuding an indescribable air of elegance.

However, in this moment, an air of solemnity enveloped the atmosphere within the pavilion in the garden. When Zhou Yi informed Zhang Zhongjin of his desire to join forces with Jin Zhanyi against the Qilian Twin Devils, the seasoned expert of the One-line Heaven revealed an expression of disbelief.

Turning to Jin Zhanyi beside him, the latter gave an apologetic gesture and said, "Zhou brother and I had a friendly spar. Nonetheless, it wasn't a life-or-death battle. Such a duel wouldn't significantly aid either of us. That's when Zhou proposed that we collaborate and face Qilian Twin Devils together."

Zhou Yi's heart surged with annoyed. This person was clearly distorting the truth. Although he was annoyed, his face remained calm and impassive, revealing none of his inner turmoil.

After a moment's contemplation, Zhang Zhongjin shook his head with a sigh, saying, "Zhou brother, are you genuinely determined to battle against the Qilian Twin Devils?"

"Of course, I genuinely do," Zhou Yi replied with a seemingly sincere demeanor. As for how much truth resided within this apparent sincerity, only the heavens knew.

A wry smile tugged at Zhang Zhongjin's lips as he continued, "Zhou brother, you are not a disciple of our Lingxiao Treasure Hall. Should you involve yourself, it might raise misunderstandings."

Zhou Yi blinked twice, his thoughts momentarily adrift before he recalled his own identity.

He hailed from one of the branches of the Northwestern's mightiest sect, the Tianchi Sect. Having departed from the Northwestern region, anyone he encountered assumed he represented the main lineage of Tianchi.

Indeed, that was the case. If Zhou Yi were merely an ordinary elder of the Hengshan Sect, it would be difficult to fathom why He Min and Xu Zili would offer guidance to him.

This time, if he were to join forces with Jin Zhanyi, in the eyes of outsiders, wouldn't it be tantamount to an alliance between the Lingxiao Treasure Hall and the Northwestern Tianchi?

As various thoughts whirled within, Zhou Yi's expression grew more serious. Suddenly, Jin Zhanyi's uninhibited laughter echoed through the air. Shaking his head, he said, "Senior Zhang, Brother Zhou, is there a need to conceal anything about the relationship between our Lingxiao Treasure Hall and the Northwestern Tianchi?" His face carried a hint of mocking smile as he continued, "Every ten years, our

Lingxiao Treasure Hall travels far and wide under the pretense of hosting contests for the new generation disciples. But do you think the powerful sects like the Qilian Mountain are blind and ignorant, clueless about the underlying schemes?"

Both Zhou Yi and Zhang Zhongjin's faces turned somewhat awkward. If such a significant matter could be concealed from the powerful sects for years on end,that would truly be incredible.

Zhou Yi's thoughts swirled as he said, "Senior Zhang, Brother Jin is correct. The relationship between our Tianchi and your esteemed faction is substantial. As such, there's no longer any need to avoid suspicion."

After a moment of hesitation, Zhang Zhongjin finally nodded. As Zhou Yi had said, even if he refrained from acting to suspicion, it wouldn't change others' perceptions.

"Very well, Brother Zhou. Since you are so keen on this battle, I will propose it to the venerables. However, whether we gain their consent is beyond my control," Zhang Zhongjin said earnestly.

The authority to decide this matter was destined to be beyond his control. He could at most offer a few favorable words.

Zhou Yi's heart was deeply vexed, yet his face displayed a thankful expression as he said, "Thank you, Senior Zhang."

After stepping out of Zhang Zhongjin's room, Zhou Yi shot a glare at Jin Zhanyi and questioned, "Are you satisfied now, Jin brother?"

Jin Zhanyi chuckled and said, "Zhou brother, are you truly not interested in this battle?" He continued with a serious tone, "If you have no interest at all, I'll go talk to Senior Zhang right now, and I guarantee he'll do me this favor. Of course, I can also lend you a look at the original manuals in the martial repository."

Zhou Yi's expression froze for a moment as he turned his head, meeting Jin Zhanyi's gaze. Within those eyes, clear as water, he saw sincerity. His heart stirred, and the words were on the brink of spilling out. After all, engaging in a battle with the Qilian Twin Devils wasn't his intention to begin with.

However, as those words reached the tip of his tongue, they lingered there for a while before ultimately not being spoken. Deep within Zhou Yi's the nation. They appeared fragmented but held intricately woven connections, ties that could never be severed. Even for the Lingxiao Treasure Hall, they held an irreplaceable position.

On this day, the convoy continued to move steadily, but there was a faint sense of excitement evident on every person's face. Perhaps many of them had left the Lingxiao Treasure Hall before, but returning home was a joyous occasion for anyone.

Jin Zhanyi gestured ahead and said, "Zhou brother, we're almost there."

Zhou Yi lifted the curtain of the carriage and gazed ahead. In the distance, the first thing he noticed was a towering structure on the ground. Although it was too far away to see clearly, he was certain it wasn't a mountain. After all, the terrain here was flat, and an abrupt mountain wouldn't just rise from it. He pondered for a moment, closed his eyes, and when he opened them again, they were sparkling, glowing with intensity.

Jin Zhanyi smiled faintly. He had grown accustomed to how newcomers to the Lingxiao Treasure Hall would be attracted to the central structure. Finally, Zhou Yi's gaze clarified, and he saw that the distant grand structure was a tower.

A genuine tower. Despite the distance obscuring its height, even a cursory glimpse filled Zhou Yi with profound awe. He was convinced that if he stood beneath the tower, the awe would be a hundredfold stronger.

Turning his head, Zhou Yi looked at Jin Zhanyi, whose smile held a mixture of amusement and intense pride. At that moment, Zhou Yi understood that the status of this tower within the Lingxiao Treasure Hall was likely comparable to the summit of the Tianchi Main Peak, hidden amidst the clouds.

This was the holy site in the hearts of all Lingxiao Treasure Hall disciples, and even in Jin Zhanyi's heart, it was no different.

Suppressing his boundless curiosity, as the carriage continued its journey, the unfolding scenery left Zhou Yi equally astounded. Before his eyes, a city gradually came into view. It was an enormous city, organized around a central tower.

Before this day, Zhou Yi could never have imagined that such a peculiar, even beautiful city existed in the world. The city's buildings seemed endless, and more importantly, it appeared to lack something vital.

As Zhou Yi's inquiring gaze wandered about, Jin Zhanyi finally spoke, "Zhou brother, what are you looking for?"

Zhou Yi hesitated for a moment before asking, "A city wall. Why doesn't this city have city walls?"

Jin Zhanyi smiled proudly and replied, "Very simple. Walls are a hassle. They impede the comings and goings of most people, so we dismantled it."

Chapter 363

"dismantled it?" A perplexed expression appeared on Zhou Yi's face; this response left him utterly bewildered. The construction of the city walls outside Zhou Family Village had consumed an immense amount of the clan's efforts and resources.

Within the Northwestern nations, those city walls of renowned cities and capitals were built over generations, reflecting countless labor and dedication.

However, Jin Zhanyi had casually mentioned tearing them down. This peculiar response stirred a strong sense of bewilderment within him.

Sensing Zhou Yi's thoughts, Jin Zhanyi smiled and continued, "brother Zhou, city walls are meant to fend off external threats. For ordinary cities and common armies, they certainly play a crucial role. But for us, do you really think mere walls can stand against true experts?"

Zhou Yi blinked, a trace of realization crossing his face. Jin Zhanyi was right; within the Lingxiao Treasure Hall, there were undoubtedly experts at the level of Venerables. With them present, no matter how many armies were deployed, they would be rendered ineffective. Similarly, the only individuals capable of posing a threat to the Lingxiao Treasure Hall were also those at the Venerable level.

Once they dared to invade the Lingxiao Treasure Hall, how could a city wall withstand their attack?

Jin Zhanyi's gaze drifted to the city in the distance as he sighed softly, "If someday a large force does come pressing in, it would spell the end of our Lingxiao Treasure Hall. With walls, escaping would be difficult. Without walls, we might just have a better chance to flee."

Zhou Yi nodded, agreeing with his perspective. Given the Lingxiao Treasure Hall's current might, no force could besiege it. However, the world was ever-changing, and nobody could guarantee eternal prosperity. Even the once-dominant Five Elements Sect, once hailed as the top faction in the East, had eventually faded into oblivion. The Lingxiao Treasure Hall might also face such a day...

As the caravan continued to approach, the city before them appeared even more colossal, especially when looking at the towering central high tower. It gave one a feeling of being small and insignificant like ants.

"Jin brother, is the Lingxiao Treasure Hall located within this city?" Zhou Yi asked in a deep voice.

Jin Zhanyi chuckled softly and replied, "brother Zhou, this is our Lingxiao Treasure Hall."

Zhou Yi was taken aback, a peculiar expression crossing his face. He couldn't help but draw a large circle with his hand, asking, "The entire city is the Lingxiao Treasure Hall?"

"Indeed," Jin Zhanyi proudly affirmed, "brother Zhou might not know, thousands of years ago, this was nothing but a barren land. Later, it was chosen by our founding ancestor, who constructed the Tower of Heaven here, and from there, the entire sect gradually developed. Over thousands of years, with the Tower of Heaven as the center, it has grown into a massive city capable of accommodating a million people."

Zhou Yi couldn't help but gasp. The Horizontal Mountain Lineage also had a history of three thousand years. However, compared to that, the Horizontal Mountain Lineage seldom communicated with the outside world. Over thousands of years, although its population had slightly increased, it remained just above two thousand people. When compared to the Lingxiao Treasure Hall, the difference was as vast as the gap between a louse and an elephant.

Silently gazing ahead at the enormous Lingxiao Treasure Hall, which housed a population of a million, Zhou Yi's heart surged. If someday Zhou Family

Village could possess a scale like this, that would truly fulfill his lifetime's ambition.

With no city walls to obstruct them, there were numerous large paths leading in and out of the city. The caravan led by Zhang Zhongjin and others was extremely conspicuous; in other cities, it would surely attract attention. However, upon entering this colossal city, it was as if a stone had been cast into the sea, creating not even a ripple.

Only when they entered it did Zhou Yi truly experience the formidable nature of this city.

Walking among the crowd on the streets, the majority of them were practitioners. While most of them had cultivation levels around the third or fourth layer of Inner Energy, just a glance would reveal practitioners with cultivation levels beyond the seventh layer of Inner Energy.

This proportion was truly terrifying. Although the same situation could be seen atop the Tianchi Main Peak, the population gap between the Lingxiao Treasure Hall and the Tianchi Main Peak was apparent, signifying the difference in overall strength.

The reputation of being the number one sect in Da Shen Empire was well-deserved.

Approaching the city's center from its outer periphery, Zhou Yi finally saw a wall about a hundred feet away from the central high tower. This wall wasn't particularly tall, only about two feet. However, there seemed to be two distinct worlds inside and outside of the wall.

As the caravan reached the entrance of the wall, similarly, no one questioned or obstructed them. However, along the broad avenue on either side of the wall, people bowed respectfully to the caravan.

Zhou Yi's gaze swept around, capturing every detail of the surroundings. Inside and outside this wall, it's clearly a division between the inner and outer city of the city. Those who can enter the inner city are undoubtedly the elite figures within the sect.

The inner city wasn't as bustling as the outer city, but as Zhou Yi moved from the wall toward the central high tower, he could sense two immense auras belonging to Venerable Realm experts. Moreover, the closer he got to the tower, the heavier his heart became. He could sense that there were even more formidable experts within.

Finally, the carriage came to a stop, and as Zhou Yi stepped out, he found himself standing beneath the towering structure. When he looked up from here, the top of the tower seemed to meld with the sky, making it impossible to see its end.

Standing there, he felt an immense pressure—a pressure that came from thousands of years of history. It seemed to descend upon him at that moment, burdening him heavily. It was as if invisible shackles were locking him in place, a weighty burden he couldn't shake off.

Although this tower wasn't as tall as the Tianchi Main Peak in the northwest, the sense of awe it invoked surpassed even that iconic peak.

While the Tianchi Main Peak soared into the clouds, it was, after all, a masterpiece of nature, one of the highest peaks in the entire northwest mountain range. The founder of Tianchi Mountain in ancient times had merely discovered that peak and established the Tianchi lineage there.

However, here was different. This towering structure wasn't naturally formed; it was built by human hands upon this flat land. It was a human-made construction, created through sheer effort.

Seeing this building, the astonishment in Zhou Yi's heart was no less intense than the feeling he had when he first saw the Tianchi Main Peak.

now that he had seen this Tower of Heaven with his own eyes, his heart was truly convinced.

There was no other explanation besides attributing it to miracles.

While Zhou Yi wasn't well-versed in architecture, he understood that the taller a structure, the more difficult it was to construct. A tower of such immense height could not have been built by contemporary craftsmen.

For a moment, Zhou Yi was overwhelmed with waves of shock and amazement. He took two steps forward, his heart brimming with reverence, and slowly reached out his hand to gently touch the surface of the tower.

The tower's surface was smooth and cool, yet it exuded a unique power. As Zhou Yi's hand made contact, he could even sense the immense energy contained within.

It was a resolute and unwavering power, not much different from the sensation he felt when facing the Tianchi Main Peak in the northwest.

Zhou Yi's face revealed an expression of incredulity. After hesitating for a moment, he slowly infused his true qi into the tower's surface. Simultaneously, an image of the Tianchi Giant Peak surfaced in his mind.

The scene before his eyes seemed to suddenly change. He felt as though he was witnessing a towering spire rising slowly from the ground, not constructed, but ascending from beneath the earth itself.

Although it was merely an illusion, Zhou Yi had a strong sensation that everything in his mind was the truth, events that had once transpired on this land.

Within this towering spire, it seemed hidden secrets that were unknown to others. And somehow, these mysteries were transmitted to his mind through a mysterious force, allowing him to witness the tower's birth and growth.

In a daze, Zhou Yi gained a clearer understanding of the Raising Heaven Seal. If the circumstances were different at this moment, he might have even felt an impatient urge to face Jin Zhanyi in battle again.

Though Zhou Yi didn't outwardly display any dramatic change, behind him, both Zhang Zhongjin and Jin

Zhanyi sensed a unique sensation emanating from him, like the aura of towering mountains.

The two exchanged a glance, perplexed by what might be happening to Zhou Yi.

After a while, Zhou Yi finally withdrew his hand, his expression becoming more peculiar.

With suspicion, Jin Zhanyi inquired, "brother Zhou, what's the matter?"

Zhou Yi pointed at the tower, uncertainly saying, "Jin Brother, the sensation I get from this tower doesn't feel like it was constructed."

Jin Zhanyi was baffled, his brow furrowing. What kind of statement was that?

Zhou Yi's gaze flickered as he stared at the tower, enunciating each word, "It's grown from beneath the ground."

Chapter 364

Zhang Zhongjin and Jin Zhanyi's faces changed slightly in unison. Jin Zhanyi spoke slowly, "Zhou Yi, have you ever heard of the miracles of the Tower of Heaven?"

"No," Zhou Yi replied without hesitation.

Jin Zhanyi's gaze shifted, his expression changing. He finally asked, "Then how did you come to know that this tower 'grew' from underground?"

Zhou Yi responded calmly, "I can feel it." Jin Zhanyi and Zhang Zhongjin exchanged looks. If anyone else had said those words, they would have dismissed it. However, coming from Zhou Yi's mouth, they felt a mixture of skepticism and belief.

"Let's go inside," Zhang Zhongjin cleared his throat and said. Zhou Yi surveyed the surroundings. Dozens of guards stood before the tower's entrance, most of them eyeing him strangely.

A sudden realization struck him. He had stood before the tower, lost in his thoughts while touching its surface. His expression must have been one of deep absorption, and in the eyes of these guards, his image was surely tarnished.

Upon Fei Tenguo's instruction, the rest of the convoy dispersed, and Zhou Yi followed Zhang Zhongjin and Jin Zhanyi into the tower.

As they entered the tower, the disciples guarding the entrance respectfully bowed to Zhang Zhongjin and Jin Zhanyi.

They displayed reverence, especially towards Jin Zhanyi, and it became even more evident when they were in his presence. Observing their expressions, Zhou Yi was reminded of the way disciples from various sects had looked at him on the Peak of Tianchi's. The similarity was uncanny.

He inwardly sighed. Just like him, Jin Zhanyi had also become a banner of the Lingxiao Treasure Hall. Regardless of circumstances, neither of them could allow for any failures to occur.

Zhou Yi wasn't aware of the tower's exact height, and Zhang Zhongjin and Jin Zhanyi didn't seem inclined to provide detailed explanations.

Led by Zhang Zhongjin and Jin Zhanyi, they arrived at a lounge on the tower's second floor.Shortly after they settled down, their attention was drawn to the doorway.

There stood a person who hadn't been there before, and Zhou Yi couldn't determine when he had arrived. The man was an elderly figure with a tall crown on his head. He exuded an aura that captured everyone's attention effortlessly. Even though he stood there casually, he managed to draw everyone's focus to him, as if he were the sole presence in the room.

Zhou Yi was taken aback by the profound presence this man exuded. It was as if his mere presence commanded attention from everyone in the room, even though he didn't intentionally release any powerful aura. It became evident that the martial arts he practiced must be truly exceptional.

"Senior Brother," both Zhang Zhongjin and Jin Zhanyi spoke respectfully in unison.

The man waved his hand gently and said, "My junior brothers, you've returned at just the right time." His gaze landed on Zhou Yi, and a hint of surprise flashed across his eyes. He inquired, "Who is this..."

Zhang Zhongjin quickly introduced, "Senior Brother, this is Zhou Yi from the Northwestern Hengshan region." Then he turned to Zhou Yi, saying, "Brother Zhou , this is our big senior brother of the Lingxiao Treasure Hall, Wei Zongjin."

Zhou Yi bowed slightly and said, " Zhou Yi pays respects to Senior Brother Wei."

Wei Zongjin's eyes lit up with a hint of realization, and he smiled gently. "So, you're Zhou Yi from the Northwestern Hengshan region. Your name is well-known indeed. I didn't expect that Zhou Brother had already reached the One-Line Heaven realm. That's truly a delightful surprise."

Zhou Yi was momentarily stunned. He had experienced something similar before, which made him smile wryly.

Zhang Zhongjin quickly added, "Senior Brother, this person is not Medicine Daoist, but a newly promoted Innate Elder from Hengshan."

Wei Zongjin's expression shifted slightly, followed by a hint of delight. He asked, "Junior Brother Zhang, has the Hengshan faction already developed a new Beauty-Retaining Pill?"

Zhang Zhongjin could only smile wryly. He had once thought the same way when he met Zhou Yi and the Medicine Daoist.

Jin Zhanyi shook his head slightly and said, "Senior Brother, you've misunderstood this time. Zhou Brother here is not in need of a Beauty-Retaining Pill to maintain his appearance. He is not yet twenty years old."

Wei Zongjin's eyes immediately lit up. His gaze swept over Zhou Yi once again, but this time, his gaze held more depth. Simultaneously, his aura, which was already intense, surged even more aggressively, as if he intended to overwhelm Zhou Yi.

Zhou Yi simply smiled calmly and met his gaze, seemingly unaffected by the overwhelming pressure he was emitting. Jin Zhanyi also maintained his smile, appearing unaffected as well.

However, Zhang Zhongjin couldn't help but retreat a step, struggling to withstand this sudden burst of pressure.

In Wei Zongjin's eyes flickered astonishment. The person before him was less than twenty years old and yet exhibited such composure under the force of his intense aura.This kind of formidable composure surpassed even Zhang Zhongjin's. To achieve this level of control, one must either possess strength comparable to or surpassing Jin Zhanyi and himself, or simply be someone who had an innate immunity to external pressures.

However, as he observed Zhou Yi's serene smile, Wei Zongjin couldn't shake the feeling that the Zhou Yi was more likely to belong to the former category.

Wei Zongjin restrained his aura and nodded, a genuine smile on his face. "I indeed misjudged. To think that the Northwestern Tianchi could possess a talent like Brother Zhou is truly enviable."

As Wei Zongjin spoke, his gaze inadvertently turned towards Jin Zhanyi. Clearly, he held a similar sentiment. To discover that in the Northwest, there existed a genius even more exceptional than Jin Zhanyi was quite a surprise.

After the four of them had taken their seats, Wei Zongjin inquired, "Junior Brothers, I trust everything has gone smoothly with your journey?"

Zhang Zhongjin quickly responded, "Senior Brother, everything went smoothly, and Brother Zhou also brought the formula for the Beauty-Retaining Pill."

Joy flickered across Wei Zongjin's face. He didn't hide his happiness, nodding appreciatively at Zhou Yi. "Thank you, Brother Zhou."

Zhou Yi's face blushed slightly. "Senior Brother Wei is too kind."

Zhang Zhongjin explained the terms of the exchange, and when he mentioned that two pills would be allocated to Zhou Yi upon the successful refinement, Wei Zongjin seemed to hesitate briefly. However, he immediately gave his approval, decisively agreeing without hesitation.

Zhou Yi admired his decisiveness. It took someone of his strength to be able to handle Zhang Zhongjin and the others and become their senior brother.

Once the matter of the Beauty-Retaining Pill was settled, Jin Zhanyi spoke up, "Senior Brother, I heard that Qilian Twin Devils have arrived at the Lingxiao Treasure Hall and want to challenge me."

Wei Zongjin's expression turned grim. "It's true. You don't need to pay them any attention." He snorted in anger and continued, "Those two old fellows are quite crafty. They're planning to use you as a stepping stone before the Great Calamity arrives. It's truly outrageous."

Zhou Yi thought to himself that judging from Wei Zongjin's expression, there probably wasn't anyone in the entire Lingxiao Treasure Hall who would support such a duel.

Jin Zhanyi smiled faintly and said, "I appreciate your concern, Senior Brother. However, since they're challenging me, I think I should have the final say in this matter."

Wei Zongjin frowned deeply, saying, "Junior Brother, those two are nearly three hundred years old. If they can't break through to the rank of a Venerable this time, they're destined to fall. Engaging with them at this moment would be extremely dangerous."

"Senior Brother, speaking of danger, could it compare to the time I went to the Western regions?" Jin Zhanyi waved his sleeve dramatically, his voice full of confidence："During that time, I faced off against a dozen opponents, finally provoking a Western Venerable who pursued me until the boundaries of the Da Shen Empire. If it weren't for my fortune in grasping the 'Horizon's Blink' technique at the brink of life and death, I might have died by his hand long ago."

Pride gleamed in Jin Zhanyi's eyes. Escaping from a Venerable's pursuit was truly a remarkable feat to be proud of.

Wei Zongjin seemed as though he wanted to retort, but in the end, he sighed and said, "Jin Junior Brother,I understand that you've chosen the path of the Asura to grow through constant battles.. However, this opportunity isn't ideal. You should think twice."

"Senior Brother, my mind is set. I humbly ask for your approval," Jin Zhanyi slightly bowed.

Wei Zongjin's expression became complex, and a powerful sense of pressure emanated from around him.

Suddenly, Zhang Zhongjin interjected, "Senior Brother, while the Venerables are in seclusion, they must have heard about this matter. How do they view it?"

A trace of helplessness flashed across Wei Zongjin's face. "The Venerables believe that it's up to Jin Junior Brother to make his own decision. However, after discussing among us senior brothers, none of us agree."

Jin Zhanyi laughed heartily and remarked, "Senior Brother, you underestimate me too much."

Wei Zongjin snorted lightly and responded, "If it were just one of them, I wouldn't intervene."

Jin Zhanyi shook his head and said, "Senior Brother, you jest. Considering the cultivation methods they've practiced, splitting them apart wouldn't even qualify as a challenge against me."

Wei Zongjin fell silent for a moment, then sighed deeply and said, "Very well, since Junior Brother has already made up his mind, I won't try to dissuade you any further. This time, I'll accompany you, Junior Brother, and we'll fight against those two old fellows together."

At first, his words seemed reluctant, but as he finished speaking, his tone became resolute, filled with an unwavering determination.

Jin Zhanyi looked at him gratefully and said, "Thank you, Senior Brother, but I have another plan in mind. There's no need to trouble you, Senior Brother."

Wei Zongjin's expression changed and he said, "I can allow you to fight against Qilian Twin Devils, but I absolutely won't agree to you facing them alone."

Jin Zhanyi chuckled and said, "Senior Brother, I'm not that arrogant, but I do have assistance now."

Wei Zongjin was taken aback, following Jin Zhanyi's gaze, his expression showing surprise as he exclaimed, "You?"

With his head held high and chest out, Zhou Yi bowed slightly, clasping his fists in salute, and said, "I am not skilled, but I am willing to join forces with Senior Jin. I ask for your blessings, Senior Wei."

Chapter 365

Wei Zongjin's expression seemed rather peculiar. In most cases, when confronted with such matters, others would have scrambled to escape. Yet this esteemed guest from the Tianchi was actively stepping forward, which was truly astonishing.

After a brief contemplation, Wei Zongjin spoke, "Brother Zhou, this is an internal matter of our Lingxiao Treasure Hall. Let us handle it ourselves."

Zhou Yi looked toward Jin Zhanyi and saw him giving a subtle glance, even though Zhou Yi couldn't quite decipher the exact message conveyed. However, he could easily guess.

Shaking his head slightly, Zhou Yi responded, "Brother Wei, the connection between Lingxiao Treasure Hall and the main branch of the Tianchi spans thousands of years. Should we quibble over such a minor matter?"

Wei Zongjin was taken aback. He thought to himself, if this was considered a minor matter, then what would be considered significant? He forced a smile, trying to be gentle, as he said, "Brother Zhou, Qilian Twin Devils had already converged Three Flowers and mastered the power of confinement forty years ago. Therefore, this time, it's best for junior Brother Jin and myself to take action."

Although his words were tactful, anyone could easily understand the underlying implication.

Jin Zhanyi stepped forward abruptly, stating, "Senior Brother, while Brother Zhou might be younger, he is the foremost cultivator beneath the Northwestern Venerables. He has already converged Three Flowers. Though he hasn't fully grasped the power of confinement, I haven't gained an upper hand in our martial exchanges."

Wei Zongjin took a deep breath, and this time his gaze at Zhou Yi became even more peculiar. Despite his two centuries of experience and unwavering composure, the muscles on his face twitched slightly at this moment.

After a long pause, he finally said, "Junior Brother Jin, do you truly believe that teaming up with Brother Zhou will ensure victory against Qilian Twin Devils?"

Jin Zhanyi's expression turned equally serious as he replied, "Senior Brother, please rest assured. The two of us, together, will surely triumph."

His words were resolute, exuding an indescribable power. Even Zhou Yi, upon hearing them, felt a surge of emotion. After giving them a deep glance, Wei Zongjin finally said, "Very well, since you've made your decision, I won't interfere. I will go report to the Duty Venerable and ask him to respond to Qilian Twin Devils."

Jin Zhanyi was overjoyed, bowing deeply as he said, "Thank you, Senior Brother, for your understanding."

Wei Zongjin waved his hand, his expression back to normal. However, the look in his eyes as he gazed at Zhou Yi still held a hint of unusual colors.

"Senior Brother, among the martial techniques Brother Zhou has learned, there is our sect's masterpiece, the 'Thirty-Six Forms of Mountain-Crushing' However, what he possesses is an incomplete version. Therefore, he wishes to borrow the complete version for observation. I humbly request Senior Brother's assistance." Jin Zhanyi said with a cheerful smile.

Wei Zongjin nodded slightly and replied, "The martial repository is open as usual. If Brother Zhou is interested, please join Junior Brother Jin to peruse it."

Jin Zhanyi burst into laughter and led Zhou Yi out of the room.

Once they left, the smile vanished from Wei Zongjin's face, his voice turning serious. "Junior Brother Zhang, is what Junior Brother Jin said true?"

Zhang Zhongjin paused for a moment, then sighed, saying, "Senior Brother, it's true that Zhou Yi is barely twenty, and his proficiency in martial arts is truly astonishing.." He recalled the scene where Zhou Yi used the Overturning Heaven Seal to bury the fox-bear spirit beast underground. The immense power he displayed seemed to have turned the heavens upside down.

Though confident in himself, Zhang Zhongjin understood that if he faced that technique, chances of survival would be slim, let alone resisting it.

With a light sigh, Zhang Zhongjin proceeded to narrate his observations in detail. While Zhou Yi was present earlier, he had naturally held back certain details. However, now he disclosed everything, like pouring out a bag of beans without any concealment. He described both Zhou Yi's incredible display of power on Tianchi Mountain and his successful defeat of the formidable Forked Sword assassin from the Yellow Springs Gate, all of which took Wei Zongjin by surprise.

Gradually, Wei Zongjin's facial expression became unpredictable. Especially upon hearing that Zhou Yi was capable of using the Earth-Tunnelling Technique, his pupils even contracted a few times.

A One-line Heaven powerhouse under twenty, with such strength, was already astounding. Yet, Zhou Yi's prowess surpassed that—he was not only a One-line Heaven powerhouse but also possessed the power of three flowers. Even without reaching the Three Flowers Gathering at the Apex realm, he had successfully connected with the power of heaven and earth and mastered the Earth-Tunnelling Technique.

Anyone hearing this for the first time, even if not driven to jealousy, would be struck silent by a sense of helplessness.

Finally, Zhang Zhongjin stopped speaking, and after careful consideration, Wei Zongjin said, "Junior Brother Zhang, instruct that regarding Zhou Yi's matters, no one is allowed to spread it outside. Otherwise, they will be dealt with according to the sect's rules."

Zhang Zhongjin was momentarily puzzled, unable to comprehend Senior Brother's intention, but he respectfully agreed nonetheless.

In reality, only those who had accompanied them to the Northwestern region were aware of this matter. As long as they were made to keep quiet, it would be sufficient.

Suddenly, a person rushed in, bowing deeply to them. "Two Ancestors, the herbs from the Northwestern region have been accounted for."

Wei Zongjin's expression immediately turned solemn as he asked, "How is it?"

"Returning to Ancestor, this time the quantity of herbs is ten percent less compared to previous years. However, when combined with the stock in the storage, it won't have a significant impact."

Wei Zongjin's countenance eased at this explanation. He said, "This time, we've advanced by a year compared to previous years, so it's only natural that the quantity is slightly reduced. Take the herbs to the pill refining room and instruct them to handle everything with care."

The person acknowledged and respectfully withdrew from the room.

Wei Zongjin nodded at Zhang Zhongjin and said, "To think that such a genius emerged in the Northwestern region. I wonder if it's fortunate or unfortunate for our Lingxiao Treasure Hall. Come with me to see the Duty Venerable and explain the situation in detail."

Zhang Zhongjin slightly bowed and replied, "Yes."

The two of them left the room and headed towards the higher levels.

Zhou Yi followed Jin Zhanyi, but he was extremely surprised. When Jin Zhanyi mentioned the manual, his expression was very relaxed, and Wei Zongjin's response was equally straightforward. It seemed that

Zhou Yi's request was for something as common as a book one could pick up from a roadside stall.

However, Zhou Yi knew that borrowing manuals preserved by other sects was a highly taboo practice. Yet, observing Jin Zhanyi and Wei Zongjin's behavior, he struggled to understand the hidden meaning.

After a moment, they arrived at a massive room on the fifth level.

At the entrance of the room, there was a unique small chamber. If this tower wasn't truly enormous, there wouldn't be such space available.

Jin Zhanyi first bowed towards the small chamber and then pushed open the door, walking inside.

Glancing at the small chamber, Zhou Yi was slightly surprised. It seemed that there was no trace of a living presence inside. He was unsure what Jin Zhanyi was paying respects to.

Hesitating for a moment, Zhou Yi also deeply bowed.

Since Jin Zhanyi had performed this action, following suit shouldn't cause any harm.

Entering the room, Zhou Yi was slightly taken aback. This room turned out to be another hall. However, in front of this hall, there were two room doors.

Jin Zhanyi gave him a faint smile and motioned for him to sit in the hall. Then, he opened one of the room doors and walked inside.

Waiting quietly for a moment, Jin Zhanyi emerged from the room, holding a small wooden box in his hand. The size of the box suggested that it likely contained a manual.

Placing the wooden box on the table, Jin Zhanyi gestured for Zhou Yi to take a seat.

After a moment's hesitation, Zhou Yi extended his hand and gently placed it on the wooden box.

The box itself was evidently a treasure, its touch cold to the hand, and its craftsmanship exquisite. Though Zhou Yi couldn't identify the wood, he had a strong sense that something significant was stored within.

Zhou Yi didn't immediately open the box. Instead, he spoke softly, "Brother Jin, I agreed to face Qilian Twins Demons in combat, which is why you're offering me the chance to peruse the complete manual.But I'm curious, why has even Senior Brother Wei become so accommodating?"

Jin Zhanyi chuckled, a hint of pride in his eyes. "Brother Zhou, to be frank, even if you hadn't agreed to join forces with me, you could still freely peruse any manual within this place."

Zhou Yi's mind raced, and he looked up suddenly. "Brother Jin, could it be that there's some agreement between Lingxiao Treasure Hall and the Tianchi Sect?"

Jin Zhanyi raised a thumb in admiration. "Impressive, Brother Zhou. You hit the nail on the head."

Listening intently, Zhou Yi took a moment to grasp the implications of this arrangement. Lingxiao Treasure

Hall, Northwestern Tianchi, Southern Lustrous Cavern, and Northern Ice Palace had a pact. Their repositories were mostly open to each other, except for the most unique and special manuals, which were restricted.

Of course, only venerable-level experts are eligible to enjoy this privilege.

Though Zhou Yi hadn't yet reached that level, he was deemed barely qualified.

Even Wei Zongjin, upon learning Zhou Yi's age and strength, had readily agreed to Jin Zhanyi's request. In his view, Zhou Yi's eventual promotion to the venerable level was almost a given. Given this, it made sense to establish a positive relationship now and extend some concessions.

After hearing his explanation, Zhou Yi couldn't help but feel a sense of being led astray.

Shaking his head with a sigh, he finally cast aside his distractions and opened the wooden box before him.

As the box opened and Zhou Yi saw the contents of the manual, his facial expression involuntarily changed, revealing a subtle surprise.

The content of the manual was far beyond his expectations...

Chapter 366

It wasn't a conventional paper book but rather a book made from some peculiar material. What truly astonished Zhou Yi was the fact that he held a similar manual in his hands—a manual crafted from the same material as the Cloud Mist Technique he possessed. Seeing Zhou Yi's expression change, Jin

Zhanyi asked in surprise, "Brother Zhou, is there something wrong?"

Zhou Yi shook his head slightly and replied, "I'm just feeling a bit ashamed. This kind of manual is something I'm seeing for the first time. Your sect's collection is truly eye-opening."

Jin Zhanyi was momentarily puzzled and said, "Brother Zhou, as far as I know, there should be a few of these manuals in the Tianchi martial library as well."

Zhou Yi expressed regret, "It's a pity, but I've never been to the Tianchi martial library."

Jin Zhanyi recalled Zhou Yi's identity as the Grand Elder of the Hengshan Sect and understood. He smiled and said, "Brother Zhou, don't be upset. Once you attain the status of a Venerable, they will definitely open the martial library for you. And honestly, if you didn't already possess the Five Elements Ring, they might have opened the martial library for you sooner."

Zhou Yi asked curiously, "What does the opening of the martial library have to do with the Five Elements Ring?"

Jin Zhanyi hesitated for a moment and said, "Brother Zhou, do you know about the secret of the Three Flowers Gathering at the Apex?"

"I do," Zhou Yi patted the Five Elements Ring and explained, "To achieve the Three Flowers Gathering at the Apex, I need to refine this item within me. It serves as a bridge for assimilating different attribute true qi and connecting with the power of heaven and earth."

Jin Zhanyi nodded slightly and continued, "Among our major sects, once we achieve the Three Flowers realm and master power of confinement, the sect's Venerables will arrange for us to enter the martial library to select suitable weapons." He paused for a moment and said with a cryptic smile, "Inside our sect's martial librarys, it's not just about storing manuals; they also house various divine weapons."

Zhou Yi's thoughts quickly connected the dots, and he said, "You mean that because I possess the Five Elements Ring, I've actually lost the qualification."

Jin Zhanyi smiled faintly. Though he didn't express agreement outright, it was clear what he meant. With a soft sigh, Zhou Yi wryly commented, "I see. I never thought that having this weapon would lead to losing the chance to enter the martial library."

Jin Zhanyi gave him a half-exasperated look and replied, "Brother Zhou, for us, we can only refine one weapon. The quality of that weapon and how well it harmonizes with our true qi are closely tied to our ultimate achievements. The selection of a weapon is a matter of utmost gravity. Despite the many divine weapons stored in the various martial librarys, not everyone can find a suitable one. Even though our four sects have a promise to exchange divine weapons among ourselves, some still traverse all four martial librarys and fail to find a weapon that aligns with their attributes. And attempting to craft a new one is an even more arduous task. Throughout history, many exceptional talents have struggled to advance to the Venerable realm due to the lack of suitable divine weapons when they reached the Three Flowers realm of their power.

Zhou Yi's expression grew solemn as he could truly empathize with the desperation those people felt. They had reached the pinnacle of their strength, only to be thwarted by the absence of a fitting divine weapon, shattering their hopes of becoming Venerables. If such a situation occurred to him, he might even consider ending his own life.

Jin Zhanyi continued, "Brother Zhou, your exceptional talent allows you to cultivate all Five Elements. The Five Elements Ring was undoubtedly crafted specifically for you. Using it to achieve the Three Flowers Gathering at the Apex is undoubtedly the best choice for you. If we were to open the martial library, that would truly hinder your progress.""

Zhou Yi bowed deeply to him and said, "Thank you for your guidance, Brother Jin."

Jin Zhanyi let out a long sigh and said, "Zhou Yi, the truth is, the Venerables of Tianchi deliberately concealed the fact about the divine weapons in the martial library. They didn't want you to be distracted from your cultivation. Don't disappoint them."

Naturally, Zhou Yi understood his implication. He smiled slightly and nodded, but a question surged in his mind. He asked, "Brother Jin, how did those divine weapons in the martial library come into being?"

Jin Zhanyi replied solemnly, "Every Venerable, before passing away, returns to the sect's main gate. When they pass away within the gate, the weapons they've condensed during their lifetime will manifest outside their bodies.. Over half of the weapons in our martial library are left behind by the past generations of elders. Of course, the remaining portion is carefully collected and crafted over thousands of years."

The smile on Zhou Yi's face suddenly became somewhat rigid. The fact that the weapons inside were left behind in the bodies of deceased individuals was quite unsettling.

He once again touched the bag at his side, and a genuine sense of relief washed over him. Fortunately, he had the Five Elements Ring with him; otherwise, selecting those weapons might have presented some psychological barriers.

Refocusing his attention on the small wooden box, Zhou Yi picked up the book and gently ran his hand over its surface, as if caressing a precious treasure. In truth, the sensation he got from touching this book was similar to what he experienced when he read the Cloud and Mist Technique that night.

Jin Brother, this book is so extraordinary; it must have a remarkable origin," Zhou Yi asked tentatively.

Jin Zhanyi nodded slightly, his eyes showing a hint of longing as he said, "This book is known as an ancient tome, also referred to as the Divine Path Scripture. It's a legacy passed down from the era of the Divine Path."

"Divine Path?" Zhou Yi's heart skipped a beat as he asked, "Could this book be related to the legendary figures of the Divine Path?"

Jin Zhanyi's face broke into an approving smile as he responded, "It is said that this book was illustrated by divine path experts. The contents are vast and profound. If one were to fully comprehend and integrate its teachings, there might be a chance for us to advance towards the path of divinity as well.

Zhou Yi nodded heavily, finally grasping the true significance of this book. Simultaneously, he recalled the reluctant expression on Xu Zili's face when he handed over this book.

He also felt secretly grateful in his heart. Gifting him this divine path manual was likely a way of showing gratitude for his past assistance in saving Xu Family Fortress.Using this book as a reward was already more than enough, and Xu Zili had also promised to accompany him to the Deep Mountain Totem twenty years later. Such gestures of repayment were already more than ample.

Vaguely, Zhou Yi seemed to understand the old man's sentiments. Perhaps, in his words, he would never admit his connection to Xu Family Fortress, but deep within his heart, the independent fortress probably still held a special place.

Jin Zhanyi stood up and said, "Brother Zhou, I'll leave first. You can read as much as you can in the next three hours. Three days from now, I'll bring you back here."

Zhou Yi smiled with understanding, replying, "I understand. Thank you, Brother Jin."

Jin Zhanyi waved his hand and re-entered the room, likely to select the scrolls he wanted to read.

Surveying his surroundings, Zhou Yi couldn't sense any other person's presence. He harbored a faint suspicion; how could a place of such importance have no guards? However, Zhou Yi also knew that the absence of guards here was impossible; he just couldn't sense them at the moment.

Shaking his head, Zhou Yi settled his mind and opened the secret manual before him. At first glance, he found an illustration of a large blade. Though it was a static image on the paper, it gave off a magical sensation as if it could leap out of the page at any moment.

Zhou Yi cradled the book and slowly observed it from different angles, revealing different scenes. If he could merge these scenes together, he would likely capture the true expression of this technique.

Injecting a thread of Gold Element True Qi into the manual, Zhou Yi's body trembled slightly. It was as if his consciousness had entered a fantastical realm. After the resonance between the Gold Element True Qi and the manual, Zhou Yi once again entered this extraordinary state.

It felt as if he now held a large Guandao in his hand, and his mind was flooded with countless blade shadows. Following a specific speed and direction, the blade's edge in Zhou Yi's hand continuously flowed, emitting a radiance that seemed to stretch for thousands of feet.

Sensing the images of the person using the large Guandao in his mind, Zhou Yi's emotions surged uncontrollably.

The first move, this is just the first move belonging to the acquired realm among the thirty-six moves of the "Thirty-Six Forms of Mountain-Crushing".But now, in his hands, the power of this move had clearly increased, reaching its peak.

Although the version of the Thirty-Six Forms of Mountain-Crushing he had previously obtained provided an extremely detailed description of this move, complete with illustrations and textual explanations, it wasn't until he touched the authentic copy that he realized only by viewing the genuine article could he clearly experience the changes and power within.

Just like this moment, his understanding of the first form had reached a new level. Though he was still far from the level of the divine path master who created this manual, in these few brief moments, there had been a drastic transformation.

He couldn't help but think that if he finished studying the first twenty-three forms and then executed them in sequence, the strength he would display would likely force even the Venerables to retreat.

Recalling his encounter with Xu Zili in the past, even though he managed to force him back with a move, half of it was thanks to Brerbo's contribution.

But if he studies the authentic version and then confronts him again, Zhou Yi is confident that he can at least force him back a step with his true strength.

Taking a deep breath, he withdrew from that mystical state and cautiously turned to the second page, fully immersing himself with devout dedication.

Chapter 367

Three whole hours passed, but in Zhou Yi's perception, it felt like merely a blink of an eye. The feeling of studying the original manual was indeed different from reading his own copy of the Thirty-Six Forms of Mountain-Crushing.

It wasn't because there was any deviation in the manual he had; rather, it was due to the subtle differences in the understanding of the Metal Element technique between him and the founding ancestor of Lingxiao Treasure Hall.

Precisely because of this difference, Zhou Yi felt an entirely distinct world. Of course, as for who had the superior understanding, that remained unknown. However, in Zhou Yi's perception, the most potent technique was the one best suited to himself.

During the first hour, Zhou Yi had completely perused forms one to twenty. In the second hour, he used his unique method to read forms twenty-one to twenty-three. He could immerse himself fully, savoring the subtle differences between the two manuals.

These differences provided him with ample room for adjustment, giving him great confidence to further enhance the Thirty-Six Forms of Mountain-Crushing.

In the final hour, Zhou Yi focused on the diagram of the twenty-fourth form in the manual.Although there were twelve more forms afterward, including the enigmatic and unpredictable final three forms, he did not peruse them.

After all, he was not the type to aimlessly pursue the unattainable. Although the images ahead were profoundly attractive to him, he managed to suppress his yearning.

Zhou Yi spent a considerable amount of time on the page depicting the twenty-fourth form. His brow furrowed as he concentrated, completely engrossed in it, yet he struggled to fully grasp the intricacies contained within.

It was like there was a semi-transparent film before him—thin and seemingly easy to tear apart, yet his hands were immobilized, making it impossible to exert any force. Naturally, he couldn't tear through that layer of film.

Suddenly, Zhou Yi felt a sensation, as if someone had approached him. His heart skipped a beat, and he quickly withdrew from the immersive state he was in.

Opening his eyes, Zhou Yi immediately saw Jin Zhanyi standing silently before him, seemingly having appeared out of nowhere.

A tinge of frustration crossed Zhou Yi's face, and he asked, "Is the time up?"

Jin Zhanyi nodded expressionlessly and replied, "Three hours."

With a sigh, Zhou Yi rose from his seated position, placed the manual back into the wooden box, closed the lid, and carefully handed it to Jin Zhanyi. If Jin Zhanyi had been cautious before when taking out the manual, Zhou Yi was even more meticulous now.

Finally, a faint smile appeared on Jin Zhanyi's face. He said, "Brother Zhou, you can come back to peruse the manual again in three days. And once you advance to the Venerable realm, you can read it here without any restrictions."

Zhou Yi gave a wry smile, knowing deep down that unless he planned to reside in the Lingxiao Treasure Hall for an extended period, this statement was essentially meaningless.

Heaved a long sigh, Zhou Yi watched as Jin Zhanyi took the manual back into the room. The intense ardor in Zhou Yi's eyes couldn't be hidden.

Leaving the martial library, Jin Zhanyi once again bowed deeply toward the small door at the entrance. Zhou Yi found it peculiar but mimicked the gesture.

His ears twitched slightly, and his expression changed subtly. He had caught a faint, almost imperceptible sound. He vaguely understood that there might be a

Venerable residing inside. However, the Venerable's concealment technique was so exceptional that even Zhou Yi struggled to pick up the slightest hint of movement while the Venerable sat perfectly still.

Following Jin Zhanyi down the stairs, he accompanied Zhou Yi out of the tower and arrived at a courtyard not far from the tower's exterior.

Here is where Jin Zhanyi resides within the Lingxiao Treasure Hall's inner city.

The closer one is to the central tower, the more central they are to the Lingxiao Treasure Hall's hierarchy.

As for those powerful Venerables, they mostly reside within the high tower. Unless their cultivation reaches a certain pinnacle or an earth-shattering event occurs outside that requires their intervention, they wouldn't leave the tower under normal circumstances.

This aspect is remarkably similar to those powerful Venerables on Tianchi Mountain.

Jin Zhanyi settled Zhou Yi in the finest guest room before bidding farewell and departing. Though he had many matters to attend to, he understood that after viewing the authentic manual of the Thirty-Six Forms of Mountain-Crushing, Zhou Yi needed ample time for comprehension.

After seeing Jin Zhanyi off, Zhou Yi immediately closed his eyes, immersing himself entirely in that extraordinary state. Time became uncertain. He remained seated with closed eyes, but he stood up after a while and moved toward the room's door.

Even though his eyes were shut, he moved as if he had an invisible pair of eyes, navigating with precision, never touching any furniture in the room. Arriving at the door, he gently pushed it open, and his steps grew even steadier.

Step by step, he walked until he stood at the center of the courtyard. Then, he assumed a stance and began to execute a series of punches and strikes, resembling slow-motion movements.

A potent surge of pinnacle-level metal-element energy emanated from him, unreservedly spreading in all directions.

Starting from the first technique of the Thirty-Six Forms of Mountain-Crushing, Zhou Yi began to execute the movements one after another in a seamless flow. His actions appeared steady and unhurried, yet the transitions between each technique were fluid, completed in the span of a few breaths, effortlessly moving from the first to the twenty-third technique.

Back in the days on Tianchi Mountain, although he had practiced the techniques one by one up to the twenty-third move, his speed at that time was far inferior to today's and the immense momentum he now gathered was also much stronger than before.

This was the result of reading the authentic manual of the Thirty-Six Forms of Mountain-Crushing. Zhou Yi's understanding of this metal-element technique had deepened. Especially in terms of transitioning between techniques, he had reached an indescribable level of proficiency. Otherwise, he wouldn't have been able to perform every technique within the span of a few breaths.

Once the twenty-third technique was executed, Zhou Yi's movement came to a sudden halt in mid-air. His inner true qi surged like a hundred-meter tall wave, reaching its pinnacle. He invested his entire being into this final technique, aiming to complete the twenty-fourth technique with the unparalleled momentum, hoping to form the Flower of Metal.

He strongly sensed that as long as he could execute the twenty-fourth technique, he would successfully condense the Metal Flower. However, despite the surging true qi and formidable momentum, he couldn't break through the thin layer of resistance in front of him.

The twenty-fourth technique had been performed countless times in his mind, yet his body couldn't control the immense power it contained. Instead, there was a constant risk of collapse.

He maintained this stance, maintaining the peak momentum, resembling a mud statue, motionless.

After a long while, he finally exhaled a deep breath. His true qi gradually receded, and a tinge of disappointment flickered across his face.

A figure flashed, and Jin Zhanyi had appeared beside him. His body stood straight as a pine, his eyes gleaming with an intense and unusual light. It seemed that Zhou Yi's prior momentum had stirred a boldness within Jin Zhanyi's heart, as if he wanted to immediately engage in a battle with him.

Sensing Jin Zhanyi's formidable fighting spirit, the disappointment Zhou Yi felt moments ago was swept away. Within his body surged a battle intent that was in no way inferior to Jin Zhanyi's.

However, as their fighting spirits were about to clash, both of them immediately reined in their emotions.

They exchanged a smile, both carrying an indescribable touch of regret.

"Zhou brother, the Senior Brother has sent a message. In five days, it will be the time for us to face Qilian Twin Devils in battle," Jin Zhanyi said in a deep voice.

Zhou Yi tightened his fists and took a deep breath. He said, "Five days, huh? I really hope they pass quickly."

Jin Zhanyi burst into laughter and said, "Zhou brother, I indeed didn't misjudge you. We are actually of the same kind."

Zhou Yi was momentarily surprised, thinking about his initial refusal and his current eagerness. He couldn't help but chuckle. Perhaps he and Jin Zhanyi were indeed of the same kind.

On the other side of the tower, in a spacious room, three elderly men sat across from each other at a table, seemingly discussing something.

Among these three individuals, two of them had identical appearances, not only in their faces and attire, but even in their expressions. It was as if there was no distinction between them.

As if sensing something, they suddenly ceased their conversation and directed their gazes toward a particular direction.

After a moment, one of the two identical-looking old men spoke with a grave tone, "With such powerful metal-element force, it must be Jin Zhanyi."

The other elderly man nodded slightly and said, "For metal-element force to become so powerful is already no easy feat. But what's even more significant is that he can maintain it for such a long time. Hehe... it's like a demonstration to the two of us."

The elderly man sitting across from them shifted his gaze and said, "Big Devil, Second Devil, what are your thoughts?"

The Big Devil immediately spoke respectfully, "Master, please rest assured. The stronger the opponent, the more advantageous it is for us."

The Second Devil followed up, "Only in moments of life and death do we have a chance to comprehend the fleeting opportunity and integrate divine weapons into our bodies. Since that Jin Zhanyi is indeed as formidable as rumored, we can only be pleased." He paused and continued, "However, who is this Zhou Yi? Why have we never heard of him before? Could it be that there are peak experts within Lingxiao Treasure Hall that we are unaware of?"

The Big Devil's thick lips curled into a grin as he said, "Regardless of who he is, since he dares to accept our challenge, let him taste the bloody flavor of hell."

The elderly man across from them sighed softly, saying, "Since Lingxiao Treasure Hall has allowed this person to participate, there must be some reliance. You mustn't underestimate him, otherwise all my efforts will be in vain."

Qilian Twin Devils exchanged a glance, nodding simultaneously as if they were one person.

The elderly man's gaze once again turned toward that direction, and he murmured, "In five days..."

Chapter 368

Back in his room, Zhou Yi's heart still couldn't calm down, and this unusual phenomenon left him deeply wary. Taking out the handwritten copy of the Thirty-Six Forms of Mountain-Crushing, Zhou Yi flipped it open, but after glancing at it for a moment, he sighed deeply and cast the book aside completely.

Having seen the original version, Zhou Yi no longer had any interest in studying the handwritten copy. After all, each person's understanding of martial arts was different, and this was especially true for someone like Zhou Yi who possessed the power of all five elements.

While the founding master of the Lingxiao Treasure Hall was incredibly powerful, it was impossible for him to have the exact same understanding as Zhou Yi. Thus, the handwritten copy could only serve as a reference at best, and it could no longer capture Zhou Yi's full attention as it once did.

Sitting down at the table, Zhou Yi's mind was still preoccupied with the original version of the Thirty-Six Forms of Mountain-Crushing. He felt an impatient urge to read the authentic original version. Of course, he knew this was nothing but wishful thinking. Even Zhou Yi himself understood that it was simply impossible.

Gazing at the tower hidden in the darkness outside the window, an aura of immense power seemed to press down on his heart, almost suffocating him. He withdrew his gaze, cursed silently in his heart, and allowed countless thoughts to race through his mind.

He intended to steal the manuals from the tower, but he understood that even if he managed to succeed, the discovery of the original manual of the Thirty-Six Forms of Mountain-Crushing missing from the tower would likely make him a prime suspect. And contemplating the immense power concealed within the tower sent a chill down Zhou Yi's spine.

After pondering for a while, Zhou Yi channeled his true qi into the silver ring, opening the ethereal and magical space within it. When he first obtained the silver ring, even merely opening this space consumed almost all of his true qi. However, now it was an effortless task. This illustrated how rapid his progress had been over the past few years.

Zhou Yi extended his hand and took out the book "Wind,Cloud and Mist" from within. As he touched the pages and felt the familiar texture, he once again marveled. Such a precious manual, Xu Zili didn't hesitate to gift it to him. Such a huge favor carried with it the potential intention of entrusting the well-being of Xu Family Fortress to him.

Besides that, Zhou Yi couldn't fathom why Xu Zili would do such a thing.

After a moment, he focused his mind, grasped the tracker given to him by Brerbo, and whispered, "Brerbo, I want to see you, without anyone noticing."

Though he didn't understand how Brerbo managed to hear his voice from afar, since the guy said it could be done, Zhou Yi was willing to give it a try.

Before long, Zhou Yi's ears caught a faint and unusual sound. He turned his head to look and saw a figure slowly flowing in through the gap in the wall.

Like water, the person appeared abruptly and mysteriously before Zhou Yi.

For Zhou Yi, who had witnessed countless mind-boggling scenes, this was nothing new. Perhaps someday, when Brerbo knocked on the door like a regular person, it would truly surprise him.

"Brerbo, where's Treasure pig?" Zhou Yi asked in a low voice.

Treasure pig, the little fellow, had gone missing again after following the caravan for a few days. As for the furnace it had left behind, it seemed to have grown tired of playing with it after a few days.

Zhou Yi stored the furnace in the ring's space and didn't mention the incident to anyone.

Though Zhang Zhongjin and Jin Zhanyi were somewhat concerned about Treasure pig, after all, the little guy was a well-known spiritual beast from the Northwestern Tianchi. If it got hurt or died within Da Shen, they would be implicated to some extent.

"It's outside the city, I've arranged for it, there won't be any issues," Brerbo said calmly.

Zhou Yi nodded slightly. Since Brerbo said so, Treasure pig must be safe.

Placing the "Wind,Cloud and Mist" manual on the table, Zhou Yi held onto a glimmer of hope and asked, "Brerbo, you possess the power of transformation. Can you try to duplicate this manual?"

Brerbo stepped forward, and his eyes immediately lit up. The radiance emitted from his eyes differed significantly from the light produced by a human concentrating; it was like a straight beam of light that struck directly onto the manual.

If there were outsiders present at this moment, they would surely suspect whether this person was some sort of forest spirit or supernatural creature.

The beam of light moved slowly over the manual's pages, and after a while, the radiance gradually disappeared.

Zhou Yi's excitement grew, and he asked, "How did it go?"

"It's feasible, with a success rate of over 80 percent," Brerbo's voice remained calm and unwavering.

Zhou Yi felt elated, but he hesitated for a moment and asked, "If it's unsuccessful, would the manual be damaged?"

"No, it won't," Brerbo answered without hesitation.

Zhou Yi instantly felt relieved, knowing that Brerbo's words were trustworthy. If he didn't have absolute certainty, Brobob wouldn't have answered so readily.

Stepping back a few paces to clear space, Zhou Yi said, "In that case, please give it a try, Brerbo, and amaze me."

Brerbo didn't refuse; he stepped forward and took the peculiar manual in his hands.

While Zhou Yi appeared relaxed on the surface, his heart was still somewhat apprehensive. Despite trusting Brerbo, he couldn't help feeling a bit uneasy.

Although there were merely ten illustrations within this manual, each one gave him a vastly different sensation. With his current level of skill, he had only managed to comprehend the first illustration. As for the rest, he had the intention but lacked the ability. Of course, this was also due to his limited time. If he were granted several years of seclusion, he might gain deeper insights.

Such a precious item, if accidentally damaged by Brerbo, would indeed be a great loss.

Under Zhou Yi's watchful gaze, Brerbo's hand holding the manual suddenly began to melt. It was as if a sparkling and translucent liquid was seeping into the illustrations. Subsequently, the exterior of the book took on a strange hue. Though no sound accompanied this transformation, it all felt rather eerie.

Zhou Yi's heart leaped.

He didn't quite understand the purpose behind Brerbo's actions, so he simply sat nearby, observing.

After a cup of tea's time, the scenery before him shifted in a peculiar way once more. The mercury-like substance began to writhe.

Brerbo extended his other arm and gently placed it atop the silvery liquid. Instantly, the mercury rushed into his arm with fervor. Almost simultaneously, his severed arm began to regenerate. By the time the liquid mercury had disappeared, his arm had fully regrown.

Zhou Yi sighed deeply, profoundly impressed.

This extraordinary ability was something only Brerbo could achieve.

Shifting his gaze back to the table, the "Wind,Cloud and Mist" manual sat there as if nothing extraordinary had occurred.

Zhou Yi extended his hand and gently placed it on the manual. He infused it with Wind-elemental true qi. After a moment, a satisfied smile graced his face. Despite Brerbo's previous manipulation, the manual remained completely undamaged, which pleased him greatly.

Looking over at Brerbo, he seemed to understand Zhou Yi's curiosity and explained, "This book was crafted using a unique method. I've come across the process in my memory, but it's tailored to the intellectual capacity of beings in this world. I can only replicate the finished product, not create it."

As he spoke, Brerbo extended his right hand and placed it on his left wrist. With a gentle twist, in front of Zhou Yi's stunned gaze, his severed left hand transformed into an identical copy of the manual.

Even though Zhou Yi knew Brerbo's body was exceptional, witnessing this scene was still difficult to comprehend.

Shaking his head slightly, Zhou Yi took the book that had been transformed from Brerbo's left hand and held it in his own hand. He attempted to infuse it with his true energy. After a moment, he opened his eyes in astonishment. The sensation these two manuals imparted was incredibly similar... no, it was practically identical.

Especially when he infused true qi into the manual, he experienced the same feeling as entering the space of swirling wind and clouds, perceiving the marvelous sensations clearly.

It was as if the manual transformed by Brerbo's hand was the true original. At least with his current level of cultivation, he couldn't discern any differences between the two manuals. If they were placed side by side, Zhou Yi was certain that after a moment, he wouldn't be able to distinguish which was the authentic version and which was Brerbo's left hand.

He tossed the manual back to Brerbo and gently touched the severed wrist, causing the manual to transform back into a hand.

"Brerbo, have you seen anyone create such manuals before?" Zhou Yi inquired thoughtfully.

"Yes, the first owner of the cave mansion once created similar books. However, after creating them, he seemed very exhausted," Brerbo responded.

Zhou Yi's eyes lit up with excitement. He asked eagerly, "Where is that manual?"

"It's inside the cave mansion."

"Why didn't you mention this earlier?" Zhou Yi reproached.

"You never asked," Brerbo replied matter-of-factly.

Zhou Yi was utterly speechless. He stared at Brerbo for a while, then finally said, "Brerbo, there's something I'd like to ask for your help with..."

After a moment, Brerbo shook his head and said, "There are too many powerful individuals here. Your chances of success in doing that are not high."

Zhou Yi's gaze shimmered with determination. He spoke slowly, emphasizing each word, "If you don't enter the tiger's den, you won't catch its cubs. I must give it a try, or I'll never be content."

Brerbo gazed at him calmly, neither agreeing nor refusing.

Chapter 369

The darkness gradually deepened, inch by inch encroaching upon everything, flowing like honey in its unhurried pace. It settled, gradually becoming one with a novel essence, denser than air, as if time itself had been partially frozen.

Amidst this swath of night, an almost ethereal silhouette gently drew near the towering edifice at the heart of the Lingxiao Treasure Hall.

Here, though masters abounded, upon this figure seemed to rest a certain mystique, melding seamlessly into the night's embrace. Despite traversing this path, not a soul discerned the trail he blazed.

The tower boasted exactly twelve entrances, each guarded by four vigilant disciples. Though their martial arts cultivation hadn't reached the pinnacle of Innate or acquired realms, their standards were still remarkably high, their synergy impeccable. One disciple, a master of Ninth Layer Inner Energy, accompanied by three of Eighth Layer.

Deploying cultivators of this caliber for nocturnal sentry duty at each of the twelve entrances was unthinkable in the Tianluo Nation. The chasm between their strengths was thus incomparably vast.

This obscure figure skulked outside the tower, revealing the visage of Zhou Yi. He cast a glance skyward at the tower, gleams of astuteness dancing in his eyes. Though his heart bore a smidgen of trepidation, his resolve stood firm—his decision having been made, he would not falter.

Drawing in a deep breath, his body promptly dwindled, soundless, the entirety of his being shrinking. The art of bone contraction, an inner energy technique he'd cultivated to the utmost in the acquired realm, had now achieved astonishing mastery in the present, yielding incredible applications.

His attire too was evidently tailored, for though his stature had diminished, his garments adhered snugly, as if imbued with remarkable elasticity.

The garment he held in his hands was none other than Sorgo's Red Wolf King leather armor. After slaying Sorgo, the armor had been mended and carefully stowed within the spatial world of Zhou Yi's silver ring. However, tonight, he has retrieved it once again.

As his figure shrank to a diminished form, Zhou Yi's visage contorted as well. The change wasn't radical, yet when compared to his original countenance, it appeared utterly distinct. No one encountering the current Zhou Yi would be able to draw a connection to his former self.

But that wasn't all—Zhou Yi produced a black cloth, shrouding his visage with it. With these carefully orchestrated preparations, he believed that if anyone could still recognize him, there would need to be ghosts in this world.

Gently placing his palm against the tower's stone surface, he sensed the icy sensation emanating from within. The power of the earth circulated slowly within his body, linking him to the tower through the medium of earth energy. Zhou Yi even began to experience a wondrous sensation akin to being a part of the tower itself.

He had never intended to enter the tower through those entrances; after all, it would be foolish not to utilize his Earth-Tunnelling Technique. However, after a brief moment, a subtle change crossed Zhou Yi's face.

To his surprise, he found himself unable to employ his Earth-Tunnelling Technique. Within this tower, an enigmatic force seemed to reside—a force exuding a formidable repulsion. While this force hadn't manifested when Zhou Yi first perceived it, the moment he attempted to infiltrate, it swiftly unleashed a robust response.

Zhou Yi swiftly retracted his true energy, abstaining from any further rash actions. For he was acutely aware that the tower, in its entirety, was woven with that very force—a force that permeated every crevice of its structure. Initially, his intrusion had been subtle, and thus the counterforce had been likewise. Yet he sensed that should he recklessly strive to breach it, he would undoubtedly provoke a monumental counterforce dwelling within the entire tower.

Back then, it wouldn't only be a matter of whether he could endure it, but it would certainly stir the formidable Venerables within the tower. If he were to attract their notice, Zhou Yi wasn't convinced that he could manage to escape.

His brow furrowed tightly as this unforeseen circumstance utterly disrupted his plans.

His gaze shifted towards a entrance, where the guards were utterly unaware that someone was attempting to infiltrate the tower.

His mind raced—simply infiltrating the tower held little challenge for him given his current prowess. To deceive a few acquired masters was a task effortlessly within his capabilities. However, the instant he contemplated the room outside the martial library, a chill gripped Zhou Yi's heart. Regardless of his self-assurance, he couldn't fathom entering the martial library without alerting the enigmatic presence within.

If he could truly achieve this, then he wouldn't need to make a twenty-year pact with the Deep Mountain Totem. He could just directly charge in and confront them.

The terrain surrounding the tower wasn't bare; it housed numerous precious flowers, plants, and trees. Except for the twelve entrances, while the rest of the area was veiled by the embrace of enchanting vegetation.

This is also the primary reason Zhou Yi can easily approach this place without worrying about being detected. Through the gaps in the flowers, plants, and trees, Zhou Yi gazes quietly at his surroundings. His facial expression shifts unpredictably, torn between two conflicting thoughts in his mind.

After this safest route was sealed off, an involuntary sense of retreat washed over Zhou Yi. After all, those formidable Venerables within were far beyond his capacity to contend with. A single misstep could result in consequences even Zhou Yi himself couldn't bear.

However, as he looked up at the towering structure once more, an intense, unwavering conviction surged within him. He'd finally made his ultimate decision. Extending his palm once more, Zhou Yi gently pressed it against the tower's surface.

This time, he didn't attempt to employ his Earth-Tunnelling Technique. Instead, he began to infuse the earth's true energy into the tower in a communicative manner. Indeed, as Zhou Yi had surmised, without the intention to forcibly invade, the latent force within the tower refrained from retaliation.

Suppressing his overwhelming delight, Zhou Yi gradually diffused his true energy, attempting to thin it out as much as possible, seeking to commune with the tower's inner force. In his perception, while the might of the force within the tower was unparalleled, it was evident that this power was ownerless.

Given that it lacked a master, Zhou Yi had confidence in finding its weak point and exploiting it. Gradually, his true energy intersected with the force within the tower, and at that moment, a familiar image reappeared in his mind.

Upon a level expanse of land, a diminutive tower tip sprouted, akin to a spring shoot emerging, gradually growing taller.

Amidst this expanse of freedom, the tower emerges from nothingness, gradually rising from the ground. The entire process is monumental, brimming with a sense of grandeur. Zhou Yi understands that even if this were a miracle, it couldn't have been accomplished in a day. The images now in his mind merely compress the passage of time, delivering the most intense sensation of awe

Although it wasn't his first time experiencing this sensation, Zhou Yi couldn't help but be swept up by the surge of emotion. If only he could one day achieve such a miracle.

However, this thought was fleeting. He was well aware that his current self had no chance of attaining such a realm. When he had encountered this vision for the first time, his excitement had forced him to sever the connection. But now, his determination was unwavering, seemingly unaffected by this monumental spectacle.

With his eyes slightly closed, he immersed himself entirely, comprehending the sensations this power bestowed upon him. It was hard to tell how much time had passed, for in Zhou Yi's perception, it felt like a century's worth of eternity, yet also as fleeting as the blink of an eye. In this time, he came to understand many things.

He had grown to understand the tower to an extent that rivaled, if not surpassed, even those mighty beings who had inhabited it for a hundred years. This understanding was pure intuition, yet it radiated with intensity.

His true energy melded gradually with the force within the tower. This wasn't an invasion, but a mutual attraction of energies. In the center of his palm, a faintly spinning flower of earth emerged. Under the control of this earth Flower, Zhou Yi's earth-based power underwent subtle adjustments, becoming increasingly akin to the attributes of the force within the tower.

Within his Dantian, the surging earth energy resonated seamlessly with the tower's force, as if the two were originally one. If the powerful beings within the tower were to learn of this situation, they would undoubtedly be rendered speechless in astonishment.

This tower was pulled out from beneath the earth by the founding ancestor of the Lingxiao Treasure Hall, was imbued with a divine power that transcended any other force.Similarly, within this tower, a residue of that ancestral divine power lingered. It is precisely due to the presence of this divine power that no one, inside or outside the entire tower, can employ the Earth-Tunnelling Technique to infiltrate it.

For the earth-based power within had already been bound by the divine power. To employ Earth-Tunnelling Techniques here, one would need a power surpassing that of the divine power, capable of forcibly dispersing it.

However, divine power remains divine power. While the latent divine power within the Tower of Heaven might not be a threat to those divine path powerhouses, for ordinary cultivators, it possesses unparalleled and formidable might.

So, even if their heads were cut off, they would still absolutely not believe that in this world where the divine path has already disappeared, there could still be someone who can use the Earth-Tunnelling Technique to enter the tower.

Zhou Yi's partially closed eyes gently rotated. He didn't sense the passage of time in the external world; his entire focus was entirely submerged in this endeavor. His Dantian, once chaotic, underwent a subtle transformation.

A strand of unique true energy unfurled slowly from his Dantian, distinctive in its nature. Finally, this strand of true energy entered the tower. Upon contact with the potent force within, it wasn't met with retaliation but rather harmonized seamlessly.

A satisfied smile graced Zhou Yi's lips. Following this, his form subtly shifted, already melding into the walls.

Chapter 370

Wandering within the tower's interior, this sensation was starkly different from traversing the depths below the earth.

Although Zhou Yi had finely calibrated his internal energy to closely mirror the potency within the tower, a subtle tinge of constrictive force lingered.

As a result, his movements were deliberate, each step a measured endeavor.

Suddenly, his surroundings brightened before him,before him, the corridor illuminated with a subdued radiance. Oil lamps punctuated the expanse, casting a gentle glow that, while not dazzling, Though the light wasn't intense, for these practitioners, it was akin to daylight.

Stepping forward, Zhou Yi had already breached the wall and entered the tower. A hint of triumph and excitement crossed his face, followed by a cat-like grace as he headed towards the second level.

Though he had ventured into the tower only once before, guided by Jin Zhanyi, Zhou Yi had already etched all the routes into his memory. The fifth level housed the martial library, but Zhou Yi refrained from ascending to that floor. Because just outside the martial library, an expert of the Venerable held vigil.

Sneaking in under their watchful gaze was beyond Zhou Yi's capabilities.

Having wandered on the fourth level for a while, Zhou Yi eventually arrived at a room that was clearly a storage chamber. Inside, an endless array of items were piled up haphazardly.

Throughout his journey, Zhou Yi proceeded with utmost caution, making sure not to alert anyone. It was clear that below the fifth level, there were no immensely powerful beings present, not even individuals of the One-line Heaven realm.

Zhou Yi had a faint intuition that the experts of the Venerable level probably resided on the upper levels of the tower. Those below the Venerable rank might not even have the qualification to dwell within the tower.

Therefore, as he moved stealthily below the fifth level, he had no worries about being detected.

Raising his head, and if his memory served him correctly, just above this storeroom was the martial library, specifically the room Jin Zhanyi had entered to retrieve a book.

During the daytime, when Jin Zhanyi had opened the door, Zhou Yi had employed the extraordinary technique of "Shunfeng Er" to listen intently for a while. He could be certain that unless there was a high-level expert of the same caliber as the one guarding the exterior room hidden inside, it would be improbable for anyone to be in this room.

Now that he had arrived here, Zhou Yi naturally couldn't leave empty-handed. He took a deep breath, and in the next moment, all the warmth in his body disappeared, even his heartbeat almost came to a halt.

This was his concealment technique, and as the "Hold Breath Technique" reached its peak, after attaining the Innate Realm, the power it exerted exceeded his imagination.

His body floated upward like a falling leaf, weightless, until he reached the ceiling. Zhou Yi extended a hand, gently touching the top of the room, and suddenly it adhered tightly.

A faint thread of Earth-aligned Qi surged from Zhou Yi's Dantian. In this moment, the wondrous effects of his experience at the bottom of the lake once again revealed themselves.

His chaotic Dantian could even simulate the astonishing power within the tower, a power that was incredibly formidable and beyond imagination.

Even though the essence of the two powers was fundamentally different, and their strengths were worlds apart, it was enough for Zhou Yi to earn the recognition of the tower's power.

However, Of course, due to the overwhelming power within the tower, the execution of his Earth-Tunnelling Technique was considerably slower. It took him an entire stick of incense's time to gradually move from the fourth level to the fifth level.

Upon entering the new room, Zhou Yi grew even more cautious. His ears twitched subtly in this silent space, capable of capturing even the faintest sound, like the fall of a speck of dust.

Finally, he ascertained it—there truly was no one in this room. His gaze swept around, capturing every facet of the chamber in his sight.

Indeed, this was a repository—a library of substantial scale. Over thirty large bookshelves lined the space, each shelf cradling hundreds of volumes. These tomes were ensconced within individual wooden cases, a testament to the meticulous care they had received.

However, it was precisely through this preservation method that the original scrolls could be retained to the greatest extent possible.

Zhou Yi's brows furrowed slightly. If he were to come in front of each bookshelf and open the wooden boxes one by one, all in complete silence, he feared that it would take until tomorrow to find the manual of the Thirty-Six Forms of Mountain-Crushing.

His gaze focused anew, and by chance, he noticed a series of tiny inscriptions preceding the wooden cases. Upon closer inspection, his delight surged.

Here, the names of the books inside the wooden boxes were actually written. He felt an instant sense of relief, realizing that without these inscriptions, even those searching for manuals here would be greatly perplexed.

His gaze shifted slightly, scanning over all the inscriptions on this shelf. To his disappointment, his desired target didn't appear among them.

Following the order of his entrance, Zhou Yi began his meticulous search. His pace wasn't hurried; rather, it was significantly slower than that of an average person. However, throughout this process, he emitted not even the faintest sound, nor did he stir up the tiniest speck of dust.

It seemed as though he had completely melded with this space, no longer distinguishing between himself and the surroundings. And so, he arrived at the final row of bookshelves.

He had already seen it — right at the top shelf of this row of bookshelves, clearly inscribed with the tiny characters "Authentic Manual of the Thirty-Six Forms of Mountain-Crushing".

Though he was overjoyed, there was no visible change in Zhou Yi's demeanor. In this moment, he was even calmer than BrerBo, almost akin to BrerBo himself. He delicately twisted his wrist, drawing a forked sword from behind him. This object seemed neither gold nor iron, yet gleamed with a texture reminiscent of human skin.

With delicate precision, he placed the forked sword atop the wooden case bearing the inscription. He didn't even deign to open the box, for he believed this object could discern what he truly sought.

Gradually, after leaving Zhou Yi's hand, the sword began to melt. It transformed into a pool of liquid mercury, seamlessly merging with the wooden box.

Zhou Yi's gaze shifted away from this sight, cautiously glancing towards the entrance of the room.Equally as a stick of incense burned away, the mercury-like substance began to change.

After about the time it takes for an incense stick to burn, the mercury finally underwent a transformation. It slowly receded from the wooden box and reshaped itself back into the form of the forked sword.

Relief washed over Zhou Yi's eyes, a feeling of burden lifted from his shoulders.Though the duration wasn't particularly protracted, in his perception, every second seemed to stretch far beyond an entire day's span. Were it not for his mastery of the Hold Breath Technique, his entire being might have been drenched in torrents of sweat akin to a rainstorm.

Finally, as the mercury returned to its original state, Zhou Yi could breathe a sigh of relief, albeit slightly. Slipping the forked sword onto his back, he gradually lowered himself, extending a hand to lightly touch the ground. Bit by bit, his inner qi flowed, merging gradually with the energies of the tower.

As his feet sank into the ground, his movements abruptly ceased. Then, in an instant, his feet withdrew soundlessly from the ground. An indescribable, potent sense of danger seeped in from the outside.

Zhou Yi's complexion turned slightly pale. The immense pressure he felt, even before seeing the person causing it, could only come from a Venerable-level expert.

Sensing this overwhelming pressure, Zhou Yi instantly abandoned the thought of using his Earth-Tunnelling Technique to escape.

After all, this tower was unlike any other. Executing the Earth-Tunnelling Technique to escape required a considerable amount of time. If he attempted it now and the person entered while he was halfway through, he would be caught in a vulnerable position with no escape route, uncertain of his fate.

Countless thoughts swirled through his mind. Finally, a determined glint sparkled in Zhou Yi's eyes. If Jin Zhanyi had managed to escape from the hands of the Western Venerable, then so could he.

With a slight movement, he had left the bookshelf and reached a corner of the room. Then, he adopted a peculiar stance, as a mist-like energy began to envelop him. Even the light seemed to bend and twist in its presence.

"Squeak..."

The door gently swung open, and a pair of ash-black cloth shoes stepped firmly inside.

It was an elderly man, a wizened figure resembling a withered tree branch. As he entered the room, his gaze swept around. In the darkness, his eyes gleamed with a piercing intensity, akin to the eyes of an owl, sending shivers down the spine.

After a brief moment, his brows furrowed slightly, as if he was contemplating something. Zhou Yi's guess was accurate; he was indeed the venerable figure from outside the room. His entry into the martial library at this very moment was not due to any discovery but rather a sudden whim.

At their level of martial cultivation, there were times when they would experience inexplicable sensations. Although enigmatic, these feelings held no rational basis. This man was naturally cautious and meticulous. If he felt such a sensation, he'd explore it.

Initially, he had been convinced that no one could infiltrate the martial library undetected, so his intention was merely to cast a cursory glance. As his gaze swept the room, everything appeared normal. Yet, for some reason, a distinct, odd sensation tingled within him, as if he had overlooked something.

After a moment's hesitation, he slowly circled the room. His hawk-like eyes emitted a faint, verdant gleam. Soon, he abruptly halted, his gaze fixed on a corner of the room. There, a flowerpot with a small tree perched atop it caught his attention. From his perspective, nothing appeared amiss, but within his mind, a tempestuous wave surged.

Given his role as the guardian of the martial library, he possessed intimate knowledge of its contents. In his recollection, that particular corner had been bare. The sudden appearance of these items was undoubtedly abnormal.

The brilliance in his eyes intensified, and he slowly uttered three words, "illusionist techniques."

Chapter 371

As those two words escaped the old man's lips, Zhou

Yi instantly realized that his presence had been

exposed. His frustration welled up within, for he

couldn't fathom how the old man had managed to unravel his concealment.

At this moment, what he was employing wasn't merely a simple illusion. Around him, there was also the ethereal power formed by the combination of the Cloud Mist Technique and the illusion technique.

With the integration of these elements, his self-assurance was unwavering.Unless facing a venerable possessing the gift of cloud and mist, he believed no one could unveil the enigma of his illusory craft.

It was precisely due to his adept combination of misty energy, the art of illusion, that Zhou Yi had the courage to venture into this place.

Yet, to his disbelief, the old man had discerned his presence with just a single glance. This outcome filled him with both chilling astonishment and deep frustration.

Could it be that the Venerable before him possessed the Cloud Mist talent? If that were the case, his luck was truly abysmal. Yet, now that he had been unequivocally singled out, Zhou Yi had no intention of remaining rooted in place.

With a slight movement, the space before him instantly warped. His figure shot toward the door like lightning.

In that instant, he had maximized his speed. However, just as he was about to burst through the door, his advancing body abruptly halted. His feet exerted a slight force, and he quickly retreated.

Simultaneously, the old man sprang into action too. His speed was unbelievably astonishing, managing to block the doorway before Zhou Yi could. Pressed tightly against the back wall, Zhou Yi couldn't help but curse inwardly.

He had attempted it before coming here, knowing full well that this tower was exceedingly mystical.Even with his full-powered strikes, he couldn't breach it. Under the watchful gaze of the old man, his only means of escape was the not-so-spacious door. However, as he looked at the old man's grim expression, Zhou Yi's heart sank.

"What a formidable illusionist techniques," the old man's voice was deep and resonant. "If it weren't for my thorough familiarity with the environment here, you might have actually slipped past me."

Zhou Yi's momentary confusion gave way to a growing sense of frustration, deepening within him. At this juncture, the truth dawned upon him — it wasn't his illusion art that had faltered, but rather his adversary's intimate knowledge of the surroundings. This knowledge extended to the placement of every object, as if etched clearly in their memory.

With a soft sigh, Zhou Yi inwardly lamented his misfortune. However, his eyes were scanning the surroundings, seemingly searching for an avenue of escape.

The old man snorted lightly, saying, "You don't need to look around. Other than the door behind me, you have no way out here."

Zhou Yi retracted his gaze and altered his tone, speaking in a slightly hoarse voice, "May I inquire about your esteemed name?"

The old man smiled arrogantly, responding, "I am Zhuo Shengfeng."

Zhou Yi's eyes narrowed as he said, "So, you're Zhuo Shengfeng. I never expected that you would remain secluded here for so many years without appearing. Your patience is quite admirable."

While he spoke, he privately wondered about Zhuo Shengfeng's origins. Judging from his demeanor, he seemed to be of considerable standing.

Zhuo Shengfeng gave Zhou Yi a cold glance and said, "I secluded myself to further my cultivation. Since you've heard my name, you should surrender obediently."

Zhou Yi shook his head slightly, crouching down a bit. His eyes squinted, exuding a fierce aura akin to a wounded wild beast.

This aura rushed forth, causing Zhuo Shengfeng's brow to furrow deeply. He let out a cold snort and suddenly asked, "Do you truly wish to fight me?"

Zhou Yi's heart stirred. "Does Senior Zhuo intend to let me go?"

"That's correct. I can spare you, but you must provide an explanation," Zhuo Shengfeng slowly stated.

Zhou Yi was greatly intrigued. The pressure on him began to diminish. Given the Venerable's identity, his promise indeed carried a certain level of credibility.

After a brief hesitation, Zhou Yi asked in a deep voice, "What kind of explanation do you seek?"

Zhuo Shengfeng stared at him deeply and enunciated each word, "How did you manage to conceal your entry into this place from me?"

Zhou Yi felt relieved. No wonder this old man hesitated to take action despite detecting him earlier. It turned out he harbored such concerns. If Zhou Yi managed to deceive him once to enter this place, he could do so again, even a third time. Even though nothing was lost this time, , it might not be the same in the future. Moreover, the adjacent area held divine weapons. From any angle, Zhuo Shengfeng needed to know how Zhou Yi entered.

With a bitter smile, Zhou Yi shook his head helplessly and said, "I'm sorry, I cannot tell you."

There was no expression on Zhuo Shengfeng's face; he seemed to have anticipated this response. Slowly, he extended his hand. As he did so, the surrounding air appeared to freeze. Despite the distance, Zhou Yi sensed an immense pressure encompassing him. His body felt as though it was firmly restrained.

Aghast, Zhou Yi realized that though he had encountered a few Venerables during his time in the Tianchi Sect, even Li Mingxuan only held the thought of giving him a lesson and didn't exert full force. However, Zhuo Shengfeng was different.

He was already using his full strength, Under the pressure of his true energy, the power of confinement like a colossal mountain, a manifestation of prowess at the level of a Venerable. This was an overwhelming force.

This was the true strength of a Venerable, an overwhelming force. When facing Jin Zhanyi's power of confinement, Zhou Yi could still engage in a head-on fight, using the formidable cutting power of the Metal element to create a path through, breaking apart the power of confinement completely.

Yet, when confronted with Zhuo Shengfeng's power, Zhou Yi abandoned such thoughts.

Unless he had the Grand Guandao in hand, he would never attempt to meet this force head-on and seek a path to his own demise.

With a swift twist of his wrist, a sinister Forked Sword materialized in his hand. The instant this eerie weapon emerged, Zhou Yi noticed a subtle shift in Zhuo Shengfeng's gaze. It was as if his eyes had momentarily narrowed, accompanied by a trace of annoyance. Strangely, this alteration in his expression seemed to ripple through the very fabric of the surroundings, affecting even the power of confinement.

Although Zhou Yi couldn't comprehend why Zhuo Shengfeng suddenly displayed such an obvious reaction, this was undoubtedly a splendid opportunity. The Forked Sword in his hand trembled, and three brilliant black sword Flowers danced through the air. These three sword Flowers seemed to possess tangible substance as they thrust forward, precisely striking the weakest points of the power of confinement

Zhuo Shengfeng's complexion slightly changed. He even revealed a hint of surprise in his eyes. Although the person before him clearly hadn't reached the level of a Venerable, his three strikes had all hit the thinnest points of the power of confinement around them. A thought flashed through Zhuo Shengfeng's mind: perhaps this person's cultivation had already reached the Three Flowers realm Peak.

Letting out a cold snort, Zhuo Shengfeng tightened his wrist, causing the remote power of confinement to intensify and converge toward the center. It was like casting a fishing net into the sea and then drawing it in, allowing the water to escape while trapping the fish within.

Since the restraining force had changed, the three strikes Zhou Yi had launched became futile. Apart from those three sword flowers colliding with the power of confinement and creating intense sparks, they had no further effect.

Although Zhuo Shengfeng's face appeared expressionless, his gaze remained locked onto Zhou Yi. He was not concerned that this person might escape his grasp; however, he was aware of the terrifying rule of the Yellow Springs Gate. If he couldn't capture this person alive and extract the method of how he infiltrated, even if he tore him apart a thousand times, it wouldn't be worth the cost.

However, just as it seemed this person was completely trapped by the power of confinement, an ominous sign suddenly emerged from Zhuo Shengfeng. Zhou Yi's body swayed slightly, like a fallen leaf swaying in the wind. Following that, he transformed into a gust of wind, flowing out through the gaps in the power of confinement net.

Zhuo Shengfeng's expression subtly shifted. His single strike seemed straightforward, yet it held his full power, utilizing every ounce of his strength. However, he never anticipated that his opponent's footwork would be so uncanny, displaying an exceptional mastery of manipulating the essence of wind. This mastery allowed them to evade Zhuo Shengfeng's strike entirely.

With a renewed glint in his eyes, Zhuo Shengfeng extended both hands simultaneously.

However, just as he was about to grasp his target, his expression suddenly changed. His eyes flared with boundless fury. The moment Zhou Yi broke free from the constraints, he darted like a soaring bird towards a bookshelf. Without sparing a glance, he seized a wooden box from the shelf and swiftly flung it. The box spun like a wheel of wind and fire, hurtling towards Zhuo Shengfeng.

Every book inside those boxes was a precious treasure. As the guardian of the martial library, if these books were destroyed, it would deal a fatal blow to his reputation.

His hands moved with gentle precision. Although Zhou Yi rained down the wooden boxes like a cascade of raindrops, under Zhuo Shengfeng's swift and agile palms, each box was deftly guided to a corner of the room. Even the hidden force Zhou Yi had exerted on the wooden boxes was effortlessly nullified by Zhuo Shengfeng's movements.

This level of control was so profound that even Zhou Yi had to admit defeat.

However, there were simply too many wooden boxes in the room, and Zhou Yi's chosen angles of attack were exceedingly cunning. Within each wooden box lay a reservoir of formidable true energy. Even a single misjudgment by Zhuo Shengfeng could result in the box shattering into pieces, inevitably leading to the destruction of the books contained within

After a moment, Zhuo Shengfeng was forced to shift his position, his footsteps moving him as he lightly pushed a few boxes against the wall.

Yet, in that brief instant, Zhou Yi had already dashed out of the room.

Glacial light gleamed in Zhuo Shengfeng's eyes, his demeanor as if he had foreseen this moment. Swiftly turning around, he extended his hand toward the empty space, making a grasping motion towards Zhou Yi.

Chapter 372

The books within this chamber were incredibly precious; even Zhuo Shengfeng would find it difficult to bear if even a single volume were truly damaged.

Thus, he intentionally stepped aside, creating a path for the intruder to escape. Yet, he held an unwavering confidence that even if the intruder managed to flee the room, he would undoubtedly be able to intercept them halfway.

At this moment, his twin claws brimmed with ture energy, unleashed with unstoppable force. Zhou Yi's mid-air form momentarily froze, as if invisible hands had tightly bound him in their grasp. Yet, he remained unfazed. With a swift twist of his wrist, two wooden boxes whirled and flew behind him.

A frosty smile on Zhuo Shengfeng's face abruptly solidified. A mélange of anger surged within him; it turned out that this individual, upon leaving, had audaciously taken away two hidden manuals. It was truly an act of audacity beyond measure.

He released one hand, gesturing in the void, and deftly moved the two wooden boxes to a corner. But in the next instant, his vision blurred again as another pair of wooden boxes came hurtling towards him like a barrage."

Zhuo Shengfeng's complexion turned ashen. Just how many manuals had this person taken with them? He secretly vowed that once he captured this individual alive ,he would make sure this person could neither seek survival nor find release in death.

With a sweep of his wrist, a gentle force diverted the trajectory of the two wooden boxes. Yet, this time he was prepared, suspecting that the intruder's cache of manuals couldn't be limited to just four. A glint of darkness flickered in the corner of his eye, confirming his suspicion.

However, as he extended his hand this time, a sudden realization dawned upon him—something was amiss. What rapidly grew larger in his eyes wasn't anything like a wooden box; it was a Forked Sword.

The Forked Sword emerged silently, akin to a venomous serpent lurking in the shadows. It unleashed its strike at the very last moment, like a snake unveiling its fangs, lunging viciously towards him.

Zhuo Shengfeng's heart skipped a beat. From this one strike, he sensed an immense power—a sharpness so keen that it almost made him feel the specter of death. Ever since his ascension to the realm of a venerable, he hadn't experienced such a sensation in over a hundred years of secluded cultivation.

His eyes darkened abruptly, and a white light materialized above his right hand, coalescing into a longsword. With a swift flick of the sword's tip, it emitted a crisp "clang" as it deflected the Forked Sword, resembling a snake, aside.

However, there was no trace of joy in Zhuo Shengfeng's heart. To have to employ a weapon against someone who wasn't even a venerable was a blow to his pride. Nevertheless, upon the sudden appearance of the Forked Sword, an intense sense of danger welled up within him. He almost instinctively wielded his weapon.

Just as he deflected the Forked Sword, at that very moment, Zhou Yi, who had been trapped in front, suddenly exerted force. Capitalizing on Zhuo Shengfeng's focus on the Forked Sword, Zhou Yi's qi surged ferociously, disrupting the power of confinement. He burst through like a soaring arrow, dashing out through another gate.

Zhuo Shengfeng snorted coldly, his figure trembling as he swiftly pursued.

As he left the room, a brief glance at the Forked Sword. He couldn't fathom why he had suddenly become so cautious toward this seemingly inconspicuous weapon. It was as if this object held a greater terror than the black-clad assailant himself.

Before his ascension to the venerable rank, he had crossed swords with Forked Sword assassins from the Yellow Springs Gate, yet he had never experienced a sensation quite like this.

At the same time, he found the actions of the black-clothed person ahead difficult to comprehend. In his memory, the Forked Sword was considered the second life for the Forked Sword Assassins.

Sword with the person, sword lost, this principle was practically ingrained in the bones of these assassins. But in the critical moment, the other party unhesitatingly used this sword as a hidden weapon and threw it out. This action was equally beyond his expectations.

However, in this moment, he had no time for such contemplation. Within the flicker of shadows, they vanished from the room.

Once they had all departed, the Forked Sword on the ground unexpectedly stirred. Transforming into a pool of water, it rapidly flowed toward the room's exit. Tracing dim corners, it vanished within the room.

The two individuals, one leading and one following, dashed out like arrows released from a bowstring. In an instant, they went from the fifth floor to the first, and then swiftly rushed out through an entrance of a particular tall tower.

The tower possessed twelve entrances. Though night had fallen, disciples of the ninth and eighth layers of internal energy stood guard at each entrance. Their gazes were fixed ahead, scrutinizing the surroundings. Suddenly, a strange sensation behind them jolted them. Before they could react, a group of four from one entrance felt a slight tightening around their necks. Swift as clouds and mist, they were propelled out from behind, letting out startled cries.

Before the cries even fully escaped their lips, they felt a gentle push on their backs, and then they stood steady.

Throughout the entire sequence, they remained oblivious to what had occurred. In the span of an eye-blink, they had vacated their original positions and found themselves standing in the middle of the tower.

Soon after, a sharp and resounding howl echoed from outside the tower.

This resolute cry pierced the silent night, igniting a commotion throughout the entire Lingxiao Treasure Hall.

Beneath Jin Zhanyi's rear end, it was as if springs had been installed, propelling him out of the room in an instant. He cast a glance toward Zhou Yi's room.

There, a rhythmic sonic break pierced the air, almost like mechanical precision.

Having witnessed Zhou Yi's display of the first few forms of the "Thirty-Six Forms of Mountain-Crushing" last night, even with his eyes closed, Jin Zhanyi knew that the young adept within the room was seamlessly transitioning from the first to the twenty-third form.

However, during this practice session, Zhou Yi refrained from utilizing his internal energy. He was simply flowing through these moves, connecting them in a continuous sequence. From the first form to the twenty-third, and then circling back to the first—a ceaseless cycle that seemed unending.

Though Jin Zhanyi didn't comprehend the benefits of such a practice, at their level of cultivation, everyone had specialized methods tailored to their own needs. Hence, Jin Zhanyi never intended to disturb Zhou Yi's training.

Yet, upon hearing the warning-like long howl, he hesitated momentarily before addressing Zhou Yi, "Brother Zhou."

The sounds of fists and feet ceased from within, followed by Zhou Yi's displeased voice, "Brother Jin, what is it?"

Jin Zhanyi clearly detected the dissatisfaction in that voice. It was a natural reaction for anyone to express when interrupted during their cultivation. He even believed that if it weren't for his words, Zhou Yi might have erupted and taken action on the spot.

With a wry smile, Jin Zhanyi said, "Brother Zhou, someone has invaded our Lingxiao Treasure Hall. Venerable Zhuo has gone in pursuit. Are you interested in joining the chase?"

Without hesitation, Zhou Yi's voice responded, " I'm not interested."

With that, the sounds of fists and feet resumed from within—the clear indication that Zhou Yi had recommenced his practice, resolutely ignoring external affairs.

Jin Zhanyi shook his head slightly, leaping into the air. Mid-flight, he took a stride, and the space around him rapidly compressed before his eyes. As he landed, he had already covered dozens of yards from his starting point.

However, Jin Zhanyi was unaware that even though the person in the room was indeed Zhou Yi, the expression on this Zhou Yi's face was unnaturally stiff.

After some time had passed, a pool of water flowed out from beneath the door, seeping into the room and converging toward Zhou Yi. He halted his movements, lowering his gaze. Suddenly, he noticed that one of his feet was missing half of its length. The water gathered around the gap, completing his foot's form.

Raising his head, Zhou Yi's eyes sparkled with a radiance akin to a small sun's glow.

On the other side of the tower, both Qilian Twin Devils stood up almost simultaneously. Their eyes turned towards the source of the long howl, radiating an eager and excited gleam.

The voice of another elderly figure resonated abruptly, "What are you planning to do? Don't forget, this is the Lingxiao Treasure Hall, not our sect realm. Don't cause unnecessary trouble."

Qilian Twin Devils exchanged glances, reluctantly sitting back down.

The big Devil's voice grew somber, "Master, judging by this howl, it seems someone is requesting aid."

Though different sects had varying signals for requesting help, most were similar in nature.

The elderly figure nodded slowly, "Indeed, this is Lingxiao Treasure Hall Hall's plea for help and warning howl. Moreover, the one emitting this howl is a venerable."

"A venerable?" Qilian Twin Devils exchanged a glance, both detecting astonishment in each other's eyes.

Even a venerable had to resort to a plea for assistance—a notion almost inconceivable.

The elderly figure furrowed his brows, softly reciting several names. Yet, the names were quickly crossed out.

While these individuals had been renowned masters in their heyday hundreds of years ago, the elderly figure remained certain that they would never come to provoke the Lingxiao Treasure Hall.

After a prolonged silence, the elderly figure sighed deeply, muttering, "Disturbances brewing in the

Western realm... Could it be the venerables of the West?"

Following Zhuo Shengfeng's resonating howl, a sensation of upheaval spread across the tower.

Although no one knew the exact number of venerable-level powerhouses within Lingxiao Treasure Hall, these old-timers more or less recognized Zhuo Shengfeng's voice.

Because he was the guardian of the martial library, even though his cultivation might not be among the most advanced among these experts, his responsibility was undeniably the most crucial.

In a matter of moments, several figures flashed before the martial library gates, entering the martial library.

Upon witnessing the chaotic state of the library, the expressions on their faces turned sour.

Two individuals exchanged a glance, wordlessly departing.

Others opened a different set of doors containing divine weapons. Their collective sigh of relief indicated that at least the divine weapons had remained unharmed.

During the subsequent cleanup, they also found that although most of the wooden boxes had fallen to the ground, the books inside them remained intact. This could be considered a fortunate turn of events amidst the unfortunate circumstances.

However, despite this, their expressions remained grim. The audacity to target the Lingxiao Treasure Hall's martial library was simply unacceptable.

Their gazes turned towards a certain direction, where three venerables had set out to chase. The intruder should have no chance of escape now.

Chapter 373

The moonlight scattered on the earth like snow, as if casting a layer of white silver frost over the land. Two figures swiftly moved beneath this pristine moonlight. Their speed had reached an unimaginable level.

The figure ahead was shrouded in a thick mist, as if rolling through the air. With each tumble, it covered dozens of yards. Behind him, an old man's footsteps glided on the ground like flowing water, appearing slow but maintaining a steady and unrelenting pace.

Several more figures followed closely behind them. Though their speeds were consistent, no one could catch up to the leading pair, and similarly, no one could shake off their pursuit.

Zhuo Shengfeng's heart was filled with shock and anger. This person's speed far surpassed his estimations, and what was even more astonishing was the increasingly dense mist surrounding the figure.

Ever since they started the chase, the person ahead was enveloped in such a dense mist. It was beneath this shroud of mist that he couldn't even discern which technique his pursuer was using to escape. Clearly, these dense mists had an incredibly powerful masking effect.

Zhuo Shengfeng even felt that this person could deceive him and silently infiltrate the martial library. It was undoubtedly connected to these mists.

If the running Zhou Yi knew what was on Zhuo Shengfeng's mind, he would surely burst into laughter.

In fact, at this moment, Zhou Yi's mood was equally joyful. Once he was beyond the city limits of the

Lingxiao Treasure Hall, his spirits immediately lifted. Inside the Tower of Heaven, the thought of the numerous experts from the Lingxiao Treasure Hall weighed on Zhou Yi's heart like a massive stone. However, at this moment, having departed from that vicinity, he felt notably different.

After he enveloped himself with a layer of mist energy and immediately utilized the Wind-Style "Two-Point, One-Line" technique to flee towards the distance, he was giving his all this time. Under his continuous execution, this powerful movement technique had been pushed to its utmost potential.

Until today, he had never attempted to continuously employ this technique for an extended period. But now that he was doing it, he felt an impulse as if he could transform into the wind at any moment.

Vaguely, he seemed to grasp the pulse of the wind. The formidable power of the wind and mist surged towards his body, completely engulfing him. At this point, even if there was no one chasing him, Zhou Yi wouldn't stop.

In this manner, he ran for a distance unknown. Suddenly, he sensed the absorption speed of the mist decreasing rapidly. He was slightly taken aback. Though his speed hadn't lessened, he raised his head and glanced around. The moon on the horizon had vanished, and the entire sky seemed incredibly dark.

He realized that dawn was approaching. The period just before the appearance of morning sunlight was undoubtedly the darkest.

With this thought, his expression changed slightly. The power of wind and mist was most formidable during the night. Once daybreak arrived, although it didn't greatly affect wind-based power, it presented significant obstacles to utilizing mist and cloud power.

His ears twitched slightly, capturing the sounds from behind. He couldn't help but smile wryly. Among the group closely following him, apart from his old friend Jin Zhanyi, there were unexpectedly three venerables. He cursed silently. He hadn't set the martial library on fire, yet these people still insisted on pursuing him relentlessly, It was truly speechless..

Surveying his surroundings, even though he stood on a plain, scattered clumps of low trees were visible at any moment. These low trees were like green ornaments on the vast plain, brimming with vitality.

Taking a deep breath, Zhou Yi suddenly changed direction and charged towards the nearest patch of greenery. With his incredible speed, it was almost a matter of a few breaths before he entered the midst of the low trees.

As he entered the dense woods, his internal energy rapidly circulated, and the power of the mist no longer absorbed into his body but burst forth in an instant. The potent misty energy filled the entire space, quickly enveloping this area of relatively small woods.

In the transition from the end of the night to the impending dawn, the air was already saturated with moisture. he cloud and mist energy acted as a catalyst, absorbing and transforming all the moisture in the air into a massive fog.

Zhuo Shengfeng inwardly cursed as he realized the situation. Although he hadn't caught up to his target and hadn't encountered this cloud and mist, as someone who had lived for hundreds of years, he was naturally knowledgeable. When the mist began to spread, he knew that this time, he might never be able to track down his target again.

Indeed, as soon as he entered the grove, he completely lost any sense of his target. This fog did possess formidable concealment properties. Trying to continue pinpointing his target's whereabouts within this mist had become beyond his capability.

Suddenly, a familiar voice came from outside the woods. "Senior Uncle Zhuo, did you catch up?"

Zhuo Shengfeng's heart leaped in joy, hastily replying, "Jin, don't come in. The fog here is strangely effective. You and the other two seniors stay outside and guard. Today, we must capture this person."

Jin Zhanbei immediately responded with a loud confirmation. He and the other two venerables who had pursued closely took up positions guarding the three directions around the grove.

The power of the Lingxiao Treasure Hall was incredibly strong. As the sun rose, nearly ten more people arrived at the scene. Although none of them were venerable-level experts, they were all at the Innate Realm or the One-line Heaven Realm.

The group scoured the dense forest for half a day, even cutting down all the low trees, but in the end, they found nothing. Despite their strong unwillingness to accept it, they ultimately had to admit that the enigmatic individual was no longer present.

After leaving the grove, the faces of everyone were rather unsightly.

The first two venerables who pursued were distinctive in appearance. One was broad-shouldered and tall, solid like a wall. The other was somewhat slender but much better off than Zhuo Shengfeng.

Although the venerables of the Lingxiao Treasure Hall generally withdrew from worldly matters and wouldn't get involved, every five years, two venerables took turns guarding the tower. If significant events occurred outside, they would intervene to coordinate.

These were the duty-bound venerables of the Lingxiao Treasure Hall.

These two were the current duty-bound venerables for this five-year term. The tall one was named Gao Weiliang, while the slightly leaner one was named Du Wenbin. Though their fame wasn't pronounced at the moment, a hundred years ago, they enjoyed considerable renown and were among the top-notch experts in Da Shen,and they were no less formidable than Jin Zhanyi is today The sands of time, however, had passed, and after a hundred years, they had retreated from the limelight.

After exchanging glances, their faces all showed frustration, and no one's expression was pleasant.

Lingxiao Treasure Hall to have such formidable strength and still let the individual escape was undoubtedly like getting slapped in the face, leaving them with a burning sensation on their cheeks.

"Senior Zhuo, what did that person look like and what cultivation technique did they use?" Gao Weiliang asked in a deep voice.

Zhuo Shengfeng's face turned ashen as he replied, "This person had a black cloth covering their face. Although I didn't see it myself, I can be certain that this person is undoubtedly from the Yellow Springs Gate."

The expressions of Jin Zhanyi and the others underwent subtle changes.

Du Wenbin hesitated before saying, "Senior Zhuo, we all know that although the Yellow Springs Gate is the number one assassin sect in the world, they have never targeted venerables for assassination. Moreover, we've never heard of them infiltrating the major sects."

While the Yellow Springs Gate was powerful, they also couldn't afford to offend all the sects in the world. They couldn't assassinate venerables, nor enter the inner sects of the major sects. This had become an accepted rule. If the Yellow Springs Gate truly acted recklessly, it would surely incite panic and hostility from all the major sects. If all the sects were to put aside their differences and unite, even if the Yellow Springs Gate remained hidden in the shadows, they would likely suffer the fate of being wiped out.

Zhuo Shengfeng snorted coldly and said, "This person's illusion has reached an extraordinary level. If I hadn't remembered the arrangement in the martial library, I would have been deceived by him as well." He paused, his face solemn as a mountain, and continued, "I feel ashamed. I didn't even know how this person entered the martial library. This level of illusion is undoubtedly derived from the authentic techniques of the Yellow Springs Gate. There can't be a second source."

Gao Weiliang's expression shifted slightly, and he asked, "He deceived even you with his illusion?"

Saying this, he turned his head to glance around.

Zhuo Shengfeng sighed wryly, "Junior Gao, we've cut down all the trees. Even if his illusion is powerful, there's no possibility of hiding."

Gao Weiliang withdrew his gaze, but a hint of reluctance remained in his eyes.

Zhuo Shengfeng continued, "This person not only excels at illusions but also uses a forked sword, a signature weapon of the Yellow Springs Gate." He paused and added, "When he escaped, I managed to retain his forked sword. It should be in the martial library."

Gao Weiliang blinked and said, "Senior Zhuo, I just came out of the martial library. Although I didn't search carefully, I don't recall seeing any forked sword."

Although the martial library was in disarray, a forked sword would be such a conspicuous target that it couldn't be overlooked. Zhuo Shengfeng's eyes gleamed, and he said, "Impossible. I personally knocked down that forked sword, right in the library."

Gao Weiliang hesitated for a moment and suggested, "In that case, let's go back and check again."

The group hurriedly returned, but when Zhuo Shengfeng learned that the forked sword indeed couldn't be found in the martial library, his expression became unpredictable. Even sparks seemed to flicker in his eyes.

The matter was indeed of great significance. Not only had the three venerables lost track of the person, but they also remained clueless about how he entered the martial library. Zhuo Shengfeng's adamant insistence that the forked sword was in the martial library added to the mystique. The sword had inexplicably vanished without a trace, leaving everyone baffled.

A day later, the martial library on the fifth floor was transferred to the tenth floor of the tower. Not only were guards stationed outside the entrance, but each library and weapon storage area also had a venerable overseeing them.

In the Lingxiao Treasure Hall, an atmosphere of tension and alarm spread as if facing a formidable enemy.

Chapter 374

The dawn's light gradually appeared, and the sun remained concealed behind the peaks, casting a faint glow around them. The soft light spread through the pale blue sky, and the sky slowly revealed its golden morning hues.

As Zhou Yi returned to the courtyard of the Lingxiao Treasure Hall, the sun was already shining brightly. Despite the atmosphere within the Lingxiao Treasure Hall being charged due to the resounding call of Zhuo Shengfeng, he silently retreated to his room.

Inside the room, another Zhou Yi was diligently practicing the "Thirty-Six Forms of Mountain-Crushing." From the first form to the twenty-third, he repeated the motions incessantly, showing no sign of stopping.

Observing this scene, an unusual thought surfaced in Zhou Yi's mind. For the first time, he was purely observing "himself" practicing the Thirty-Six Forms of Mountain-Crushing an outsider's perspective.

This set of metal-element martial arts appeared to be filled with flaws, as if a simple wave of the hand could break the entire set of techniques. He shook his head slightly and sighed, knowing that this was because when using this set of techniques, there was no synergy with Metal Element true qi. The lack of true qi or inner energy coordination was precisely what gave rise to the feeling of a superficial display.

However, upon further reflection, Zhou Yi chuckled to himself. Not only this set of metal-element martial arts, but any martial arts would become mere forms if not paired with the corresponding true qi. The real power of martial techniques stemmed from the synergy between the technique and the user's energy.

He shook his head again and muttered, "Brerbo, I'm back."

The Zhou Yi who had been performing the dance-like routine suddenly came to a halt, and a strange fluctuation rippled through him. Then, Zhou Yi disappeared, transforming into Brerbo.

As Zhou Yi looked at him, his eyes were filled with envy. If only he had such a miraculous ability, things would undoubtedly be much more convenient for him.However, the thought of Brerbo's inhuman identity sent shivers down Zhou Yi's spine. This notion seemed to grow wings and vanished from his mind in an instant.

"Brerbo, did you succeed?" Zhou Yi inquired.

Brerbo didn't answer verbally. Instead, he extended his right hand and directly detached his left wrist, tossing it to Zhou Yi.

As he caught the bloodless severed hand, the muscles on Zhou Yi's face involuntarily twitched. He sighed wryly and placed it on the table.

The left hand immediately began to dissolve. Upon recongealing, it transformed into a divine tome.

A faint gleam appeared in Zhou Yi's eyes. He extended his hand to pick up the book, directly flipping to the twenty-fourth page.

However, a strange expression immediately crossed his face. On this page, although it was still one of the Thirty-Six Forms of Mountain-Crushing, it wasn't the twenty-fourth form but rather the fourteenth form.

He looked up in astonishment, gazing at Brerbo expressionlessly. A realization dawned upon him, and he casually flipped to the first page.

His face displayed a mix of laughter and tears. On this page, indeed, was the first page of the Wind,Cloud and Mist Manual.

He shook his head wordlessly, combining the contents of two completely different systems of divine

Manuals into a single book. Perhaps only Brerbo would do something like this.

"I'm leaving."

Seemingly unaffected by Zhou Yi's puzzled expression, Brerbo's calm voice resounded.

"Where are you going?" Zhou Yi asked in confusion.

"The treasure pig is still outside the city," Brerbo replied succinctly.

Zhou Yi sighed inwardly, truly not understanding why Brerbo and the treasure pig, two entirely different non-human entities, were so close. But since Brerbo was with the treasure pig, the little fellow must be safe and sound.

His gaze then fell on Brerbo's severed hand, and he glanced at the manual in his hand. A hint of hesitation appeared on Zhou Yi's face.

Brerbo extended his hand, and his hand slowly regrew from the broken part, instantly restoring to its normal state.

Zhou Yi opened his mouth, then finally waved his hand gently and said with a bitter smile, "Go on, take care."

Brerbo reached the doorway, seeming to pause for a moment before saying, "You too." With that, his entire form dissolved and vanished through the crack in the door, as if he had turned into flowing water.

Zhou Yi stared at the spot where he had disappeared, dumbfounded. After a moment, he pinched his arm, feeling the pain, indicating that he wasn't daydreaming.

However, considering Brerbo's personality, it was truly astonishing that he would say such words.

Shaking his head to dismiss the thought, Zhou Yi reopened the divine path manual in his hand.

The first page of this book is the "Wind,Cloud and Mist Manual," and its immense power is something Zhou Yi deeply understands. He had relied on the formidable concealing abilities of the Cloud Mist power to escape from the noses of those venerables.

Especially within the dwarf forest, after severing the connection to Zhuo Shengfeng's sensing, he immediately employed the Earth-Tunnelling Technique to distance himself.

Of course, while employing the Earth-Tunnelling Technique, he shrouded himself with a layer of Cloud Mist power, fully concealing his aura.

If not for that, attempting to escape under the joint pursuit of the three venerables would undoubtedly be a foolish and unrealistic idea

This showcased the incredible potency of the Cloud Mist power. Particularly for someone like Zhou Yi who had yet to reach the venerable stage, it was undoubtedly the first choice for preserving his life.

However, at this moment, Zhou Yi wasn't studying the Cloud Mist power. Instead, he directly turned to the thirty-fourth page.

Sure enough, there was the illustration of the twenty-fourth stance of the "Thirty-Six Forms of Mountain-Crushing."

Zhou Yi's eyes immediately lit up. A strand of Metal energy from his hand flowed into the manual. After a moment, through a mysterious method, Zhou Yi seemed to enter a strange space.

In this realm, there were boundless expanses in all directions, Moreover, this space was filled with a unique pressure that was both sharp and keen.

This was the power of the Metal element, the manifestation of the ultimate potency of the Metal element's power.

In the next moment, Zhou Yi's hand held a terrifying large Guandao.

The entire blade exuded a mystical power, especially the tip of the blade, which radiated brilliance, akin to a small sun.

Zhou Yi's heart was filled with doubt. He had borrowed the original copy of the "Thirty-Six Forms of Mountain-Crushing" before, but in that world, the Guandao certainly didn't possess such an exaggerated power.

He had a strange thought in his mind. Could it be that within the manual transformed by Brerbo, the power of this Guandao had increased tenfold?

Shaking his head to dispel such notions, Zhou Yi let go of distractions and began to move his body. He started from the first stance, gradually executing each one until the twenty-third stance.

Throughout this process, Zhou Yi didn't pause in the slightest. The sequence of movements flowed like water, executed seamlessly from one stance to the next. However, every time he reached the twenty-third stance, he felt a sense of powerlessness. Despite his momentum reaching its pinnacle, executing the twenty-fourth stance was an impossibility.

Yet, Zhou Yi wasn't discouraged. In this peculiar space, he continued to swing his guandao, one stance after another, with an unyielding determination. He seemed to possess an immensely resolute heart, unwavering despite numerous failures.

Here, there was no wind, no air, no sunlight—only boundless emptiness. The only sound that broke the silence was the noise generated by the swinging of the large Guandao. If Zhou Yi ceased his practice, this place would fall into complete stillness, devoid of any sound.

In such an environment, those lacking strong determination would quickly break down. But for those with steadfast willpower, this environment without any interference was the perfect place for cultivation.

He couldn't ascertain how much time had passed. In Zhou Yi's perception, no matter how long he practiced, it seemed to be only a moment.

Even though Zhou Yi had immersed himself in this peculiar method of cultivation, it didn't mean he was completely unaware of the outside world.

A peculiar sensation welled up in his heart, prompting Zhou Yi to promptly exit this extraordinary state without hesitation.

His ears twitched slightly, and Zhou Yi immediately heard the footsteps of Jin Zhanyi. Of course, this was because Jin Zhanyi wasn't making any effort to conceal his footsteps. If Jin Zhanyi had been stealthily approaching, even Zhou Yi wouldn't confidently claim to easily detect his presence.

Glancing at the manual in his hand, Zhou Yi's eyes reflected a tinge of surprise. He realized that at some point, the manual had become scorching hot, resembling the temperature of flames. However, this heat couldn't harm Zhou Yi, as he had already manifested the Fire Flower within himself. Thus, while he was wholeheartedly engrossed in the manual, he hadn't noticed the change.

Pausing for a moment, Zhou Yi gently rubbed the manual with his hand. As he did so, the manual seemed to transform like soft clay, forming a round ball with a metallic luster. .

Openly, Zhou Yi held this metallic-colored sphere in his hand. He firmly believed that no one could deduce that this was, in fact, a divine path manual hidden within it. Surveying the room with a complete sweep of his gaze, he found no possibility of exposure.

Taking a deep breath, Zhou Yi's heart settled. As he completed these actions, a composed knocking sounded at the door.

Deliberately stalling for a moment, Zhou Yi responded with a displeased tone, "Brother Jin, come in."

Waving his hand, an invisible force swung the tightly closed door open. As the door swung open, Zhou Yi caught sight of the light outside, but to his surprise, it was not the morning light breaking through. Instead, it was the twilight glow of the setting sun.

He instantly understood that he had been practicing within the room for an entire day. Outside the door indeed stood Jin Zhanyi, but in contrast to before, his face now held a peculiar expression.

Zhou Yi's heart skipped a beat, and a horrifying thought flashed through his mind: Could it be that Jin Zhanyi had figured it out?

Yet, the words that Jin Zhanyi spoke next completely dispelled this notion from his mind.

Chapter 375

Jin Zhany let out a long sigh and said, "Brother Zhou, there's something I need to apologize for."

Zhou Yi looked up and replied, "Please,Brother Jin, go ahead."

Jin Zhanyi's face showed a hint of embarrassment as he said, "Zhou Brother, an unexpected incident occurred in our Lingxiao Treasure Hall last night."

Confusion crossed Zhou Yi's eyes as he asked, "What kind of incident?"

Jin Zhanyi sighed wryly. He had mentioned this to Zhou Yi before he left last night, but he understood that at that time, Zhou Yi was deeply engrossed in his unique cultivation method and probably didn't take his words to heart.

Of course, such a situation wasn't unusual; Jin Zhanyi had experienced it many times before, so he wasn't suspicious at all.

"Brother Zhou, last night someone infiltrated our Lingxiao Treasure Hall's martial library, seemingly attempting to steal the collection of books stored there," Jin Zhanyi said slowly.

Zhou Yi's face immediately changed, and he anxiously asked, "Brother Jin, was the 'Thirty-Six Forms of Mountain-Crushing' stolen?"

Jin Zhanyi waved his hand reassuringly and said, "Brother Zhou, please calm down. The original copy of the 'Thirty-Six Forms of Mountain-Crushing' is intact."

Zhou Yi's face relaxed at once as he sighed, "That's a relief."

Seeing Zhou Yi's expression, Jin Zhanyi couldn't help but smile wryly. He understood Zhou Yi's thought process— as long as that particular book was safe, the rest of the books wouldn't matter to him.

Shaking his head slightly, Jin Zhanyi continued with a serious tone, "Zhou Brother, due to this incident, the two venerables within the sect have discussed it and decided to temporarily close the martial library. As a result, Zhou Brother, you won't be able to access the original copies of the manuals for the time being."

Furrows appeared on Zhou Yi's brow, and his expression immediately turned serious.

Jin Zhanyi wore a helpless expression as he said, "Zhou Brother, once the martial library reopens in the future, I promise you'll have free access to the 'Thirty-Six Forms of Mountain-Crushing'."

After a moment, Zhou Yi let out a long breath and said, "Since the venerables of your sect have made this decision, I can only comply. I just hope that your sect can reopen the martial library as soon as possible."

Jin Zhanyi immediately patted his chest and assured, "Within a month, we will definitely reopen the martial library."

Zhou Yi nodded and seemed to suddenly remember something. He asked, "Brother Jin, who could possibly have the audacity to infiltrate your sect's martial library? Could it be that there's no one guarding outside the library?"

Jin Zhanyi's face reddened slightly. The martial library was of utmost importance to a sect, so how could it be left unguarded?There was always a powerful venerable stationed in the room outside the martial library.

However, no one had anticipated that the assassin from the Yellow Springs Gate would have perfected the art of illusionist techniques to such an extent. When he entered the martial library, not even Venerable Zhuo Shengfeng had detected any flaws. Fortunately, Venerable Zhuo Shengfeng's instincts led him to sense something amiss and he discovered the intruder's presence by chance. Otherwise, this incident would have been a major embarrassment.

But Jin Zhanyi couldn't reveal these details to Zhou Yi. He could only force a laugh and vaguely replied, "Brother Zhou , the person who intruded this time is actually not unfamiliar to you."

Zhou Yi's expression immediately shifted, and he hesitantly said, "The Deep Mountain Totem?"

Jin Zhanyi opened his mouth but felt somewhat helpless. However, considering the strained relationship between Zhou Yi and the Deep Mountain Totem, it wasn't surprising.

He waved his sleeve and said, "While the Deep Mountain Totem possesses formidable strength, they rarely leave the northwest region and are even less likely to come challenge our Lingxiao Treasure Hall."

Zhou Yi nodded and thought for a moment before asking, "Is it someone from the western region or the Yellow Springs Gate?"

Jin Zhanyi's tone turned serious as he replied, "It's the Yellow Springs Gate."

Zhou Yi furrowed his brows slightly and inquired, "How can you be so sure?"

"The technique employed by the intruder this time is clearly the Yellow Springs Gate's highly secret 'illusionist techniques.' Only those who have attained the level of a Forked Sword Assassin or higher could have learned this technique. Moreover..." Jin Zhanyi paused and then shifted the topic, "Based on all the evidence, it's undoubtedly one of the top experts from the Yellow Springs Gate."

He had originally wanted to mention that Venerable Zhuo Shengfeng vowed that he had taken away the intruder's Forked Sword, but the problem was that everyone had searched the room thoroughly, and not even a dagger was found, let alone a sword.

Naturally, this led to suspicions of an insider. Venerable Zhuo Shengfeng wouldn't lie about such a matter. As a result, the disciples responsible for cleaning and organizing the martial library were immediately under suspicion.

Those granted the honor of entering the martial library for cleaning were all core disciples of the Lingxiao Treasure Hall. Although there were no innate realm experts among them, there were several post-heaven realm disciples with peak internal energy cultivation.

The fact that an insider might be among these disciples was both astonishing and deeply distressing, considering their clean backgrounds and varying degrees of blood ties with previous venerables. It wouldn't be feasible to take drastic measures against them all without proper investigation. However, until the Forked Sword was found or Venerable Zhuo Shengfeng's statement changed, the futures of these disciples would be affected.

Of course, Jin Zhanyi couldn't possibly inform Zhou Yi about this matter either.

Zhou Yi's face was full of surprise, but his heart was genuinely relieved. When Jin Zhanyi had initially arrived, Zhou Yi appeared calm on the surface, yet he was still somewhat anxious deep down. Despite his confidence in his series of arrangements, the Lingxiao Treasure Hall was filled with experts, and who knew if someone might discern the underlying complexities.

If someone were to find any clues and trace them back to him, Zhou Yi didn't believe he could easily evade Zhuo Shengfeng and the others a second time.

"Jin Brother, now that you've determined it was the work of Yellow Springs Gate, how do you plan to handle this?" Zhou Yi asked.

"We will report to the sect master and seek his decision," Jin Zhanyi's expression wasn't pleasant.

Zhou Yi's heart skipped a beat, "For just the Yellow Springs Gate, do you really need the sect master to personally intervene? Can't you handle it?"

Jin Zhanyi hesitated for a moment, "Brother Zhou, you might not know this, but the Yellow Springs Ancestor of Yellow Springs Gate is a peer of our sect master. His strength is unfathomable, and without this level of power, the Yellow Springs Gate wouldn't have been so audacious and able to maintain their dominance in the world of assassins."

Zhou Yi nodded slightly, but honestly, he wasn't very interested in the negotiations between the two major factions.

Although shifting the blame to Yellow Springs Gate seemed a bit unfair, thinking about how Sima Yin had attempted to assassinate him for no apparent reason, he felt at ease.

Given that Yellow Springs Gate could try to assassinate him, causing them a bit of trouble could be seen as a form of retribution.

Simultaneously, both of them naturally veered away from the topic.

Jin Zhanyi certainly didn't want to say more, and Zhou Yi was eager to avoid it as well.

"Brother Zhou, the day after tomorrow is the showdown with Qilian Twin Devils. In the next two days, it's better for you to rest more. Perhaps during the battle, you might be able to perform exceptionally and break through your limits," Jin Zhanyi advised.

Zhou Yi sighed bitterly, "Thank you for your kind words,Brother Jin."

Jin Zhanyi put away his smile, "As the saying goes, 'know thyself, know thy enemy, and you will never be defeated.' Since Brother Zhou is new to the Da Shen, you probably don't know the background of Qilian Twin Devils."

Zhou Yi shook his head and genuinely asked, "I'm not aware, so I would appreciate it ifBrother Jin could enlighten me."

Jin Zhanyi's expression turned serious as he spoke, "Qilian Twin Devils became renowned two hundred years ago. They were orphaned and abandoned by their parents, but through fortunate circumstances, they entered a mystical realm of Qilian Mountain. From that point on, their reputation grew, and their path in martial arts took them further. They are ruthless in their methods and cultivate the path of demons, seeking breakthroughs through battles with formidable opponents. Over the past century, countless strong individuals have fallen to their hands, contributing to the Twin Demons' formidable reputation. But after they achieved the Three Flowers forty years ago, they naturally went into seclusion until now when they challenged you and me."

Zhou Yi thought to himself that they challenged you, and I'm just a backdrop. However, he knew that Jin Zhanyi's explanation wouldn't be so simple.

As expected, Jin Zhanyi continued, "Although Qilian Twin Devils both reached the Three Flowers realm, their the Three Flowers realm is quite distinct from ordinary individuals." At this point, he gave a meaningful glance at Zhou Yi and said, "Brother Zhou, when we face them in battle, it's best not to use weapons, especially your Five Elements Ring. No matter what, do not reveal it."

Zhou Yi was puzzled, "Why?"

Jin Zhanyi spoke earnestly, "Have you heard of the Five Elements Sect?"

Zhou Yi's heart skipped a beat, "Is the mystical realm of Qilian Mountain also a branch of the Five Elements Sect?

Jin Zhanyi nodded emphatically, "Exactly, the mystical realm of Qilian Mountain is indeed a splinter faction that split from the Five Elements Sect, and it happens to be the strongest branch."

Zhou Yi nodded solemnly, understanding that a camel is bigger than a horse. He naturally grasped this principle. If those guys saw the Five Elements Ring, it would surely lead to countless troubles.

"Although Qilian Twin Devils are twin brothers, their Five Elements attributes are not the same. The elder Devil possesses attributes of Metal, Water, and Wood, while the younger Devil possesses attributes of Fire, Earth, and Metal."

Jin Zhanyi's voice resounded with enthusiasm and a potent, sharp power. Particularly when he touched upon the Qilian Twin Devils' cultivation attributes, a gleam of fervor danced in his eyes. Evidently, there was no trace of psychological pressure in his heart regarding the imminent duel.

This ability to transform pressure into motivation was indeed impressive to Zhou Yi.

After pondering for a moment, Zhou Yi said, "When they join forces, it's the Five Elements Cycle."

A hint of a smile curved Jin Zhanyi's lips as he responded, "Exactly. Due to the Five Elements Cycle, their power increases significantly when they team up. However, if they're separated, their strength diminishes considerably."

Observing Jin Zhanyi's confident demeanor, Zhou Yi couldn't help but shake his head slightly. Perhaps in

Jin Zhanyi's eyes, once these two were separated, they could hardly be considered opponents. However, in reality, becoming a Three Flower-level powerhouse wasn't something easily accomplished.

Jin Zhanyi met Zhou Yi's gaze and continued in a calm voice, "Brother Zhou, that night I saw you practicing the Thirty-Six Forms of Mountain-Crushing. From the first form to the twenty-third, your momentum gradually increased, and your power multiplied. I have a proposal; I wonder what you think..."

His voice gradually lowered, and as Zhou Yi listened intently, a unique radiance began to shine in his eyes, growing brighter and brighter.

Chapter 376

When Jin Zhanyi paused, a tumultuous storm surged in Zhou Yi's heart. His proposal had indeed stirred his interest, but executing it during the decisive battle was fraught with uncertainty.If he could accomplish it in one go, everyone would rejoice, but if he faltered midway, he would become the subject of ridicule.

As Zhou Yi remained silent, Jin Zhanyi gently shook his head and asked, "Brother Zhou, have you made any progress during your solitary cultivation?"

Zhou Yi shook his head with a sense of desolation, saying, "difficult."

This short word seemed to encapsulate the countless hardships of his cultivation journey, and it also seemed to strike a chord within Jin Zhanyi, whose expression mirrored his sentiments.

"The path of martial arts is like rowing against the current. If you can't consistently make breakthroughs, you will gradually regress and end up with nothing," Jin Zhanyi's voice resonated with the stability of a mountain. "Brother Zhou, neither of us is inherently inclined to seek comfort. Only in the fiercest battles can we truly make breakthroughs. My proposal might seem perilous, but only through it can we fully tap into our potential and take that crucial step forward."

Zhou Yi opened his mouth as if to speak but ultimately didn't utter a word.

Jin Zhanyi sighed deeply, saying, "Brother Zhou, you're also an outstanding practitioner in the realm of martial arts. You should understand the sorrow of being unable to take that final step."

Zhou Yi blinked, giving him a sidelong glance.

He had a profound understanding of what Jin Zhanyi referred to as that final step. When one had cultivated a certain realm to its pinnacle, a distinct sensation of impending breakthrough would arise. This feeling would grip the cultivator's heart tightly, filling them with boundless hope. Yet, actually transcending that threshold was an immensely elusive task.

Regardless of the realm, there were countless individuals trapped on the precipice of that final step. They remain stuck at the pinnacle of a certain realm, unable to make a smooth breakthrough no matter what they do.

After Zhou Yi's extraordinary encounter at the bottom of the lake, he has been progressing steadily, overcoming challenges one after another. Even when he encountered obstacles, he managed to overcome them within a few months. However, not everyone was as fortunate. Even someone like Jin Zhanyi, hailed by the Da Shen as one of the fastest cultivators in history, also found himself lingering before those barriers, unable to take that final step.

Jin Zhanyi continued, "Although facing Qilian Twin Devils carries its dangers, it's also one of our greatest opportunities. To achieve a breakthrough here, we must shatter their strongest attacks. If we lack even this modicum of confidence, there's no point in us joining the battle at all."

His words carried a sincere tone, and his gaze was clear and transparent. What he said was straightforward and insightful. Zhou Yi finally let out a breath, saying, "Since you propose this, Brother Jin, I shall obey."

A joyful expression instantly appeared in Jin Zhanyi's eyes, unmasked and genuine. He slapped Zhou Yi's shoulder enthusiastically and said, "I knew Brother Zhou would agree. May this battle lead to your successful condensation of the Metal Flower and an early breakthrough to the Three Flowers Gathering at the Apex Realm."

Zhou Yi offered a faint smile, saying, "Thank you for your kind words." Then, he looked at Jin Zhanyi with an enigmatic expression and asked, "Brother Jin, you seem to have great expectations for this battle.Could it be that you're pinning your hopes on this for reaching the Three Flowers Gathering at the Apex Realm?"

Jin Zhanyi chuckled, neither confirming nor denying, but his tacit acknowledgment was evident.

After a short while, Jin Zhanyi left with a graceful exit, while Zhou Yi remained lost in thought. His constitution was completely different from ordinary people. Even if individuals like Jin Zhanyi had reached his current level, they couldn't guarantee the successful refinement of the Metal Flower.

However, Zhou Yi had never harbored such concerns. Despite numerous unsuccessful attempts, he had an intuitive feeling that each effort added a bit more weight to his understanding and mastery of the power of gold.

He faintly sensed that his inability to make the breakthrough was because he hadn't truly reached the pinnacle of this realm. Given more time, if he were to practice from the first technique to the twenty-third technique repeatedly, there would certainly be a day when everything fell into place. However, following this method step by step would demand a considerable amount of time.

Perhaps it would take a year, or maybe two, or even longer. This gradual method of cultivation was indeed not very suitable for Zhou Yi, who was bound by the Twenty-Year Pact.

He turned his head and looked in the direction that Jin Zhanyi had left, slowly clenching his fists. Since Jin Zhanyi was willing to accompany him in this battle, what harm was there in taking a risk?

Gradually, his fluctuating emotions settled. Zhou Yi placed the orb, which had already cooled down, on the table. Jin Zhanyi also noticed the orb in Zhou Yi's hand, but he didn't ask anything. He couldn't fathom its true purpose at all.

Applying a gentle pressure with his hand, guided by the potent force of his golden True Qi, the orb gradually changed shape and finally transformed into the form of a book. As it assumed this shape, a faint, sparkling and translucent light danced across its surface. When the light dissipated, the secret manual reappeared before him.

Zhou Yi picked up the manual and held it in his hand, a hint of perplexity surfacing within him. Gently tapping the manual in his hand, he suddenly spoke up, asking, "Brerbo, where does the space within this manual come from? How is it different from the outside world?"

A faint voice resonated from the manual in his hand, "Within the divine path scripture, there exists the power of space. However, the manner in which this power is employed is incredibly intricate. As a result, I can only achieve flawless replication, but I cannot make improvements or innovations."

A glint of excitement flashed in Zhou Yi's eyes as his other hand reached for his chest, where he had another spatial silver ring.

Although the space within the silver ring and the space within the Divine Path Scripture were not the same, they had their differences. One could store items, while the other seemed to exist purely in the realm of the mind. However, it was undeniable that these two kinds of space shared a faint similarity – they both operated on the foundation of spatial energy.

Vaguely, Zhou Yi seemed to grasp something. He inquired in a deep voice, "Breibo, is the mastery of spatial power restricted to divine path powerhouses?"

"Insufficient data to confirm," Breibo replied promptly.

Frowning deeply, Zhou Yi shook his head slightly. Half-closing his eyes, he carefully contemplated every bit of his experiences in that miraculous realm. While he was well aware that the seemingly boundless space within the Divine Path Scripture was an illusion, merely a product of his mental imagery, that space had imparted a powerful sense of tangible existence.

Recalling his practice within that realm, it seemed to hold no difference from the outside world for him. This training sanctum was truly alluring, enough to tempt countless individuals.

With a shift of thought, Zhou Yi remembered Breibo mentioning that the first owner of the cave was a divine powerhouse.

After creating the Divine Path Scripture, that person had appeared extremely fatigued. From this, it was evident how precious this artifact was – even for divine path powerhouses, crafting it wasn't an easy feat.

With a thread of Metal qi flowing from his hand, Zhou Yi once again entered that boundless space. Inside this space, he meticulously executed the Thirty-Six Forms of Mountain-Crushing, one move after another, methodical and earnest. Through his tireless practice, he gained a clearer understanding of this combat technique. However, every time he executed up to the Twenty-Third Technique, that sensation of complexity, so close yet just out of reach, would surge back, causing him to have to abandon his attempt to execute the Twenty-Fourth Technique.

The feeling of powerlessness his efforts saddened him, but it didn't shake his confidence. On the contrary, his confidence grew stronger. He realized that with each practice session, his aura became more potent. Perhaps when his aura reached its peak, the Twenty-Fourth Technique would finally manifest as he wished.

Suddenly, a dangerous signal entered his mind. Zhou Yi's heart skipped a beat. He had a vague sense that this wasn't due to someone approaching. Scanning his surroundings, his expression changed. Somehow and at an unknown time, faint cracks had appeared in this endless spatial realm.

Though the cracks were small, he sensed a strong feeling that these were caused by the spatial repulsion force. If he remained here, this space might collapse.

Not daring to be careless, Zhou Yi promptly exited the space.His gaze fell upon the Divine Path Scripture, which had a faint metallic sheen. Surprisingly, it also bore subtle cracks. However, this thing was transformed by Breibo's magic; after Zhou Yi exited that space, it began to automatically repair itself.

After a brief moment, the book returned to its original state. Aside from the lingering scalding sensation in his hand, everything seemed normal.

Frowning slightly, Zhou Yi asked, "Breibo, why did the Divine Path Scripture heat up? Is the collapse of the spatial world related to it?"

"The spiritual space within the Divine Path manual is not meant for your cultivation. If you were to use the original manual for practice, it would have been rendered useless long ago," Breibo's voice sounded, maintaining its calm tone, yet Zhou Yi seemed to sense a hint of reproach in it.

It was only now that Zhou Yi realized that the extended practice had caused this.

However, he also came to understand one thing: why the Lingxiao Treasure Hall did not use the space world within the Divine Path Scripture for cultivation, despite possessing it. That was because prolonged cultivation would cause significant damage to this kind of space. It would be fine if they merely comprehended the contained power system, but if they treated this spiritual space as a normal cultivation ground like the outside world, the inevitable result would be the destruction of the manual.

Realizing this, Zhou Yi's admiration for Breibo's abilities grew. This fellow not only possesses the ability to perfectly replicate the Divine Path Scripture, but also holds the power to mend the spiritual world within the scripture.

This non-human entity truly had abilities far beyond what humans could reach. Zhou Yi stepped to a window, gently pushing it open. As he breathed in the cool air, a sudden sense of anticipation for the impending battle filled his heart.

Chapter 377

The slanting sunlight illuminated the ground, casting a

vibrant glow on clusters of white flowers against the

backdrop of green. Zhou Yi focused his mind and

calmed his breath, his heart seemingly devoid of any ripples. With his ears slightly twitching, he effortlessly picked up all the sounds from outside, stood up, and walked to the door, opening it.

As he stepped out, the door across from his swung open almost simultaneously, and the sharp-eyed gaze of Jin Zhanyi immediately met his. The two exchanged a smile, a moment of unusual tacit understanding between them.

They walked out together, heading towards the central tower. Walking side by side, their auras seemed to be gradually shifting. Their every step seemed to be precisely measured, devoid of any differences. Faintly, their deepening harmony resembled that of a single entity.

When they reached the central tower, Zhang ZhongJin had been waiting there for a while. He looked at the two before him in surprise, a sense of bewilderment in his heart. He couldn't fathom when their rapport had grown so profound.

Nevertheless, for today's decisive battle, their remarkable understanding of each other was undoubtedly an immensely advantageous factor. Nodding slightly, Zhang ZhongJin led the way, guiding them to the seventh floor of the tower.

On this level was an expansive arena, where the Venerables sparred and honed their martial skills. The power possessed by these Venerables was unquestionably formidable, and their battles could greatly impact their surroundings. However, the tower itself possessed a mystical power, ensuring that no one could cause any harm to it during combat. Therefore, the members of the Lingxiao Treasure Hall had established a vast arena within the tower, making the most of the available space for martial contests.

At this moment, there were already over twenty people gathered on the arena. Zhou Yi's gaze shifted and immediately focused on the three figures directly in front of him. Among them, two elderly men looked virtually identical in appearance. They were seated with their eyes closed, seemingly unresponsive to the external world. However, the moment Zhou Yi's gaze fell on them, both of them simultaneously opened their eyes, revealing four powerful and intense gazes.

In that instant, Zhou Yi even felt a burning sensation in his eyeballs. A faint curve formed at the corner of his mouth, showing a hint of indifference as he calmly averted his gaze. On the other hand, Jin Zhanyi raised an eyebrow, and his sharp gaze shot out like arrows. The gazes of the three parties converged in the air, and the atmosphere in the arena seemed to grow tense.

Furrowing his brow slightly, Zhou Yi cleared his throat. Understanding his intention, Jin Zhanyi gave a muted smile and retracted his gaze. The two of them settled onto chairs on the opposite side, comfortably taking their seats. They acted as if they were completely ignorant of the provocative gazes ahead, as if those two figures didn't exist at all.

The Qilian Twin Devils displayed a faint trace of anger in their eyes. They had traversed the world for two hundred years, and such blatant disregard for them was indeed extremely rare. However, these two were also shrewd and experienced individuals who had been through countless battles. They exchanged a glance, and the fleeting anger within them subsided, replaced by absolute calmness.

As Zhou Yi sat down next to Jin Zhanyi, he continued to calmly observe the others on this floor. Apart from the three figures across from them, the remaining twenty or so individuals had all reached the One-Line Heaven realm. Among them were Zhang ZhongJin and Wei ZongJin.

Seeing Zhou Yi's gaze shifting towards them, most of these individuals wore faint smiles on their faces. However, Zhou Yi still detected a sense of skepticism in their eyes. It was clear that many of them were doubtful about him and Jin Zhanyi, or perhaps about him.

Because the gazes of everyone, when directed at Jin Zhanyi, were filled with confidence.

Finally, Zhou Yi's gaze settled on the Qilian Twin Devils. However, this time his attention wasn't on the imminent opponents but rather on the elderly man sitting above them, an old man who seemed as fragile as a wooden carving. As Zhou Yi caught sight of this aged figure, a feeling of extreme danger suddenly surged in his heart. It was akin to the intense sense of crisis he had experienced during his encounter with Zhuo ShengFeng that night in the Lingxiao Treasure Hall's martial library.

Seemingly sensing Zhou Yi's gaze, the old man opened his eyes and offered him a faint smile. Within that smile, there was no hint of enmity; instead, it bore a gentle air, reminiscent of how an elder might regard an outstanding disciple within a family, radiating a sense of warmth.

Zhou Yi was slightly taken aback, and then he heard Jin Zhanyi's voice whispering in his ear like a murmuring insect, "Brother Zhou, this person is the master of the Qilian Twin Devils, the most renowned venerable expert in the Qilian Mountain, Fan Shuo."

Nodding almost imperceptibly, Zhou Yi imprinted the man's visage firmly in his memory.

Two distinct sets of footsteps became audible, and as soon as these sounds reached their ears, all the One-Line Heaven experts within the Lingxiao Treasure Hall stood up almost as if it were prearranged, including Jin Zhanyi and the Qilian Twin Devils.

Zhou Yi naturally stood up without neglecting proper etiquette. However, his ears twitched slightly as he speculated about the origins of these two individuals. For some reason, he found a faint sense of familiarity from them, as if he had encountered them somewhere before.

When Gao Weiliang and the other entered, it was quite straightforward, One was robustly built, while the other was relatively shorter. Despite their differences in stature, they exuded a commanding presence, radiating an aura of dominance that seemed to encompass their surroundings.

All present bowed in unison as they entered. The burly figure waved his sleeve and said, "Please, everyone, take your seats."

In a hushed voice, Jin Zhanyi informed Zhou Yi, "Brother Zhou, these two are the appointed duty elders of our sect this year, Gao WeiLiang and Du WenBin."

Zhou Yi's gaze shifted to them, and a sudden realization flashed through his mind. The two Venerables who accompanied Zhuo Shengfeng that night as he left the Lingxiao Treasure Hall were most likely them.

With a light chuckle, Fan Shuo said, "Brother Gao, Brother Du, thank you for your trouble. It's quite embarrassing."

Brother Gao and Brother Du exchanged a knowing smile. Brother Gao replied, "Brother Fan, please don't mention it. This competition was personally approved by the Sect Master. We're just carrying out the task."

A trace of surprise flickered in Zhou Yi's eyes. While Gao WeiLiang and Du Wenbin were also venerable-level experts, their demeanor indicated a deep sense of wariness toward Fan Shuo.

Suddenly, Zhou Yi's ears twitched as he caught a faint sound of footsteps approaching.

When Gao WeiLiang and Du Wenbin entered, their arrival was conspicuous, but this person's approach was stealthy, as if he wanted to conceal his presence from everyone.

However, if Zhou Yi wasn't mistaken, this person was trying his utmost to hide, and her Lightness Technique was commendable—his footsteps barely made a sound upon landing. But the problem was that this person's cultivation level was rather unimpressive, failing even to reach the Innate Realm.

Regardless of how carefully she moved, it was unlikely they could remain unnoticed by anyone here.. Yet, when Zhou Yi looked around, he found that everyone was wearing an expression of calmness, as if they hadn't heard the footsteps at all.

Doubts swirled within Zhou Yi's mind. While today's battle wasn't a life-or-death struggle between the two factions, those present were at least One-line Heaven-level experts. Even ordinary Innate experts were denied entry, so how could this regular person, who hadn't even reached the innate realm, dare to come here?

Fan Shuo glanced at the entrance and chuckled, "Miss Qiu is here as well. Please come in."

The faint footsteps immediately grew louder, and a graceful young lady appeared at the entrance.

She possessed bright eyes and white teeth, dressed in a flowing emerald green robe that cascaded all the way to her feet. Especially striking were her curved eyebrows and large eyes, which exuded a captivating radiance.

As she emerged from the entrance, a gentle smile appeared on everyone's faces. Zhou Yi could clearly sense a hint of helplessness in their eyes, even the two Venerables. It was as if everyone felt helpless in the face of this young lady. However, within that helpless expression, there was also a deep sense of indulgence. These two conflicting emotions intertwined, leaving Zhou Yi greatly surprised.

"Qiu, why are you here? When Zhanyi and the others engage in combat later, if you accidentally get injured by the aftermath, what are we going to do?" Gao WeiLiang sighed and said.

The young lady, Qiu, playfully rolled her bright eyes, revealing a mischievous charm. She replied, "Uncle Gao, with you and Uncle Du here, how could I get hurt?"

Zhou Yi's eyes widened, and he almost began to doubt his own ears. This young lady actually referred to the two venerables as uncles. What kind of status did she have?

After a careful examination, it was confirmed—she hadn't even reached the Innate Realm.

Jin Zhanyi shrugged slightly and said, "Brother Zhou, this is our sect master's young daughter and his only heir. If there's nothing urgent, it's best not to provoke her."

Zhou Yi nodded slightly, mentally noting to avoid any unnecessary interactions with this young lady.

Gao WeiLiang let out a hearty laugh and remarked, "The two of us are here, so of course, we won't let you get hurt. However, your martial cultivation is still low, and watching this battle might not be beneficial for you."

With a mischievous smile, Miss Qiu replied, "Uncle Gao, I've watched before as my father and the three uncles from the upper levels sparred. Is Brother Jin even more formidable than my father and them?"

Gao WeiLiang was left completely speechless. He shook his head and said, "Since you're interested in watching, then sit down properly and don't move around."

Miss Qiu's smile grew brighter as she settled beside the two venerables and quietly took her seat.

As she sat down, her whole demeanor underwent a transformation, resembling that of a refined young lady. The agile and clever aura she had displayed earlier was nowhere to be seen.

Chapter 378

Zhou Yi marveled at the change in the woman's temperament, but this was just a minor interlude. ; everyone's attention returned to the arena simultaneously.

Fan Shuo smiled and said, "Brother Gao, receiving a response from your sect this time, I am truly grateful. After this battle, regardless of victory or defeat, I will present two Jiahuang Pills as a token of appreciation."

Gao Weiliang's expression slightly changed as he said, "Brother Fan, with your generosity, I thank you on their behalf."

The eyes of Jin Zhanyi brightened, clearly filled with excitement as well.

Although Zhou Yi had the intention to inquire a bit more, he understood that it wasn't suitable to be distracted right before the competition. With a slight shift of his thoughts, he suppressed all his musings.

Qilian Twin Devils stood up suddenly and walked towards the central arena. Their footsteps were synchronized as they walked together, creating an illusion that they were just one person.

Zhou Yi's heart skipped a beat, and he held Qilian Twin Devils in higher regard.

While he shared a certain level of understanding with Jin Zhanyi, it could be said that in comparison to these two individuals, it wasn't even worth mentioning.

Turning his head, he exchanged a glance with Jin Zhanyi, both of them recognizing the burning determination in each other's eyes. Sharing a smile, they stood up as well and confidently stepped onto the arena.

Fan Shuo's gaze remained fixed on Zhou Yi, and he straightforwardly inquired, "Brother Gao, this young man Zhou Yi seems extraordinary. I wonder which esteemed master he's a disciple of?"

Gao Weiliang shook his head and chuckled, "Brother Fan, Zhou Xian is not a disciple of our Lingxiao Treasure Hall. He comes from the Northwest Tianchi and formed an unbreakable bond with Jin Zhanyi. Hearing that the twin devils wished to challenge Jin Zhanyi, he volunteered to fight. We did try to advise against it, but he was determined, and there was nothing more we could do." He sighed lightly, expressing helplessness.

Fan Shuo's face still wore a hearty smile, but his mind had already turned over countless thoughts. The challenge posed by the twin devils was aimed at the Three Flowers disciples of the Lingxiao Treasure Hall. However, a disciple from the Northwest Tianchi ended up getting involved. Considering the intricate relationships that the Lingxiao Treasure Hall had maintained with the most powerful sects across the lands over the millennia, Fan Shuo's heart couldn't find peace.

A faint smile lingered in Gao Weiliang's eyes. He knew that news of Zhou Yi representing the Lingxiao Treasure Hall in the battle was certain to spread after this bout. Once this information circulated, the outcome of this contest would become insignificant. Even if Jin Zhanyi's side were to be defeated, no one would genuinely believe that Jin Zhanyi was inferior to Qilian Twin Devils. Because everyone would assume that it must be Zhou Yi's insufficient strength that led to their ultimate defeat.

In the center of the arena, Zhou Yi had long since focused all his attention. His mind was completely composed, and his spirit was intensely concentrated. He gazed keenly at the twin devils before him.

These two identical old men, even the wrinkles between their brows held no distinction. Prior to making a move, it was impossible to differentiate their identities.

Standing several meters apart, after sizing each other up for a moment, the elder on the opposite side spoke, "Please... be cautious."

As he uttered this "Please", the four palms of the two simultaneously rose, causing an intense and extreme surge of heat to fill the air. This heatwave rushed unhesitatingly towards Zhou Yi and his companions.

Only at this moment did the old man utter the words "be cautious."

Zhou Yi inwardly cursed, even though he had prepared for it, there was still a sense of being caught off guard. With a snort of anger, he flicked his wrist, and a similarly potent surge of fire-type True Qi surged forth.

Between them, it seemed as if two fiery-red dragons had appeared. This is the tangible form born from the condensation of the Fire Flower, transformed by the pure essence of fire. The intense heat within the Fire

Dragon instantly diffused, causing the temperature of the seventh level to seemingly rise significantly in an instant.

"Gao Weiliang's sleeves swayed intentionally or unintentionally, and a gentle breeze wafted by. The temperature around his body remained unaffected by the Fire Dragon's influence."

Qiu, the young lady, sweetly smiled at Gao Weiliang, yet her eyes harbored a strong shade of envy.

"Boom..."

Two powerful fire-type forces clashed fiercely in midair. After a moment of standoff, they continued surging toward Zhou Yi's direction.

Zhou Yi's expression slightly changed, as the immense fire-type power displayed by the opposing side indeed exceeded his imagination. After all, they had already reached the Three Flowers realm forty years ago. Now, they were just a step away from the Three Flowers Gathering at the Apex. Not to mention the power of confinement within their fire-based techniques, even when considering their fire-based strength alone, they outmatched Zhou Yi by more than just a step.

Seeing the massive fire-type energy about to press down on him, a cold smile suddenly appeared on Zhou Yi's face. He opened his mouth and forcefully expelled a green-colored flower.

Everyone here, except for Qiu, was at least a One-line Heaven expert. Naturally, they recognized this as a tangible flower, and even more remarkably, the rare Windflower.

However, most of them couldn't fathom its purpose at this juncture.

"Break..."

With a soft shout from Zhou Yi, the Windflower before him abruptly burst into countless specks, blending into the fire dragons.

In the next moment, the flames in front of him seemed to undergo an extremely subtle change. Amid the fiery red hue, an abrupt hint of green emerged. This mixed fire dragon suspended in midair momentarily halted before rapidly expanding. In just a blink of an eye, this crimson and green intertwined fire dragon seized the absolute advantage, suppressing the Qilian twin devils' initially advantageous fire dragon entirely.

Everyone present displayed astonishment on their faces, especially the three Venerables. As they looked at the intersecting green and red fire dragon, they couldn't contain their profound sense of shock.

Gao Weiliang exchanged a glance with Du Wenbin. Although they had heard Zhang Zhongjin introduce Zhou Yi's achievements and his battles with the Totem Clan's Bear Wuji, However, even Zhang Zhongjin himself was unaware of the Firewind Flower, so it's even more impossible for them to know. Now, witnessing the fusion of wind and fire, their shock surpassed even the One-line Heaven experts'.

Someone had actually combined wind and fire even before achieving the Three Flowers Gathering at the Apex realm...

A thought simultaneously crossed the minds of the three Venerables: What kind of freak is this?

Indeed, from the body of this peculiar fire dragon emanated a potent fusion of wind and fire energies. It wasn't merely the power of fire; it was fused with the force of wind.

With the wind aiding the fire's might and the fire harnessing the momentum of the wind, their fusion resulted in a power several times stronger. When these two elements merged, their combined power surged several times over, instantly overwhelming the opponent's mighty yet purely elemental fire power.

A hint of fanaticism gleamed in the eyes of Qilian twin devils. Confronted with this sudden twist of events, their fighting spirit swelled even further.

As the green and red fire dragon lunged before them with fangs and claws bared, their aura abruptly shifted. The fire dragon manipulated by the Qilian twin devils split into two and dispersed on both sides, releasing a surging water power in the process. Like gigantic waves, it surged toward Zhou Yi and Jin Zhanyi.

The seamless coordination between the twin devils was nothing short of remarkable. They masterfully manipulated two opposing forces, water and fire, and their collaboration unleashed an overwhelming and unparalleled power.

However, just as the immense water wave surged forward, the airborne green and red fire dragon suddenly vanished into thin air.

The enormous fusion of wind and fire power seemed to dissipate in an instant. At that moment, Zhou Yi took a step forward, his hands forming an intricate seal. Amidst the torrent of water and fire power, he lifted his hands above his head.

This was the power of earth. The potent force of earth spread instantaneously to every corner of this layer.

At this point, everyone finally realized that Zhou Yi had instantly converted the power of the Windfire Flower into the power of Earth.

This time, not only were all the spectators amazed, even the Qilian Twin Devils in the arena momentarily showed a stunned expression.

Almost every person had a question in their mind: How could he achieve such a rapid conversion speed?

Jin Zhanyi, who had been concealed behind Zhou Yi all this time, had his eyes light up. He hadn't intervened initially; he was waiting for this opportunity.

At this moment, his body arched slightly, and he suddenly shot forward like an arrow released from a bow, heading straight towards Qilian Twin Devils.

The direction Jin Zhanyi's attack was aimed at wasn't a specific person among the Qilian Twin Devils; it was directed at the space between them.

When the Qilian Twin Devils took action, they maintained a subtle distance between each other. Within this distance, their attacks were clever and varied.

However, at this moment, when Jin Zhanyi seized the opportunity and struck in an instant, they suddenly felt an obstruction within the flow of the Five Elements.

In that moment, Jin Zhanyi seemed to transform into a long spear, striking at their vital point, causing them to experience an extreme sense of discomfort. The combined power of the Qilian Twin Devils was utterly suppressed at this moment.

In an instant, the water and fire powers in the air significantly weakened. The two entirely opposing forces no longer exhibited the clever coordination they had just demonstrated. Instead, they seemed to be conflicting with each other, subtly showing signs of internal discord.

"Whoosh..."

As Zhou Yi raised his hand seal high, a tremendous force surged in reverse, forcefully dispelling the twin devils' combined water and fire power in an instant.

In the eyes of the onlookers, it was as if they saw a peak breaking through the water and fire blockade, rising tall and majestic from nothingness. What astonished the experts of the Lingxiao Treasure Hall even more was that watching this process evoked a sense of familiarity and intimacy within them.

This is the result of Zhou Yi combining the insights from the Tianchi Main Peak and the Tower of Heaven.

Under this technique, the power of the Raising Heaven Seal reached its utmost expression. Even if the united force of Qilian Twin Devils had not been shattered by Jin Zhanyi's attack, and even if their water and fire powers were intact, it might not necessarily be enough to suppress Zhou Yi's Raising Heaven Seal technique.

Amidst the awe of the crowd, Zhou Yi's Raising Heaven Seal had reached its limit.

Just when everyone thought he was about to stop, Zhou Yi's eyes sparkled, and his hand seal Overturning upward

In the blink of an eye, the wind swept through the clouds,

In the blink of an eye, the heavens and earth turned

upside down...

Chapter 379

The eyes of all the onlookers lit up, and in most of

their eyes, there was a trace of astonishment mixed

with a hint of fear.

Among these One-line Heaven experts of Lingxiao Treasure Hall, they only truly understood Zhou Yi's terrifying strength at this moment. In their minds, the image of this young man suddenly grew tall and full, and no one dared to scrutinize him with any hint of doubt anymore.

n the presence of these martial arts experts, only by using even more formidable strength could one earn their respect.Zhou Yi had undoubtedly achieved this.

Overturning Heaven Seal

As the Raising Heaven Seal reached its zenith, Zhou Yi's palm flipped, naturally and effortlessly unleashing the final and most powerful technique of the earth-based hand seal.

A massive dark cloud took shape in the mid-air, created by Zhou Yi's Overturning Heaven Seal. It transformed the intangible into the tangible, utilizing powerful true energy as a guide to draw external forces and condense into a vast expanse of "Heaven"...

Within this process, there is more than just his inherent Earth-element power; there is even a trace of the Earth-element energy from within the tower itself. As this expanse of "Heaven" takes form, a potent upsurge of air currents bursts forth, causing ripples that even make the entire tower quiver slightly.

Of course, this is merely an illusion caused by the swirling air currents. In reality, even if it were a combined effort of everyone here, including Zhou Yi, they wouldn't be able to truly shake the tower.

However, despite that, the Overturning Heaven Seal, empowered by the Raising Heaven Seal, had gathered its might to its utmost point. Even Qilian Twin Devils couldn't afford to underestimate it.

Moreover, amidst them, there was Jin Zhanyi, who was like a thorn in their side. It was precisely due to his sudden attack that they had shattered the unity of Qilian Twin Devils and forced them into an absolute disadvantage.

Zhou Yi's aggressive assault and Jin Zhanyi's covert attack worked in such perfect harmony that it surpassed even the coordination of Qilian Twin Devils, leaving everyone astonished.

The faces of Qilian Twin Devils changed simultaneously; the big devil turned as red as blood, while the Second one turned as dark as iron. Then, they both exhaled a breath.

In front of the onlookers, five distinct colored tangible flowers suddenly appeared out of nowhere. At the moment of their formation, these tangible flowers swiftly merged together, intertwining and creating a natural cycle of the Five Elements, forming a Reincarnation Flower of Five Elements.

Subsequently, the immense Reincarnation Flower fiercely descended towards Jin Zhanyi.

With a loud shout, Jin Zhanyi, no matter how confident he was, didn't believe that he alone could withstand the Qilian Twin Devils' Five Elements Reincarnation Flower. He exerted a slight force with his feet and swiftly retreated, moving as if he were flying.

With the removal of this obstacle in the middle, Qilian Twin Devils both breathed a sigh of relief. They stepped toward each other's direction, instantly standing side by side. Each of them extended a hand to rest upon the other's shoulder, and then raised their other hands, striking towards the black cloud above them.

A tremendous rumble ensued, as the black cloud descended. Whatever stood in its path was pulverized to dust. While Qilian Twin Devils' striking hands and the Reincarnation Flower above their heads impacted the sky, it was like a mantis trying to stop a chariot, showing no effect whatsoever.

Instantly, this expanse of sky had enveloped everything beneath it. Whether it was the Qilian Twin Devils or their Reincarnation Flower of Five Elements, all appeared dim and and were completely overwhelmed under this sky.

Both inside and outside the arena, silence reigned, and even Miss Qiu, who was accustomed to watching clashes among master-level experts, wore a bewildered expression on her face.

Before the clash between the two sides, nobody had anticipated such an outcome. With just a few moves, Qilian Twin Devils had already suffered a defeat, even without fully utilizing their true strength.

And it's not just a simple failure – under the immense power of this black cloud, the question of whether they can even preserve their lives becomes uncertain."

"The power displayed by Zhou Yi's flip of the hand was so immense possessing a force that seemed to suppress everything. Not only were the top-tier experts of the One-line Heaven astounded, even the three venerable figures of the Three Flowers Gathering at the Apex level felt a chill in their hearts. If they were to encounter this dark cloud, could they withstand its force?"

Even in the hearts of Gao Weiliang and the others, a question arose this time: Could it be that this guy was originally a Venerable from the start?

Jin Zhanyi's eyes flickered with a tinge of shock. Such a thunderous strike was not something achievable by a Three Flowers Realm cultivator; it was doubtful that even the Venerable-level individuals could manage it.

Zhou Yi, too, stared strangely at his own palm. He seemed to be pondering something peculiar, yet in his eyes gleamed a spark of excitement, indicating that whatever it was, it was a good thing.

Indeed, as Zhou Yi executed the Raising Heaven Seal, he unexpectedly sensed a mysterious force emanating from beneath his feet. This power originated from the earth itself, a culmination of the Earth Element's energy.

However, this particular force was distinct; it seemed to be the hidden power within the tower. Because of its presence, Zhou Yi found it challenging to employ Earth-Tunnelling Technique to enter the tower. Yet, as this unique force traveled from his feet into his chaotic-like Dantian before being concentrated into his hand seal, the power of his earth-based technique underwent an exponential enhancement.

As he smoothly executed the Overturning Heaven Seal,this strand of power erupted alongside it. In the face of this force, everything else was as insignificant as chicken feathers and dog hair.

The unfortunate duo, Qilian Twin Devils, found themselves inevitably suppressed beneath it. Even their life-saving technique, the Reincarnation Flower of Five Elements, failed to have any effect.

He let out a deep breath, feeling the mysterious power in his Dantian. Zhou Yi's heart was filled with mixed emotions, making it hard for him to describe the overwhelming sensations he experienced.

The black clouds on the ground dispersed.Although this was a technique conjured by Zhou Yi, the construct was ultimately intangible. Once it lost the support of power, it instantly became unable to condense back into shape.

"Huh...?"

Sounds of astonishment echoed from various places outside the arena. Everyone's eyes were filled with disbelief and shock.

Qilian Twin Devils hadn't been crushed into a pulp as everyone had expected. Around them, there appeared something like a mesh that covered them like a net.

Around them, there seemed to be something like a net-like cover that enveloped them. Although the immense force pressed them to the ground, they remained unharmed under the protective power of this net-like shield.

Gao Weiliang widened his eyes and angrily shouted, "Seamless Heaven Garment... Brother Fan, you've gone too far."

Upon hearing the term "Seamless Heaven Garment," everyone's expressions changed, particularly Jin Zhanyi, whose face turned even uglier.

Though Zhou Yi didn't know exactly what the Seamless Heaven Garment was, seeing the net-like shield above Qilian Twin Devils' heads made it clear that the origin of this item was beyond astonishing.

Fan Shuo's face turned extremely awkward, and he reached out. The net-like shield above Qilian Twin Devils' bodies instantly leaped up, flying back into his hand.

Fan Shuo cupped his fists and said, "Please calm down, everyone. Ten Jiahuang Pills."

In an instant, all the discontented voices vanished. Even Jin Zhanyi's expression returned to normal after a few changes.

Zhou Yi became even more curious, wondering what this thing was that possessed such incredible power.

Qilian Twin Devils stared at Zhou Yi with their four eyes, and slowly a red light glowed in them. Zhou Yi suddenly felt a chill run down his spine.

Not killing these two just now had indeed brought on bigger troubles.

Qilian Twin Devils leaped up from the ground, their bodies pressed closely together, mouths open. Five differently colored tangible flowers once again formed before them.

The Five Elements Reincarnation Flower...

Instantly, the pressure in the air doubled, and everyone felt a powerful power of confinement. With all five flowers in place, Zhou Yi even sensed a pressure not inferior to Zhuo Shengfeng's. The Five Elements Reincarnation was enough for them to challenge beyond their current level.

Jin Zhanyi suddenly let out a low roar. Zhou Yi nodded heavily, raising a hand high above his head.

He executed the Twenty-three Forms move of the Thirty-Six Forms of Mountain-Crushing, releasing its full power in that moment.

Though this strike was far less terrifying than the Overturning Heaven Seal that had integrated a trace of the divine power from the tower, its activation speed was just as incomparable.

Almost at the moment his palm was raised high, it came crashing down.

Simultaneously, Jin Zhanyi arched his body once again and shot out like a lightning bolt.

Jin Zhanyi transformed into a long spear, while Zhou Yi's transformed palm became a blade, both striking towards the same point. Violent energy fluctuations spread through the air. With their combined efforts, even a true venerable wouldn't be able to completely seal them using only the power of confinement.

Although Qilian Twin Devils' Five Elements Grand Reincarnation was formidable, it couldn't truly surpass the power of a venerable.

However, to everyone's surprise, Zhou Yi and the others didn't attack forward as expected. Instead, they directed their assault towards the weakest point of the Five Elements power behind them. This strategic move allowed them to easily create a clear path through.

Following that, they swiftly moved, already arriving at the entrance of the seventh floor.

Chapter 380

Jin Zhanyi laughed loudly, "Brothers of the Twin Devils, this venue is too small. How about we take the fight outside?"

The big devil snorted in anger, "You plan to escape without a fight, what skill is that?"

Gao WeiLiang and the others exchanged confused glances, not understanding what the two of them were up to.

Jin Zhanyi grinned, "Even the Seamless Heavenly Garment was used. Can't we two brothers find a new battleground?"

The Qilian Twin Devils were suddenly rendered speechless. Everyone had witnessed the previous scene. Without the miraculous treasure of the Seamless Heavenly Garment, the Qilian Twin Devils would likely have been crushed to pieces long ago. They wouldn't be here, unscathed, talking as they were.

That pitch-black cloud, which could easily suppress even the Reincarnation of the Five Elements Flower, how could any physical body withstand it?

Since they had employed such a heaven-defying treasure, Jin Zhanyi's proposal to change the battleground and engage in a fair duel wasn't a big deal at all.

The Qilian Twin Devils glanced at each other. Although they knew that the suggested location would definitely favor their opponents, they had no room for refusal anymore.

After all, as formidable experts with a reputation spanning over two hundred years, they couldn't possibly object in this situation.

With a cold snort, the big devil said, "Lead the way."

Zhou Yi and Jin Zhanyi nodded to each other and turned, leaving the entrance and dashing towards the outer part of the tower. The Qilian Twin Devils followed without hesitation. Though they were extremely cautious and wary, they displayed an indifferent demeanor on the surface.

The experts on the seventh level exchanged glances, Gao WeiLiang let out a bitter laugh, and with a wave of his hand, he said, "Go."

Having received his permission, everyone stood up and followed suit.

This martial contest was incredibly splendid, and even though it hadn't concluded yet, it had already left a profound impact on everyone. As long as there was a glimmer of possibility, no one was willing to choose to stop watching.

In the blink of an eye, only three Venerables and Miss Qiu remained on the seventh level.

The reason Miss Qiu chose not to join is because she's well aware of her limitations. Without relying on the power of the two Venerables by her side, there was no way she could catch up with Jin Zhanyi and the others on her own.

Fan Shuo stood up, a hint of hesitation flickering across his face. He finally asked, "Brother Gao, did Zhou Yi really come from the Northwest Tianchi?"

"Yes."

Fan Shuo's eyes brightened, and he enunciated slowly, "Has he... reached the respected figure realm?"

Gao WeiLiang had intended to firmly deny it, but an incredible scene of "heaven" suddenly appeared in his mind.

After a moment of contemplation, he sighed and said, "Brother Fan, your insight is wide-ranging, your perception keen as lightning. Can't you see for yourself?"

Fan Shuo replied with a touch of annoyance, "I'm asking because I can't see clearly. That's why I'm trying to find out whether he has ascended to the respected figure realm and is playing a tiger-eating-the-pig role here."

Gao WeiLiang's expression turned serious, and he finally shook his head, saying, "He isn't a Venerable." He looked up and under Fan Shuo's skeptical gaze, continued, "Brother Fan, do you really think a Venerable would have the leisure to play with the youngsters down here?"

Fan Shuo hesitated for a moment, then slowly nodded.

Taking a step forward, Fan Shuo had already arrived at the entrance of the seventh level. His face had regained its usual friendly smile as he said, "I'm curious about the location that Nephew Jin proposed. Let's go together and take a look."

Gao WeiLiang and his companion shared a slight smile and took Miss Qiu's hand, following the crowd. Despite being the last to come out, they caught up with everyone in a matter of moments. What surprised them, however, was that Jin Zhanyi's group seemed to be running farther and farther ahead and had already left the grand and enormous city of Lingxiao Treasure Hall.

After almost half an hour, Jin Zhanyi's group finally stopped in a broad valley. Although the area was mostly flat, it featured numerous towering peaks. While not comparable to the vast mountain range that spanned the northwest, finding suitable valleys wasn't difficult.

A hearty laugh echoed from Jin Zhanyi's mouth. He grinned and said, "Gentlemen, let's decide the outcome here."

The Qilian Twin Devils surveyed the valley, their eyes filled with confusion.

The only notable characteristic of this valley was its size—compared to it, the seventh level of the tower seemed small. Their doubts arose: could it be that Jin Zhanyi had chosen this location because he found the seventh level too cramped?

Within this momentary delay,the powerful individuals who were originally on the seventh level had already arrived, and a few more had joined as well.These individuals were well-known within Lingxiao Treasure Hall. These individuals were all renowned figures within Lingxiao Treasure Hall. Once they saw them all rushing out, it naturally attracted some experts of the Innate Realm to follow suit.

Jin Zhanyi and Zhou Yi weren't moving at a fast pace, so catching up with them was only natural.

Upon their arrival, these people voluntarily spread out and stood at a distance to observe, leaving ample space for the impending clash.

The big devil's voice was cold as he said, "Since you've chosen your battleground, let's begin."

His words had barely faded when both of them simultaneously exhaled tangible flowers. Neatly arranged, five kinds of colored tangible flowers revolved in front of them, forming a massive Five

Elements Reincarnation Flower in the order of the five phases.

When the Five elemental forces coalesced once more into a singular mass, that formidable power of confinement manifested again in an instant.

However, in that very moment, Jin Zhanyi abruptly crouched down and took a sidelong step.

One of his feet extended diagonally, and his movement wasn't so fast as to become a blur; it was just slightly quicker, that's all. Everyone could clearly observe each of his actions, even the movement of his hair being lifted by the wind was distinctly visible.

But when his foot touched the ground, he had already covered dozens of yards, leaving the confinement radius of the distant Reincarnation of the Five Elements Flower.

Fan Shuo's gaze sharpened, and he whispered, "Horizon's Blink."

Gao WeiLiang and the Lingxiao Treasure Hall members showed satisfaction or excitement. They understood that such an earth-based movement technique was typically reserved for respected figure-level experts. Jin Zhanyi mastering it at such a young age was a remarkable achievement and a testament to his incredible talents and limitless potential.

At this point, everyone finally understood a crucial matter—why Jin ZhanYi proposed leaving the Tower of Heaven and coming here. It was because the seventh level of the tower indeed impeded his capabilities. Engaging the Qilian Twin Devils, who possessed the Reincarnation of the Five Elements Flower, there and here yielded vastly different outcomes.

Yet, at the next moment, a question arose in everyone's minds.

Jin Zhanyi possessed the swift earth-based Lightness Technique of Horizon's Blink. But what about Zhou Yi, the powerhouse from the Northwest Tianchi? Did he also possess a similar top-tier Lightness Technique?

All eyes turned towards Zhou Yi, curious to see what surprises the young man, who had already displayed the incredible power of the Overturning Heaven Seal, might bring next.

Jin Zhanyi's instantaneous departure had genuinely astonished the Qilian Twin Devils, but being seasoned warriors, they immediately shifted their attention to Zhou Yi.

The Five Elements Reincarnation Flower flew towards Zhou Yi like shooting stars. The closer they got, the more intense the overwhelming pressure became, making it increasingly difficult to withstand.

While they had once suffered greatly under Zhou Yi's Overturning Heaven Seal, they understood that such an immensely potent earth-based martial technique couldn't be employed so effortlessly. If Zhou Yi could truly manipulate it with ease, then he couldn't possibly belong to the same level as them; he would have to be a genuine Venerable

The Five Elements Reincarnation Flower emitted intense radiance as they pressed down. The overpowering pressure converged from all directions, as if trying to immobilize him at the center.

Zhou Yi's expression turned quite solemn, yet he remained standing in his place, resolutely unmoving.

The faces of the Qilian Twin Devils shifted slightly and they simultaneously thought, could it be that this guy is about to use that incredible Overturning Heaven Seal again?

With this thought, the speed of the flowers in the air doubled, and they descended with increased pressure. Of course, this meant that the immense power of confinement had diminished somewhat.

In martial arts, one can't have it both ways. This principle held true here as well.

A faint ripple coursed through Zhou Yi's body, and a powerful aura burst forth from him. However, he didn't employ a rapid Lightness Technique like the Horizon's Blink to escape from beneath the Five Elements Reincarnation Flower. Instead, he stood tall and held his head high, his gaze sharp and unwavering as he fixed it straight ahead. It seemed as if he paid no heed to the Five Elements Reincarnation Flower above his head.

In truth, Zhou Yi did consider using the Overturning Heaven Seal. However, he hadn't fully mastered the peculiar power within his Dantian. To utilize it, he needed time to accumulate energy, and he had to transition from the Raising Heaven Seal to the

Overturning Heaven Seal to unleash its full potential.
So, at this moment, he had no intention of using the
Overturning Heaven Seal again.

In the span of a breath, the Five Elements
Reincarnation Flower had reached just above his
head, an unending Reincarnation of creation and birth.
The immense pressure descended like Mount Tai.
Around his body, countless forces surged incessantly,
the overwhelming aura reaching its apex.

Yet, at this very moment, a sardonic smile formed at
the corners of Zhou Yi's mouth. This smirk caused the
Qilian Twin Devils, who were already astonished, to
feel their hearts sink.

Then, in front of everyone's gaze, Zhou Yi's body
steadily sank into the ground, unaffected by the

immense power of the Reincarnation of the Five Elements Flower. No matter how potent the flower's strength was, it couldn't harm him in the slightest.

In an instant, the entire valley fell into silence, devoid of any sound save for rustling leaves.

Fan Shuo muttered slowly, four words escaping his lips, "He... is... a... Venerable..."

Chapter 381

"He's a Venerable..."

These four words hit the crowd's hearts like a heavy hammer. Among them, the most significant reaction came from Qilian Twin Devils. Their initially confident expressions, the strong aura they exuded even before engaging in combat, carried a hint of disdain for the world. Despite showing respect to the renowned Jin Zhanyi of Da Shen, their actions clearly conveyed an immense confidence in their victory for this battle.

However, after the initial exchange, Zhou Yi's Overturning Heaven Seal had left them dumbfounded. Though this earth-based hand seal had rendered everyone disoriented, Qilian Twin Devils were undoubtedly the most affected. If it weren't for the protection of the priceless treasure, Seamless Heaven Garment., they might have perished on the spot.

However, their hearts were as steady as rocks, and they rallied their spirits once again to face Jin Zhanyi and Zhou Yi. Yet, at this moment, witnessing Jin Zhanyi display the pinnacle speed achievable only by a Venerable through connecting with the power of heaven and earth, and seeing Zhou Yi's even more distinct mastery of the Earth-Tunnelling Technique, a trace of despair truly welled up in their hearts.

What kind of opponents had they encountered?

Were these two individuals even human? The Five Elements Reincarnation Flower immediately turned back around, enveloping Qilian Twin Devils within its bounds. They stood back to back, their eyes filled with a profound bitterness.

In a sudden flicker, Zhou Yi emerged from beneath the ground, his face still bearing a smirk. YHowever, in the eyes of everyone watching, there was now an added layer of deep fear. Some even recalled their initial arrogance when they had first met him and lowered their heads in unease.

Upon seeing Zhou Yi, the expressions of Qilian Twin Devils changed slightly. The big Devil immediately bowed deeply and said, " Venerable Zhou, we concede."

Zhou Yi was slightly taken aback, feeling a mixture of amusement and exasperation rising within him.

Fan Shuo took a deep breath, his gaze turning cold, and he said, "Brother Gao, Brother Du, you've gone too far this time."

Initially, when they first encountered this elderly man, he appeared to be friendly and amiable, resembling a kind and gentle individual. However, as he revealed his awe-inspiring aura, a sense of fear gripped everyone. It was only then that they realized this man was far from ordinary; he wielded power beyond that of typical Venerables.

.

"Brother Zhou, I apologize on behalf of my two disciples for any offense caused. However, I'm feeling a bit itchy for some action now. How about we spar a bit?" Fan Shuo said calmly.

In an instant, the air in the valley seemed to solidify. It wasn't the power of confinement of a Venerable, but rather the overwhelming pressure stemming from the hearts of all present. No one could have anticipated that this day would evolve into a battle among Venerables.

Mixed with the excitement in their eyes was a hint of fervor. Witnessing a battle between Venerables was an extremely rare opportunity.

Zhou Yi stared at Fan Shuo in astonishment, a chill running down his spine. Without hesitation, he firmly and unequivocally refused, "I decline."

A bizarre thought crossed his mind: Could this old man be going insane? Such a proposition would be categorically rejected unless one was utterly foolish.

Fan Shuo burst into hearty laughter, saying, "Brother Gao, this is the Venerable your Lingxiao Treasure

Hall invited? He only bullies juniors. If news of this gets out, wouldn't it become the subject of ridicule?"

Though his words were full of laughter, there was no trace of amusement in his expression. In an instant, the faces of most of the Lingxiao Treasure Hall's experts turned red-hot.

Even if they lost this martial contest, or if Jin Zhanyi met his end here, it shouldn't have caused them this much embarrassment. Qilian Twin Devils weren't Venerables, and while the Lingxiao Treasure Hall had dispatched an unfamiliar Venerable to compete, if news of this truly spread, the colossal reputation the Lingxiao Treasure Hall had meticulously built up over thousands of years, would crumble overnight.

Gao WeiLiang shook his head with a serious expression. While he was uncertain , he understood that there was no room for hesitation at this moment. He spoke slowly, his clear voice ringing out for all to hear, "Brother Fan, you're mistaken."

"Where did I go wrong?" came the cold response from Fan Shuo.

Gao WeiLiang's gaze was sharp as lightning, his voice like a blade, "Zhou Yi is a Three Flowers Realm expert from the Northwest Tianchi. "He hasn't even mastered the power of confinement, so how could he possibly achieve Three Flowers Gathering at the Apex?"

His voice paused slightly, before he continued, "Could it be that Brother Fan has been in seclusion for too long, to the point where you can't even sense his aura?"

While there was a touch of sarcasm and mockery in Gao Weiliang's words, this unreserved display of dominance actually caused Fan Shuo to hesitate. If Gao Weiliang didn't possess absolute confidence, how could he be so fearless and self-assured?

Fan Shuo calmed his mind, carefully sensing the aura emanating from Zhou Yi. His expression grew increasingly surprised and uncertain. The person's aura didn't truly reach the level of a Venerable. Moreover, deep down, Fan Shuo himself couldn't believe that the Lingxiao Treasure Hall would commit such an outrageous act.

However, that Overturning Heaven Seal and the Earth-Tunnelling Technique, like two enormous hands, firmly clutched at his heart, leaving him restless.

Jin Zhanyi flew to Zhou Yi's side like an arrow, and the two stood shoulder to shoulder. Facing Fan Shuo's gaze as sharp as a blade's edge, Jin Zhanyi respectfully bowed deeply and said, "Respected Venerable Fan, Brother Zhou and I have traveled a long way from the Northwest. I vouch with my life and honor that Brother Zhou hasn't reached the Venerable realm."

Fan Shuo pondered for a moment, and the formidable aura in his eyes subsided. Suddenly, he asked, "Since he hasn't reached the Venerable realm, how can he use the Earth-Tunnelling Technique?"

Jin Zhanyi smiled faintly and replied, "Respected Venerable Fan, I am not a Venerable either, but I've also mastered the Horizon's Blink technique."

Fan Shuo's expression remained neutral, but his voice held a hint of inquiry, "Jin, you should be aware that Horizon's Blink and the Earth-Tunnelling Technique hold entirely different meanings. According to my knowledge, throughout history, there have been individuals who mastered Horizon's Blink even within the Innate Realm." As he said this, a trace of peculiar light flickered in his eyes. Zhou Yi noticed that most people's eyes held a similar gleam, indicating that this matter had indeed spread widely.

Innate Realm, Horizon's Blink...

It was truly difficult for Zhou Yi to associate these two terms. With a fleeting thought, he recalled Shui XuanJin, who had similarly comprehended the essence of the Wind Element at the end of his life. Regrettably, he hadn't survived. If he had broken through to the One-line Heaven level, wouldn't he have become a legend of similar proportions?

After a brief pause, the tone of Fan Shuo's voice intensified slightly, carrying a hint of severity: "Throughout history, even the ancient divine path cultivators, none of them were rumored to have mastered the Earth-Tunnelling Technique while being below the Venerable realm. And yet, you're implying, Jin, that this Mr. Zhou's talent could surpass even those divine path ancestors of the past? Are you suggesting he is a peerless figure, unmatched in history?"

The crowd fell into silence, all eyes fixed on Jin Zhanyi. Yet, his face remained placid, his eyes filled with an indescribable determination. The intense questioning from Fan Shuo seemed to leave no ripples in his heart.

Bowing deeply to Fan Shuo, Jin Zhanyi proclaimed loudly, "Respected Venerable Fan, the martial talent of Brother Zhou is truly unparalleled in history. No one can surpass him."

Fan Shuo was briefly taken aback, and around him, everyone except the two Venerables from the Lingxiao Treasure Hall, Zhang Zhongju, and Wei

Zongjin exchanged glances involuntarily. The atmosphere in the arena suddenly turned eerie.

Fan Shuo's gaze turned cold as he questioned, "And how can you be so sure?"

Jin Zhanyi held his head high, his voice resonating clearly, "Brother Zhou is not yet twenty years old. Respected Venerable Fan, has there ever been anyone among the illustrious cultivators throughout history who achieved such accomplishments at his age?"

Fan Shuo's expression froze, and it wasn't just him — even those few who were privy to the inside story were struggling to maintain their composure.

From the display of Zhou Yi's Dragon of Wind and Fire, along with his Earth-Tunnelling Technique, it was evident that he was at least at the Third Flower level.

While this level of expertise couldn't be compared to that of a Venerable, the thought of his age sent a strange sensation rippling through everyone's hearts. Among these feelings were envy, suspicion, admiration, jealousy, and even a strong sense of loss.

Fan Shuo stared deeply at Zhou Yi and asked in a soft voice, "Mr. Zhou, may I inquire about your age this year?"

A wry smile played on Zhou Yi's face as he replied, "Nineteen."

At this point, whether he was willing or not, he had to speak the truth.

Fan Shuo's facial muscles twitched slightly, and he let out a long sigh. He said, "I was reckless just now. I ask for your forgiveness, Mr. Zhou."

Zhou Yi's heart skipped a beat. A venerable figure like Fan Shuo actually bowed his head in apology before him, in front of everyone. While this might seem honorable, Zhou Yi couldn't help but feel a chill. The man before him could either be a genuinely noble person or a manipulative schemer.

Onlookers were also filled with mixed emotions. They had come to terms with the fact that Zhou Yi wasn't a Venerable. To have achieved the Three Flowers Realm at his age was already incredible, and considering the miraculous events that had unfolded, accepting this reality was easier.

Fan Shuo waved his hand grandly, stating, "Today's contest concludes. We admit defeat."

However, Jin Zhanyi raised an eyebrow, suddenly interjecting, "Hold on..."

Chapter 382

As Fan Shuo conceded, the tension that had lingered

among the spectators finally dissipated. Although they

hadn't witnessed overly thrilling battles since leaving the Tower of Heaven, witnessing the Five Elements Reincarnation Flower of Qilian Twin Devils, Jin Zhanyi's Horizon's Blink, and Zhou Yi's Earth-Tunnelling Techniquehad opened their eyes and made their journey worthwhile.

With Fan Shuo's surrender, it meant that the Lingxiao Treasure Hall had won this duel and secured ten Jiahuang Pills. For the members of the Lingxiao Treasure Hall, this outcome was more than satisfactory.

However, as soon as Jin Zhanyi began to speak, the unease among the crowd resurfaced. Their gazes turned towards Jin Zhanyi, now tinted with curiosity and uncertainty.

Fan Shuo's expression slightly darkened as he asked, "Jin Zhanyi, do you have any further dissatisfaction?"

Jin Zhanyi met his gaze fearlessly and then bowed slightly before speaking loudly, "Respected Venerable Fan, I've long heard of the fame of the Five Elements Reincarnation Flower, especially the Metal Flower, created by the Qilian Twin Devils. It's truly exceptional.His voice suddenly rose, carrying an unmatched and fierce battle intent, "I may be lacking in skill, but I wish to experience it firsthand."

With these words, the crowd understood his intention. If you've come to challenge, then you must show your true strength; otherwise, don't even think about leaving.

Thinking about Jin Zhanyi's personality and his notorious habit of seeking challenges everywhere, the spectators couldn't help but find it amusing. Qilian Twin Devils seemed to have kicked a hornet's nest, and it wouldn't be so easy for them to shake off Jin Zhanyi now.

Fan Shuo's gaze shifted slightly between the two challengers and he calmly stated, "Both of you possess the Horizon's Blink and Earth-Tunnelling Technique. In this duel, you are already in an invincible position. Even if the Qilian Twin Devils' martial techniques are powerful, they won't be able to reach you. What's the use?"

Jin Zhanyi glanced at Zhou Yi, who nodded subtly.

"Venerable Fan Shuo, we can assure you that in the upcoming battles, we won't employ the Horizon's Blink and the Earth-Tunnelling Technique," Jin Zhanyi spoke with a composed tone.

These words caused even the initially cheerful Gao and Du, the other two Venerables, to slightly change their expressions.

"This won't do..." A clear and melodious voice rang out. It was Miss Qiu, who had remained silent since leaving the tower. She couldn't hold back anymore and spoke up, "Senior Brother Jin, since it's a decisive battle, why would using ultimate techniques not be allowed? If you insist on conceding, you might as well tie up your hands and feet to fight them."

Both Fan Shuo and Qilian Twin Devils blushed slightly. However, they chose to remain silent in unison. Miss Qiu's authority was truly formidable; even they dared not provoke her.

Jin Zhanyi shook his head slightly and said, "Junior Sister Qiu, Zhou and I only wish to test our skills against the Qilian Twin Devils without any restrictions. Please refrain from intervening."

Though his words were polite, the underlying message was clear.

A hint of irritation flickered in Miss Qiu's eyes, but it quickly gave way to concern. Despite her irritation, she eventually restrained herself from voicing further objections.

Fan Shuo's gaze swept over the four individuals and then, without any further action, he turned around and returned to his original position.

A chill ran down Zhou Yi's spine as he realized that Fan Shuo's speed was even faster than his own.

He had a faint thought in his mind that if this old man had been among the pursuing Venerables that night, it would have been difficult for him to escape easily.

Since Fan Shuo had departed, the crowd naturally understood his intention. Qilian Twin Devils bowed respectfully. Their expressions were now extremely serious, and both sides' auras had subtly shifted after the recent incident.

The Qilian Twin Devils' momentum had been greatly suppressed. Launching an attack now might not be a favorable outcome for them. But Fan Shuo was also helpless; the battle between Zhou Yi, Jin Zhanyi, and the Qilian Twin Devils was even more crucial for the Qilian Twin Devils. If they missed this opportunity, who knew if they would still have the chance to break through their limits.

Both parties took their positions. Qilian Twin Devils uttered a low shout, standing side by side once again. However, this time there was a slight difference from before. The Big Devil's body was positioned slightly behind that of the Second Devil, not standing on the same plane.

The Five Elements Flower, which had been hovering above their heads, swooped down again towards Zhou Yi and Jin Zhanyi. Simultaneously, the Qilian

Twin Devils' bodies moved subtly, following closely behind the Flower, closing the distance.

Jin Zhanyi burst into hearty laughter, his eyes filling with unwavering determination. His hands clasped the empty air, and a strong metallic hue shimmered within his palms. He then opened his mouth and exhaled, expelling a Metal Flower.

The Metal Flower drifted downwards, exploding between his hands. Immense golden energy emanated from his palms, merging with the shattered petals of the Metal Flower. In just a single breath, a golden spear had appeared between his hands.

This wasn't his Dragon Spear; it was the astounding effect created by condensing his entire Metal energy into a single point.

Zhou Yi glanced at him with envy. While he was also skilled in manipulating Metal energy, he couldn't achieve this level without forming the Metal Flowers.

However, facing the incoming Five Elements Flower with its overwhelming force, Zhou Yi refused to be outdone. He, too, opened his mouth, and three distinct flowers manifested before him.

With a gentle exhalation, the three flowers burst apart, releasing boundless energy that whirled around him. Swiftly, the energy converged into three distinct beams of light, each shimmering with a different hue – representing the Wind, Fire, and Earth elements.

These three streams of light merged yet remained distinct, forming an intricate balance of the Wind, Fire, and Earth elements. His Three Flowers United seemed somewhat similar to Qilian Twin Devils' Five Elements Flower, but most of the experts present could discern the essential difference.

Qilian Twin Devil's Five Elements Flower was an amalgamation formed by harnessing the mutually enhancing power of the Five Elements. If any one element was missing, the technique would fall apart. However, Zhou Yi's three flowers melded together in complete unity, a sensation of seamless integration that was a novel experience for most observers.

While others might have only grasped the visual distinction, for Fan Shuo and the other two Venerables, it bore an entirely different significance. Since Zhou Yi hadn't integrated any divine weapon into his body, he hadn't reached the status of a Venerable.

But even so, the fusion of three distinct elemental flowers into one by Zhou Yi was incredibly astonishing to them. This act shattered their understanding, even inducing a strong sense of unease. Ultimately, a thought they couldn't suppress arose within them: Could it be possible that the lost divine path of thousands of years might have a chance of resurgence?

Unaware of the intense impact his integration of the Three Flowers was having on the three Venerables, Zhou Yi had only one goal in mind – to collaborate with Jin Zhanyi and force the Qilian Twin Devils to unleash their strongest attack.

In the next moment, the Five Elements Reincarnation Flower collided with the golden spear in Jin Zhanyi's hand, and then it struck the three-colored barrier in front of Zhou Yi.

This was the first genuine confrontation between the four of them after their duel.

In the Tower of Heaven, Zhou Yi and his companion had cleverly seized an advantage and been aided by the tower's mysterious power. This made Jin Zhanyi and his partner appear formidable, as if they could easily defeat Qilian Twin Devils with a mere wave of their hands.

However, now that the Qilian Twin Devils were fully coordinated, and Zhou Yi lacked the infusion of the tower's mystical energy, the current clash was a true test of their respective strengths.

"A boom..."

Following a tremendous roar, a powerful shockwave emanated from the four of them, causing the soil beneath their feet to be ejected outward like bullets.

Gao Weiliang took a step forward, positioning himself in front of Qiu Girl.

With his strength, he naturally cared little about the impact of the flying debris and powerful shockwave. But even he, sensing the formidable power of the four in the scene, felt a touch of apprehension. He didn't dare to be reckless any longer; if he were to inadvertently fail to protect miss Qiu   and she got hurt, he wouldn't be able to withstand the wrath of the Sect Master.

The onlookers around were immediately thrown into chaos by the powerful shockwave. Even ordinary

One-line Heaven realm experts felt unsteady in the face of this immense force. When the chunks of earth and debris were sent flying, apart from the two Three Flower powerhouses who had formed their foothold, the rest subconsciously dodged. If they were truly unable to avoid the debris, they would use their own strength to shatter it.

As for the ordinary innate experts who had luckily arrived at the scene, their fortune had just turned sour. They struggled to withstand the residual impact, and three of them even sustained minor injuries.

At this moment, they truly grasped the immense disparity between themselves and the established experts. This gap was insurmountable at their current stage, leaving them with a profound sense of defeat.

When the dust finally settled, they were able to see

the changes that had taken place in the arena...

Chapter 383

At this moment, a sharp contrast emerged between

Zhou Yi and his companion and the Qilian Twin Devils.

The Twin Devils stood back to back, and though their

movements weren't swift, every strike they made

carried a weighty force, steady and powerful, as if the

entire force of space converged towards them.

Meanwhile, Zhou Yi and Jin Zhanyi darted around like lightning, circling Qilian Twin Devils like spinning wheels of wind and fire. Occasionally, they would reach out and strike, disrupting the Twin Devils' actions and preventing them from building up their momentum.

In secret, Fan Shuo let out a sigh of relief – Zhou Yi was indeed not a Venerable . The full-force blow just now had revealed the true strength of both sides. Despite appearing evenly matched, no one could claim absolute dominance over the other in this head-to-head clash.

However, the three venerable experts could easily discern that Zhou Yi was undoubtedly the weakest link among the four. His ability to display such dominance stemmed from his complete fusion of the three elemental forces. By harnessing the true unity of the three elements, he was barely able to match the Metal elemental power of Jin Zhanyi.

This collision had immediately exposed his true strength, bringing a slight sense of relief to the hearts of the three venerable experts. If Zhou Yi possessed not only the Three Flowers United skill but also formidable true energy comparable to Jin Zhanyi's, their confidence might have been truly shaken.

Similarly, as the four engaged in battle, this exchange gave them a rough assessment of each other's strengths. Accordingly, their strategic approaches began to diverge.

Leveraging their strong synergy, the Qilian Twin Devils consistently unleashed the power of confinement of the Five Elements Reincarnation Flower. They took a steady approach, showing no signs of impatience, and aimed to wear down Zhou Yi and his companion through sheer endurance.

Yet, Zhou Yi and his companion, aware of their slight disadvantage in absolute strength, maneuvered lightly. They circled around the Qilian Twin Devils, and both Jin Zhanyi's Dragon Spear and Zhou Yi's united three-element power were not to be underestimated. The immense counterforce posed an equally troublesome challenge for the Twin Devils.

For a while, the two sides remained entangled, displaying extreme caution and patience, as if they aimed to prolong this battle endlessly.

Suddenly, Fan Shuo's brows furrowed. He faintly sensed that something was amiss. His eyes lit up as he realized the reason – when Jin Zhanyi issued the challenge earlier, he wanted to experience the shared gold power of the Qilian Twin Devils. However, by dragging the battle out like this, they might not have the chance to go all out.

A vague feeling told him that Zhou Yi and his companion were plotting something. After that initial strike, the Qilian Twin Devils unknowingly fell into their trap. Even Fan Shuo himself couldn't discern the true intentions of Zhou Yi and his companion.

After a few more moments of continuous clashes and confrontations, the momentum among the four escalated like sesame flowers in full bloom. The pressure exerted by their immense momentum gradually grew and spread. Fortunately, the valley was spacious enough, and at least everyone present was at the Innate level. While they couldn't completely resist this overpowering pressure, they had enough space to retreat.

However, with each step back, their awe of the four combatants deepened. After this battle today, it had a significant impact on those innate strength experts. It fueled their desire for higher levels of martial arts and deepened their yearning for advanced stages of the martial path.

As Zhou Yi and his companion sped up, their movements grew more frantic, resembling two shooting stars revolving around the Qilian Twin Devils.

Finally, the momentum of all four had reached its peak, nearly reaching an unimaginable height.

In the hearts of the three venerable figures including Fan Shuo, there arose a sense of astonishment. The four individuals present were clearly not on the level of true revered experts, yet when their powers were pushed to their limits, the overwhelming aura they produced was no less intense than the ferocity seen in the life-and-death battles of two true venerable beings.

However, at this point, determining a winner between the four of them could be extremely dangerous.

During their swift movements, Zhou Yi and Jin Zhanyi exchanged a glance in midair and nodded almost simultaneously.

Following this, Zhou Yi flipped backward and leaped away, while Jin Zhanyi's speed increased even further. The tangible spear in his hand was like lightning, thrusting towards the Twin Devils. Each spear shadow seemed to be a coiled-up viper finally unleashed, revealing terrifying fangs, sweeping like a mountain of snakes.

Although Qilian Twin Devils were taken aback by Zhou Yi's sudden withdrawal, under Jin Zhanyi's burst of speed, they were temporarily suppressed by him alone.

Of course, it was evident to all that such a wild offensive couldn't be sustained for long. Perhaps in a matter of a few breaths, Jin Zhanyi would exhaust himself and have to retreat. At that moment, he would face the full-force counterattack from Qilian Twin

Devils, which would undoubtedly be perilous and highly dangerous.

All eyes were fixed on Zhou Yi. Everyone knew there was a reason for their actions. Most people were speculating whether Zhou Yi intended to continue deploying his near-unstoppable Overturning Heaven Seal.

However, what astonished them was that Zhou Yi unexpectedly began to throw punches.

At such a crucial juncture, he actually ignored the ongoing battle and started to throw punches as if he were alone.

The thirty-Six Forms of Mountain-Crushing, the first move, the second move, the third move...

A hint of doubt appeared in everyone's eyes. At this point in the battle, it was clear to everyone that Zhou Yi hadn't condensed the Metal Flower. If that was the case, why would he use a set of Metal-element combat techniques? Could he possibly have lost his mind?

However, the thirty-Six Forms of Mountain-Crushing were not unfamiliar to most. Even though they hadn't chosen to cultivate this technique, this set of Metal-based combat techniques was renowned even in the martial repository, and many had browsed through it to some extent.

Zhou Yi seemed to recognize that Jin Zhanyi couldn't hold out for much longer, so he was clearly moving much faster while executing this technique.

In just a couple of breaths, he had already completed twelve moves of post-celestial fist techniques.

The thirteenth move!

As this move was executed, a piercing sound of air being torn apart resounded in the atmosphere.

The immense momentum that had pervaded the atmosphere seemed to be drawn towards this technique, surging fiercely towards Zhou Yi. The dense and loud cracking sound was like the popping of beans, exploding in the air.

Once the innate techniques of the thirty-Six Forms of Mountain-Crushing were initiated, they instantly stirred the qi of heaven and earth. In the perception of everyone present, Zhou Yi seemed to transform into a massive blade. His intent harmonized perfectly with the innate technique, creating a seamless fusion.

The expressions of the Qilian Twin Devils changed slightly. They vaguely grasped Zhou Yi's intention. Zhou Yi was clearly accumulating the momentum of a certain martial technique. When he fully executed this set of techniques, it would erupt with a tremendous power surpassing ordinary combat techniques.

This kind of slow and accumulative immense force through each move and technique should not have appeared in actual combat. However, with Jin Zhanyi's impact, everything had become possible.

The Twin Devils suddenly roared loudly, moving at twice their previous speed. At the same time, their expressions underwent a stark change.

The big Devil stepped back a pace, his body curling up, seemingly shrinking a whole round to conceal himself entirely behind his brother. A powerful water-based energy surged from his body. Meanwhile, the water flower within the Five Elements Reincarnation Flower, which had been hovering above their heads, also shone brightly. The entire space was filled with an overwhelming water-based energy.

Jin Zhanyi's gaze sharpened. He accelerated even more, seemingly attempting to disrupt the Twin Devils' technique. However, the second Devil's hands spun like flying wheels. It appeared as if he had grown by a whole circle, unexpectedly fully absorbing Jin Zhanyi's onslaught.

The atmosphere in the arena grew increasingly tense. Everyone felt the same way. The battle between the four of them was reaching its climax, with victory or defeat hanging in the balance.

Unconsciously, the hearts of all present were suspended in anticipation. They wanted to see who would ultimately emerge victorious.

Zhou Yi's movements became faster and faster, seemingly responding to the changes in the Five Elements Flower. The momentum emanating from him also underwent corresponding changes. The latent potential within him was being forced out bit by bit. His skin even took on a metallic hue.

The Five Elements Flower above the Qilian Twin Devils' heads once again underwent subtle changes. The light of the wood element gradually intensified. Then, the position of the Qilian Twin Devils underwent an incredibly rapid shift. The flowers representing the fire and earth elements illuminated, converging their energies toward the golden flower.

Although Qilian Twin Devils practiced different techniques, when they joined forces, they possessed the entire power of the five elements. Moreover, they shared the gold-based power. As their true energy gathered together, the flowers of the other four elements rushed into the golden flower, making it expand to an enormous size.

A gleam of excitement and anticipation flashed in Jin Zhanyi's eyes. His body moved like lightning, retreating to the rear, standing like a spear on the side.

Zhou Yi's techniques had already been pushed to their limits. The twenty-third stance of the "Thirty-Six

Forms of Mountain-Crushing" had successfully been manifested in his hands. In the past few days of training, whenever he reached this point, Zhou Yi often felt inadequate, causing him to gradually disperse the gathered true energy and momentum.

Instead of showing any intention to stop, he turned his gaze towards the Qilian Twin Devils and took a step forward.

His footfall wasn't forceful, yet as it landed on the ground, it sent shivers down everyone's spines. Then, the boundless momentum in the air surged wildly toward him, as if igniting dry wood, it burst into a thunderous explosion.

His hands separated, forming an odd posture.

"Twenty-Fourth Stance of Mountain-Crushing..."

Chapter 384

As the unimaginably powerful aura from all directions converged and erupted due to Zhou Yi's performance of the Thirty-Six Forms of Mountain-Crushing, he finally took that last step forward.

Previously, when practicing these twenty-three forms, he always fell short at the critical moment. This wasn't due to Zhou Yi's lack of effort; rather, his cultivation hadn't been sufficient. Although he had been building momentum from the First Technique onwards, gradually approaching the minimum requirement to execute the Twenty-Fourth Technique, there had always been a slight deficiency in his attempts.

However, this time was different. When he executed the Twenty-Third Technique, the overwhelming aura around him became his greatest aid. At that moment, his body seemed to transform into his own Dantian, like an alternate black hole, avidly absorbing all the surrounding aura. It transformed into a chaotic force before being infused into his fist techniques.

Zhou Yi extended his hand high, and the edges of his palm seemed to narrow slightly, resembling the sharp edge of a big blade. Carrying boundless momentum, he viciously slashed towards the Qilian Twin Devils. Almost simultaneously, Jin Zhanyi's eyes radiated brilliance, and his body lunged forward like a spear, piercing ahead. The coordination between this slash and thrust was flawless, as if they had rehearsed it countless times, leaving people in awe.

In an instant, the force of the blade and spear collided forcefully with the massive Metal Flower.

Both were razor-sharp forces of the Metal element. When these similar yet distinct manifestations of the same element collided, a chilling sense of foreboding spread through everyone, even from the aftermath of their clash.

A piercing friction sound filled the air as the clash between the blade and spear and the Metal flower reached a temporary stalemate. However, this lasted only for a brief moment. The unparalleled force could no longer be contained, resulting in a violent explosion in the air.

The aftermath of this explosion was far more powerful than their initial collision. Cold gusts emanated from the center, like enormous, sharp blades slicing through everything within sight. On the ground, deep furrows, half a foot wide and several zhang long, appeared, spreading out like a spiderweb around the four combatants and extending into the distance.

Simultaneously, numerous sharp blade winds blew towards the onlookers.

"Use your weapons," Gao Weiliang's voice resonated with gravity.

The words of the venerable individual were promptly followed by everyone. They all took out their suitable weapons and erected flawless energy barriers in front of them.

Especially the innate experts, they gathered together, united in their efforts to resist the immense destructive force caused by the clash of the four central top experts engaged in their combat.

After a moment, the sporadic blade-like residual gusts finally subsided. As everyone breathed a sigh of relief, they turned their gaze back to the center.

The four individuals in the field were not in good condition either. Their clothes were torn and tattered, as if they had been slashed by countless sharp blades, leaving them looking disheveled and worn.

However, amidst the tattered outer garments, a glimmer of light seemed to flicker. Those who could advance to the Innate Realm were certainly not fools. They immediately understood that this was because all four of them had unconsciously put on protective armor. Therefore, during the previous impact, they had only shielded vital areas like their heads and faces.

However, what truly surprised everyone was that the intense combat intent between them seemed to inexplicably disappear. Instead, the four of them furrowed their brows and appeared to be deep in thought. Occasionally, they exchanged glances, then quickly averted their gazes, entering their own world of contemplation.

Fan Shuo and the other two venerables secretly breathed a sigh of relief. At the moment when the four of them went all-out, their greatest fear was mutual destruction, with all four losing their lives on the spot. If that had truly happened, it would have had profound consequences for the Lingxiao Treasure Hall and the Qilian Mountain.

However, after this exchange, even though neither side had emerged as the clear victor, it seemed that both parties had gained some insights from the confrontation. The three venerables exchanged a glance and saw a hint of gratification in each other's eyes.

The entire valley gradually quieted down. Apart from the chaotic aftermath, there was no sound left. Most people gazed at them in silence. Wei Zongjin and the other expert who had reached the One-line Heaven of their level were savoring the scene that had just unfolded.

The collision of the four experts' Metal powers intersected. Apart from the intense impact they felt as participants, for other high-level experts of similar caliber, it was a rare experience as well.

After a long while, Qilian Twin Devils were the first to let out a sigh. Excitement flickered in their eyes. The second Devil's body trembled slightly, and he coughed up a mouthful of blood. Although the big Devil managed to hold on, his face turned as pale as snow.

Fan Shuo took a step forward and stood beside them. He retrieved a pill bottle from his person and handed it directly to them. The Twin Devils didn't stand on ceremony and immediately swallowed the pills.

In just a few breaths, their complexions improved significantly. Everyone gazed at the bottle of pills in Fan Shuo's hand with envy, but no one dared to harbor thoughts of snatching it.

Jin Zhanyi also let out a sigh. However, as he exhaled, his body seemed to sway unsteadily. Du Wenbin rushed over to his side and saw that Jin Zhanyi had managed to steady himself, his eyes brimming with intense joy.

Jin Zhanyi didn't ingest any pills; instead, he sat cross-legged on the ground and began absorbing the qi of heaven and earth as if no one else was present. As a peak expert, his absorption speed was incredibly fast. After a moment, he opened his eyes, leaped up from the ground, and although his complexion was somewhat pale, his spirit was revived.

Qilian Twin Devils exchanged a profound glance, a hint of unusual sentiment on their faces. They all envied Jin Zhanyi's youth, which allowed him to endure solely by absorbing the qi of heaven and earth in this situation. If it were a hundred years ago, they might have achieved the same, but now they had to rely on precious pills to preserve their vital energy.

Finally, another long exhale echoed through the air. The gazes of the people once again converged on the young powerhouse.

When Zhou Yi exhaled, his breath was noticeably different from Jin Zhanyi andQilian Twin Devils. The breath he expelled carried a hint of metallic luster. Everyone, including the three venerables, was slightly taken aback. They scrutinized the peculiar light closely, a sense of realization dawning upon them, and their expressions turning somewhat strange. Envy and jealousy mingled in their eyes.

As Zhou Yi's breath was completely expelled, the myriad metallic glimmers instantly converged. In the blink of an eye, a tangible flower took form in midair.

The Metal Flower...

A heartfelt chorus of sighs emanated from all around. Anyone could tell that the tangible flower that had appeared was the result of Zhou Yi's recent enlightenment and mastery.

The combined force For Qi Lian's dual demons' attack finally enabled Zhou Yi to unleash the Twenty-Fourth Technique from the "Thirty-Six Forms of Mountain-Crushing" form.

Moreover, in the ultimate clash, the collision of their powerful metallic forces had granted them a fresh understanding of this power.

What exactly the other three had comprehended, Zhou Yi wasn't sure. Yet, the only thing he could be certain of was that he had touched the essence of metallic power, which enabled him to ride the momentum and execute the Twenty-Fourth Technique, culminating in the successful formation of the Metal Flower.

Seeing the Metal flower hovering in the sky, , a subtle change crossed Qilian Twin Devils' expressions.

In their perception, this Metal Flower didn't merely contain metallic power; much like their Five Elements Reincarnation Flower, it seemed to carry the essence of all five elemental powers.

Of course, the other four elemental forces were faint, almost negligible. Even Fan Shuo didn't notice. If it weren't for their hundreds of years of companionship and possession of the entire spectrum of elemental forces, they wouldn't have picked up on this subtle change.

Zhou Yi exhaled and then took a deep breath. With his inhalation, the Metal Flower that had formed dissipated instantly in the air, transmuting into the five elemental powers that he absorbed into his abdomen.

A thought flashed across the mind of the Big Devil. He bowed deeply, saying, "Brother Jin, Brother Zhou, I am greatly indebted to both of you."

Jin Zhanyi waved his hand and chuckled, "Mutually beneficial. If you two ever feel like sparring again in the future, we can always have another contest."

Inwardly, everyone couldn't help but sigh. If anyone else were to be challenged by Qilian Twin Devils, they would avoid it like the plague. Only someone like Jin Zhanyi, a madman of sorts, would look forward to such a contest.

The Big Devil let out a wry smile. Although both he and his brother walked the path of cultivation through challenges with powerful adversaries, allowing them to progress rapidly, when compared, Jin Zhanyi seemed even more daring.

Clearing his throat, the Big Devil turned his gaze to Zhou Yi and said, "Brother Zhou, congratulations."

Zhou Yi smiled faintly and sincerely replied, "The battle with both of you has been greatly enlightening.

If there's an opportunity in the future, I'd be glad to exchange moves again."

The Big Devil blinked in surprise, and laughter echoed from those around. Unexpectedly, it seemed that another troublesome fellow like Jin Zhanyi had emerged.

Shaking his head lightly, the bloodthirsty nature within the Big Devil was finally ignited. He spoke, "Gentlemen, from today onward, my brother and I go into seclusion for cultivation. Within two years, we will either achieve the status of Venerable or be reduced to dust. If we're fortunate enough to survive..." A hint of a smile appeared on his face as he continued, "Three years later, my brother and I will head to the Realm of Life and Death. However, I wonder if at that time, we'll still be able to journey alongside both of you."

Jin Zhanyi's eyes suddenly glinted, and he said in a deep voice, "You two have comprehended it?"

Qilian Twin Devils exchanged a glance, both revealing a touch of proud smiles on their faces simultaneously.

Chapter 385

Jin Zhanyi observed them and, after a moment, nodded deeply, saying, "Congratulations."

Qilian Twin Devils simultaneously shook their heads. It was evident that their nearly three-hundred-year companionship as twin brothers had made them incredibly synchronized in their actions. They seemed as if they were one person, moving in perfect harmony with each other.

During their battle just now, they displayed deep enmity towards each other, as if they wished to annihilate their opponent completely. However, as soon as the battle ended, they immediately relaxed and quickly formed a camaraderie.

Despite the significant age difference among the four of them, they treated each other as equals and their interactions seemed completely natural. After reaching the Innate Realm, their interactions were based on their individual martial cultivation.

For a Venerable, it was impossible to truly bond with a group of One-Line Heaven"experts, even if those experts were Three Flower experts. As long as these experts had not advanced to the Venerable Realm, they wouldn't receive recognition from Venerable powerhouses.

Strength is everything in the world of martial arts.

A smile impossible to conceal appeared on Fan Shuo's face. He extended his wrist, revealing another jade bottle, and handed it over to Jin Zhanyi with a cheerful demeanor. He said, "Nephew Jin, I was trouble the two of you this time.Here are ten Jiahuang Pills. Please accept them."

Jin Zhanyi carefully received the jade bottle, his excitement barely hidden even with his composure.

Jin Zhanyi received the jade bottle with great care, and despite his strong self-control, a faint trace of excitement could be seen in his expression. With a deep bow, he said, "I sincerely thank Senior Fan for this generous gift."

Fan Shuo waved his hand and said, "I can tell that you've gained a lot just now. Do you also have the confidence to break through your limits?"

Jin Zhanyi let out a bitter laugh and replied, "Although I've had some insights, it still seems quite challenging to overcome that final barrier."

Fan Shuo nodded slightly, his response from Jin Zhanyi falling well within his expectations. It would only feel balanced if Jin Zhanyi managed to reach that level.

Big Devil hesitated for a moment and suddenly spoke, "Brother Jin, I have a suggestion, though it might seem abrupt. I hope you won't take offense."

Jin Zhanyi laughed heartily and replied, "You don't need to be so polite. Please, go ahead and speak."

big Devil spoke solemnly, "Given the turmoil rising in the Western regions, with numerous experts flocking to the Central Great Plains, Brother Jin, if you could participate in this battle, perhaps your long-cherished wish could be fulfilled."

Fan Shuo furrowed his brow slightly and said, "Big Devil, please don't speak recklessly."

Participating in the battle between the Eastern and Western regions was indeed an excellent opportunity to break through martial barriers. However, it also came with significant risks. Whether Jin Zhanyi would be willing to go wasn't solely his decision; it would surely require the deliberation of the Venerables from the Lingxiao Treasure Hall. Regardless of the intentions behind Qilian Twin Devils' proposal, it seemed to tread on sensitive ground.

Jin Zhanyi naturally understood this. He gave a faint smile and said, "Esteemed Venerable Fan, I made up my mind long ago.After this battle, I will head to the Central Great Plains."

He turned his head, his gaze intense as he looked at Qilian Twin Devils, and continued, "In three years, I, Jin Zhanyi, will head to the Realm of Life and Death. I hope to meet the two of you there."

Gao Wei Liang burst into laughter, echoing agreement, and the others from the Lingxiao Treasure Hall displayed expressions of joy. Jin Zhanyi's bold words seemed to have ignited unparalleled excitement among them.

Qilian Twin Devils nodded slightly, their gazes meeting once again, seemingly regaining their sharpness.

Zhou Yi was uncertain in his heart. He had heard of the Realm of Life and Death and knew that it had a close connection with the Totem Clan. However, he didn't understand why Jin Zhanyi and the others kept mentioning it. Could it be that they also intended to provoke the Totem Clan?

If that were the case, Zhou Yi wouldn't mind adding fuel to the fire, or even stepping in directly.

Qilian Twin Devils' gaze gradually softened. big Devil turned his head and said, "Brother Zhou, if I'm not mistaken, you've already condensed the fourth tangible flower."

Zhou Yi nodded with a smile and replied, "That's correct. I have indeed condensed the fourth tangible flower."

TFor most people, being able to condense three tangible flowers is already considered a limit. Once reaching this stage, one would begin to master the power of confinement and prepare for the ultimate Three Flowers Gathering at the Apex.

However, Zhou Yi had managed to possess four tangible flowers without even having fully mastered the power of confinement. This was truly an extraordinary feat.

With a gleam of excitement in his eyes, Big Devil inquired, "I would like to ask, Brother Zhou, which three tangible flowers do you intend to use as the foundation for the Three Flowers Gathering at the Apex?"

Without any hesitation, Zhou Yi responded, "Naturally, it would be the Five Elements Flowers."

His response was swift and confident, without a trace of hesitation. After all, this wasn't some secretive matter; once he became renowned in the world, it would naturally become common knowledge.

big Devil's expression suddenly froze, and he said, "Brother Zhou, I noticed something peculiar about your Metal flower earlier. It seems to contain the power of the Five Elements. Am I correct?"

Fan Shuo's eyebrows twitched slightly, a barely noticeable movement. Then, he fixed his gaze intently on Zhou Yi.

Fan Shuo wasn't a practitioner of all five elements. Despite his strength and keen insight, he still fell short of being able to discern the Five Elements' power within the Metal flower.

Zhou Yi hesitated for a moment. However, he realized that this matter was impossible to conceal from those who were truly attentive. If he were to deny it vehemently, he would truly be looked down upon.

A faint smile appeared at the corner of his mouth as he responded, "Brother big Devil has sharp eyes."

Qilian Twin Devils and Fan Shuo, the three of them, fixed their gazes on Zhou Yi, their expressions showing a hint of bewilderment.

"Brother Zhou, how did you achieve this?" big Devil asked solemnly.

With a slight shrug of his shoulders, Zhou Yi said, 'I have always practiced the five elements together. After seeing your Five Elements Reincarnation Flowers, I gained some insights and blended in the powers of the other four elements. However, it's just a superficial technique, far from being comparable to a genuine Five Elements Reincarnation Flower.

He said this sentence absolutely sincerely, and the power of the Metal Flower he condensed is far inferior when compared to the huge Metal Flower that Qilian Twin Devils had just formed.

However, after hearing his explanation, the expressions of Fan Shuo and Qilian Twin Devils turned increasingly peculiar. Gao Weiliang and Du Wenbin exchanged a helpless look, shaking their heads slightly, opting for silence.

Fan Shuo's gaze shifted unpredictably, and he finally regained a cordial smile, saying, "Mr. Zhou, after arriving from the northwest to Da Shen, are you planning to travel the world?"

As Zhou Yi looked at the smile on Fan Shuo's face, for some inexplicable reason, he felt a tingling sensation on his scalp. Moreover, being addressed as "Mr. Zhou" by a Venerable made him mutter to himself internally. Thankfully, after all he had been through, he wouldn't outwardly show his unease, even if he felt any.

"Indeed, I've come to Da Shen from the northwest with the intention of experiencing a different atmosphere," Zhou Yi replied honestly.

Fan Shuo's smile grew even gentler as he said, "Well said. As an outstanding martial artist, staying secluded doesn't yield results as good as traveling the world. Mr. Zhou, you truly have broad perspectives."

Zhou Yi's expression remained unchanged, and he slightly bowed, saying, "Respected Venerable Fan, your praise is too kind."

Deep inside, however, he mused, Is this esteemed person flattering me or scolding me to my face? These are the accumulated experiences of countless predecessors, something every cultivator knows, especially those who have reached the Innate realm.

Fan Shuo waved his hand and said, "Mr. Zhou, the Da Shen region is vast with countless famous sites and deep mountains and valleys. However, our Qilian

Mountain is undoubtedly one of the best places in the world. Among them, the Five Elements Sanctuary is recognized as the number one cultivation sanctuary in the world. For those with a Five Elements constitution, the speed of cultivation there is more than ten times faster than in other areas." As he spoke, he put away his smiling face and continued solemnly, "Mr. Zhou, I'd like to invite you to visit Qilian. What are your thoughts?"

While Zhou Yi's heart was indeed moved by the enticing description of Qilian Mountain, he became even more cautious. Fan Shuo's enthusiastic introduction and persistent invitation had to have some hidden motive, and Zhou Yi wouldn't believe otherwise even if you killed him.

With a faint smile, Zhou Yi showed a grateful expression but regretfully said, "Thank you very much, Elder Fan. However, I already have prior commitments at the moment, so I'm unable to visit."

While he spoke politely, he had already decided in his heart that he wouldn't visit no matter what.

Fan Shuo hesitated for a moment and then inquired, "May I ask about Mr. Zhou's recent plans?"

Zhou Yi was slightly taken aback, not expecting this person to be so persistent, seemingly determined to continue until he achieved his goal. His heart skipped a beat, and his gaze turned toward the smiling Jin Zhanyi. His eyes brightened involuntarily, and he said, "Master Fan, I have already made an agreement with Brother Jin to join the expedition to the west and face the enemy together. This is a rare opportunity for experience. I hope you can understand, senior."

Fan Shuo's gaze turned toward Jin Zhanyi. In his heart, Jin Zhanyi was cursing, but when faced with Fan Shuo's inquiring gaze, he still nodded firmly and said, "Indeed, the two of us have an agreement. After the battle with Qilian Twin Devils , we will immediately head to the Central Great Plains."

Fan Shuo let out a disappointed sigh and then said, "Mr. Zhou, you practicing all five elements is indeed a unique gift. However, practicing all five elements requires specific complementary techniques to fully unleash the most powerful potential. If Mr. Zhou decides to come to Qilian Mountain in the future, please seek me out. I will be more than happy to welcome you and discuss our cultivation together."

Zhou Yi's heart was immediately stirred. Despite all that Fan Shuo had said, it was this particular statement that truly captured Zhou Yi's attention.

He understood deep down that perhaps this Venerable had sensed his dismissive attitude earlier, which was why he was offering such an enticing bait.

Even though he had already made up his mind not to visit Qilian Mountain, the temptation was still strong at this moment, especially for someone like him who possessed the power of all five elements. He couldn't help but feel moved.

Finally, he heaved a long sigh and composedly replied, "Venerable Fan, after I return from the Central Great Plains, I will definitely come to Qilian Mountain to pay my respects to you."

A faint smile of satisfaction appeared on Fan Shuo's face, and he burst into laughter, saying, "I'll be waiting on Qilian Mountain. Just don't keep me waiting too long, I hope."

Zhou Yi responded with an awkward smile.

After a brief hesitation, Fan Shuo eventually tossed another vial in his hand to Zhou Yi, saying, "The journey to the west is quite perilous. Please carry this elixir with you. It might come in handy."

With that said, he cupped his hands slightly in a farewell gesture to the surrounding crowd and departed in great strides. Following closely behind him, Qilian Twin Devils nodded slightly at Zhou Yi and Jin Zhanyi before disappearing from view along with Fan Shuo.

After a while, the three of them had vanished from the sight of the others and were nowhere to be seen.

Chapter 386

From a distance, a gentle breeze swept by, as if it was this breeze that roused the people in the valley from their thoughts. After the departure of the Venerable Fan Shuo and the master-disciple duo Qilian Twin Devils, the attention of the many experts turned towards Zhou Yi and Jin Zhanyi. Their eyes revealed unconcealed envy.

Zhou Yi's accomplishment of condensing the Metal Flower was noteworthy, but Jin Zhanyi was the true focus of attention. Gao Weiliang walked towards them with measured steps and asked, "Nephew Jin, are you truly confident?"

Jin Zhanyi's expression tightened, and a definite look appeared on his face. He reached his hand to his waist and lightly patted it, causing a flash of cold light. The dragon spear appeared before everyone's eyes.

At this moment, the legendary dragon-skin crafted spear shaft stood tall, emanating a dazzling cold radiance that was almost painful to the eyes

The people were momentarily taken aback, not quite understanding what he was doing. Only Gao and Du, the two venerable experts, and the highly perceptive Zhou Yi, faintly sensed that behind the cold gleam, a faint white mist seemed to hover, as if the dragon spear was on the verge of misting away.

"Please rest assured, Senior Uncles. The only step I lack is the final one, and I've already had some premonitions," Jin Zhanyi said calmly.

Zhou Yi was surprised, but Gao and Du were overjoyed. They exchanged a glance and nodded at each other. Gao Weiliang let out a long sigh and said, "Nephew Jin, your choice is the right one. Today's battle has indeed brought you considerable benefits."

Jin Zhanyi, composed and unhurried, inquired, "When should I set out for the Central Plains?"

Gao Weiliang hesitated for a moment and replied, "Although the Western forces have begun mobilizing their troops, according to past patterns, it will be at least after the New Year when the Holy Knights will appear on the main battlefield. you wait here for three more months, consolidate what you've learned, and build up your strength. This will allow you to be well-prepared for the battles against the real powerhouses."

Jin Zhanyi nodded slightly and said, "I'll defer to Senior's decision." With a flick of his wrist, the dragon spear swiftly coiled back to his waist, the entire movement as smooth as flowing water, leaving a pleasing sensation.

Zhou Yi couldn't help but marvel at the display. Just then, a person slowly walked forward – it was the smiling Qiu Miss. She greeted warmly, "Senior Brother Jin."

Jin Zhanyi's demeanor lost the earlier ease and he replied with a slight smile, "Junior Sister Qiu."

Zhou Yi's gaze shifted between the two of them, a faint trace of curiosity coloring his thoughts.

Gao Weiliang cleared his throat and suggested, "Nephew Jin, how about you escort Junior Sister Qiu back to the Tower of Heaven?" He then gestured grandly towards Zhou Yi and said with a smile, "Mr. Zhou... how about I accompany you back to the sect?"

Originally, Gao Weiliang intended to address Zhou Yi as 'Junior Nephew Zhou', which considering his rapport with several other venerable experts from Tianchi, wouldn't have posed any problems. However, recalling Zhou Yi's demeanor today and how Fan Shuo addressed him, the term 'Junior Nephew Zhou' felt like a bone stuck in his throat. No matter how he tried, he couldn't bring himself to say it.

At the eleventh hour, he chose to follow Fan Shuo's example and referred to Zhou Yi as 'Mr. Zhou'.

Jin Zhanyi's expression changed slightly and he quickly added, "Senior Uncle Gao, it was Nephew who greeted Mr. Zhou upon his arrival at the Lingxiao Treasure Hall."

Immediately, a hint of sadness crossed Qiu Miss's eyes, as if silently reproaching something.

Gao Weiliang's face turned a bit stiff as he said, "Since Mr. Zhou has come to the Lingxiao Treasure Hall, he's a guest of our entire sect. Would Senior Uncle's hospitality not be sufficient?" He turned his face and softened his tone, saying, "What do you think, Mr. Zhou?"

Zhou Yi glanced around and noticed the peculiar expressions on everyone's faces. He understood the underlying meaning very well. Ignoring the pleading look Jin Zhanyi cast his way, he maintained a composed expression and said with earnestness, "Senior Gao is right. I am currently interested in visiting the Tower of Heaven. I kindly request Senior Gao's permission."

Gao Weiliang burst into laughter and responded, "It's a small matter, Mr. Zhou. Please follow me." With that, he turned around, his figure shifting as if igniting a wildfire. In an instant, his presence dimmed and brightened, and he was already far away.

Zhou Yi smiled apologetically at Jin Zhanyi and gave a discreet signal, indicating that he would take his leave. Jin Zhanyi, despite his displeased glare, understood the situation and allowed Zhou Yi to escape.

While Jin Zhanyi was well-liked within the Lingxiao Treasure Hall and held a promising future, Zhou Yi was not willing to offend the sole daughter of the Sect Master for his sake. .

Du Wenbin shot a fierce glare around the surroundings and bellowed, "What are you all waiting for? Go back and focus on your cultivation. Reflect on what you've witnessed today. Perhaps you'll make a breakthrough." The crowd respectfully acknowledged and in an instant, the valley was filled with a scramble of activity as dozens of people rushed out, as if they were being chased by some ancient and ferocious beast.

Du Wenbin nodded slowly, quite satisfied with the performance of these young disciples. Then, without acknowledging Jin Zhanyi and Zhou Yi, he departed as if he hadn't even noticed them, drifting away.

When Zhou Yi returned to the Lingxiao Treasure Hall, Gao Weiliang had been waiting there for a while. Zhou Yi didn't employ any high-level Wind-based Lightness Technique, so his speed wasn't as exaggerated as his counterpart's. After all, he was wary of this Senior Gao who had relentlessly pursued him that night. He wouldn't give him the chance to see through him if he could avoid it.

Gao Weiliang accompanied Zhou Yi into the Tower of Heaven, but for half an hour, they only moved around below the fifth level. Despite Gao Weiliang's polite demeanor, he steadfastly refused to take Zhou Yi any further up.

Zhou Yi naturally understood the underlying reason and made a tactful retreat, returning to his temporary lodgings within the Lingxiao Treasure Hall.

As he pushed open the door, Zhou Yi's ears twitched, prompting him to exert force on his toes and swiftly evade. Just as he moved, a tree branch pierced through the afterimage of his previous position.

Turning around, Zhou Yi awkwardly said, "Brother Jin, this matter had nothing to do with me. It was Senior Gao's instruction for me to leave. How could I dare to disobey?"

Jin Zhanyi snorted coldly, discarding the branch in his hand. He remarked, "I'm not unaware of your thoughts.It's probably because you've learned about Miss Qiu's background that you don't want to offend her, right?"

Zhou Yi smirked, not denying it. He looked at the weather and curiously asked, "Brother Jin, since it's a rendezvous with a beauty, why did you come back so early? If it were me, I'd willingly spend the entire day with her, no matter what."

He wanted to make a couple of teasing remarks, but seeing the other's eyebrows seemingly furrowing, he quickly lowered his expression and said, "Brother Jin, truth be told, I really want to visit the Ice Palace in the Northern Territory. If it weren't for your invitation to the Lingxiao Treasure Hall, I would definitely be on my way there."

Jin Zhanyi indeed seemed startled. He opened his mouth, feeling a vague sense of guilt rise within him. He responded, "Brother Zhou, since Miss Yuan has been brought to the Northern Territory Ice Palace, there must be significant benefits awaiting her. This temporary separation is just a preparation for a lasting future. You should rest assured."

Zhou Yi nodded slightly, as if recalling something, and asked, "Brother Jin, is that Miss Qiu truly the daughter of the Sect Master?"

Jin Zhanyi gave him a look of impatience, saying, "Can this matter still be lied about?"

Zhou Yi chuckled, "Since Miss Qiu is the Sect Master's daughter, then why hasn't she even reached the Innate Realm?"

Back when Zhou Yi had just started practicing martial arts, he held a strong yearning for the Innate Realm, regarding it as the pinnacle of martial achievements. However, as he progressed in his martial journey and encountered more people and experiences, his perspectives on certain matters underwent a complete transformation.

Although he had only met miss Qiu once, he had already sensed her remarkable talent. While not as extraordinary as Jin Zhanyi's, she was undoubtedly not inferior to most of the One-line Heaven experts present.

But with such talent and status, she was merely an acquired cultivator. That fact was rather perplexing.

Jin Zhanyi waved his hand nonchalantly and explained, "Sister Qiu is only twenty-five years old this year. She has already reached the peak of the 9th layer of Inner Qi in three different elements, a speed that ranks among the top records in the history of the Lingxiao Treasure Hall. As for stepping into the Innate Realm, it would take at least another ten years of cultivation.

He looked at Zhou Yi with a strange expression and continued, "Zhou Brother, do you think there's anyone else who can achieve the Three Flowers Realm at your age?"

Zhou Yi was taken aback for a moment, then chuckled and said, "Qiu Miss is only twenty-five years old? May I ask the age of your esteemed Sect Master this year?"

Jin Zhanyi hesitated for a moment and replied, "I don't know either, but I've heard from Senior Gao that when he joined the Lingxiao Treasure Hall and began practicing martial arts, the Sect Master was already in charge of our sect. The Sect Master often goes into seclusion, and most matters within the sect are handled by the Duty Elders."

Zhou Yi widened his eyes in astonishment and then used his two hands to gesture, clearly showing his confusion.

Jin Zhanyi chuckled helplessly and explained, "Brother Zhou, it's not a secret. It's quite simple, actually. The Sect Master remarried thirty years ago, and his new wife was around the same age as Miss Qiu at the time. Five years later, Miss Qiu was born. That's the story."

Zhou Yi finally understood and couldn't help but admire the Sect Master's boldness.

Changing the topic, Zhou Yi asked, "Brother Jin, I can tell that Miss Qiu regards you quite highly. What are your intentions?"

Jin Zhanyi smiled wryly and said, "Brother Zhou, I'm nearly 150 years old this year. Do you really think I'd have such thoughts?"

He paused for a moment and continued, "Ever since the day I started practicing martial arts, I've decided to devote myself completely to the path of martial arts. I won't get entangled in love affairs. And now, especially as I'm on the verge of breaking through to the Venerable Realm, how can I afford to be distracted?"

Zhou Yi nodded slightly. At this moment, Jin Zhanyi had to devote all his energy to martial arts. But what about after he reached the Venerable Realm?

Subtly, Zhou Yi found himself eagerly anticipating the future development between them.

As for the matter of age, he guessed that within the Lingxiao Treasure Hall, no one really cared about it. As long as they considered the actions of the Sect Master, everything became reasonable and justified.

Chapter 387

The atmosphere in the courtyard immediately relaxed a lot. Once the two of them had an open and honest conversation, everything returned to normal.

Suddenly, Zhou Yi remembered something and asked in a low voice, "Brother Jin, what is the Jiahuang Pill?"

Jin Zhanyi lowered his voice and replied, "The Jiahuang Pill is a type of invigorating elixir. Upon ingestion, it triggers the latent potential of the body, causing the essence, energy, and spirit to reach an unparalleled peak within a matter of days."

Zhou Yi's brows slightly furrowed as he inquired, "Such a medicine must surely have adverse effects on the body."

Jin Zhanyi nodded slightly and said, "Indeed, there are some side effects. After the effects of the medicine wear off, the person who took it will feel extremely fatigued, requiring about a month of rest and the consumption of replenishing elixirs daily to gradually recover."

Zhou Yi's surprise grew, and he questioned, "Since there are drawbacks to taking this medicine, why do you all value it so much?"

During their time on the seventh level of the Tower of Heaven, the attitude of everyone towards the Jiahuang Pill was clearly evident.

Even when the Qilian Twin Devils used the mysterious artifact "Seamless Heaven Garment" to withstand Zhou Yi's formidable attack, stirring up resentment among the crowd, a single mention of the " Jiahuang Pills" from the venerable Fan Shuo was enough to quell all discontent. Even Jin Zhanyi looked forward with eagerness, his previous resentment completely dissipated.

Their reactions were definitely genuine, and Zhou Yi could see that. It was evident that the value of the Jiahuang Pill was absolutely extraordinary.

However, from what Jin Zhanyi was saying now, the effects of this item seemed to be nothing more than that, and it didn't appear to have a significant purpose at all.

A mysterious light flashed across Jin Zhanyi's face as he spoke, "Brother Zhou, the Jiahuang Pill isn't meant for us to use when we're fighting for our lives. Once this elixir is consumed, its effects last for several days, and it won't pose a life-threatening risk. You should understand when it's best to use it, right?"

Zhou Yi looked at his expression, a sudden realization dawning upon him. He exclaimed, "Limit Barrier..."

Jin Zhanyi solemnly nodded, saying, "Exactly, it's the best elixir we use when breaking through the barrier. If an acquired peak expert consumes it while breaking through to the Innate level, success is almost certain. Similarly, it's highly effective when breaking through from Innate to the One-line Heaven level. Besides that, if we aim to attain the Three Flowers Gathering at the Apex and break through that final barrier, this item is of immense use."

At this point, he spoke with seriousness, "Brother Zhou, what do you think the value of this elixir is?"

Without hesitation, Zhou Yi nodded affirmatively and sincerely said, "Priceless."

Looking towards Jin Zhanyi's embrace, he found Jin Zhanyi extending his hands, saying, "Don't bother looking. Such a high-level elixir isn't something I can distribute. I already had Qiu Miss deliver them to Sect Master."

Zhou Yi sighed in regret, shaking his head slightly.

A strange smile flashed across Jin Zhanyi's face. With a flick of his wrist, a smaller jade bottle appeared.

He looked at the slightly dazed Zhou Yi and said, "But Venerable Fan Shuo mentioned that two of these ten Jiahuang Pills belong to you and me."

Zhou Yi's excitement surged, hastily snatching the jade bottle from Jin Zhanyi's hand. Upon opening it, he saw a yellow pill resting quietly inside. He sniffed it, detecting a fragrance reminiscent of various flowers and herbs. Of course, the composition of the pill was far more intricate than that, but without the formula, it was impossible to reproduce it.

He carefully put away the Jiahuang Pills and took out the vial that Fan Shuo had given him, asking, "What is this?"

Jin Zhanyi couldn't help but reveal a tinge of envy and said, "This is a specially made elixir from the Qilian Mountain, called Hui Ming Pill. Not only can it rapidly replenish Innate True Qi, but it also has remarkable effects on internal injuries. Venerable Fan Shuo has indeed invested a lot for you to enter the Qilian Mountain."

Zhou Yi's expression tightened as he inquired, "Brother Jin, why is Venerable Fan Shuo so persistent? Could it be that he knows I possess the Five Elements Ring?"

Shaking his head, Jin Zhanyi explained, "Senior Brother mentioned that anything related to you should not be divulged to outsiders. Hence, they couldn't possibly know about your possession of the Five Elements Ring. However, having the talent to cultivate all five elements simultaneously is something they can't overlook either."

A chill ran down Zhou Yi's spine as he asked, "Do you know what they want to do?"

Jin Zhanyi hesitated for a moment and replied, "I'm not sure. But the precursor of the Qilian Mountain was the Five Elements Sect, and it was the main branch of the Five Elements Sect. What Venerable Fan said is true,since you possess the Five Elements Ring, the best cultivation method for you would be the Five Elements technique passed down from the main branch. Such techniques are only possible to acquire within the Qilian Mountain or among the sects that branched off from the Five Elements Sect thousands of years ago."

Nodding slightly, Zhou Yi's mind raced through countless thoughts. He then asked, "Brother Jin, do you know which sects split from the Five Elements Sect apart from the Qilian Mountain?"

Jin Zhanyi hesitated for a moment, shaking his head, and said, "When the Five Elements Sect split in the past, there were dozens of influential sects that emerged for a time. However, after thousands of years of development and attrition, to my knowledge, only two major sects have endured."

Zhou Yi's eyes gleamed slightly as he had made up his mind. If there was even a slight possibility, he wouldn't go to the Qilian Mountain. If there was another option, he'd naturally set his sights on that one.

Jin Zhanyi continued with a solemn tone, "Apart from the Qilian Mountain, the only other sect that carries on the legacy of the ancient Five Elements Sect is the Da Shen Imperial Family."

Zhou Yi was taken aback and asked, "The imperial family?"

Jin Zhanyi seemed to have understood his thoughts and said, "Senior Brother Zhou, the Da Shen Imperial Family is different from the northwestern region. Less than a thousand years ago, they replaced the previous dynasty. Now, the imperial family is filled with experts, including several at the level of Venerable. So, if you truly wish to inherit the Five Elements technique, it's best to accept Venerable Fan's invitation."

Zhou Yi's brows furrowed deeply in contemplation.

Jin Zhanyi smiled faintly and continued, "Senior Brother, you are a distinguished guest of our Lingxiao Treasure Hall, and you are also under the Tianchi Sect, the number one sect in the northwest. Although the influence of the Qilian Mountain is formidable, they won't easily trouble you unless they've gone mad. However..." He hesitated for a moment and said, "If you are determined to go to the Qilian Mountain, it's better to hide the Five Elements Ring first or wait until you become a Venerable. By then, you won't have as many concerns."

This time, Zhou Yi nodded in genuine agreement. He had already condensed the Metal Flower and was capable of attempting the Three Flowers Gathering at the Apex. As long as he could eventually achieve the Three Flowers Gathering at the Apex, even if the Qilian Mountain had malicious intentions, he had the confidence to extricate himself from any situation.

Jin Zhanyi suddenly slapped his forehead and exclaimed, "I've been so focused on preparing for battle that I forgot about this important matter."

Zhou Yi was puzzled and asked, "What is it?"

Jin Zhanyi smiled wryly and said, " Brother Zhou, we invited you to Lingxiao Treasure Hall for a reason.

Could it be, as you mentioned, that you're planning to go to the Central Great Plains?"

Zhou Yi's face blushed slightly. Jin Zhanyi had helped cover up for him in front of Venerable Fan, yet he had ignored Jin Zhanyi's subtle signals for help at a critical moment. This action of his felt somewhat unfair.

He quickly changed the subject and said, "I understand, Brother Jin. Are you planning to start refining the Beauty-Retaining Pill soon?"

Jin Zhanyi said proudly, "Exactly, in three days, we will start refining the elixir. Make sure you don't miss it."

Zhou Yi agreed with a response but was inwardly amazed. Since coming to the Lingxiao Treasure Hall, he had given the prescription to Jin Zhanyi. On that prescription were countless rare herbs. According to Zhou Yi's original estimate, even if they emptied the entire medicinal store of the Lingxiao Treasure Hall, they would likely be missing one or two ingredients. Despite their influence spanning the entire world, collecting everything would probably take several years.

However, it was astonishing that they were about to start refining the elixir in just a few days. This indicated that the wealth of the Lingxiao Treasure Hall's medicinal resources far surpassed his expectations. Such profound reserves truly lived up to the reputation of being the number one sect in the Da Shen Empire.

Jin Zhanyi let out a sigh and said, "In the field of alchemy, there is no one under the heavens who can compare to the experts of the Qilian Mountain. Venerable Fan, in particular, is renowned as an exceptional alchemist. However, we can't request their assistance; it's truly regrettable."

As the top sect in the eastern region, the Lingxiao Treasure Hall naturally had its own alchemists. They wouldn't seek assistance unless there was no other option, much like the Tianchi Sect in the northwestern region.

Zhou Yi hesitated for a moment and asked, "Brother Jin, what is the certainty level of success if your sect's alchemist takes action?"

Without any hesitation, Jin Zhanyi replied, "Around fifty percent."

Zhou Yi let go of his worries and chuckled, "Having a fifty percent chance is already quite remarkable. If it were our Hengshan Sect attempting to refine the Pill, I'm afraid we wouldn't even have a ten percent chance."

Jin Zhanyi shook his head slightly and said, "The one responsible for alchemy in our Lingxiao Treasure Hall is a senior who has secluded himself for many years. He is also the foremost alchemist in our sect. But according to him, if we can get Venerable Fan Shuo to help, there would be at least a seventy percent chance of success."

Zhou Yi's expression finally changed a little. It turned out that this senior, Venerable Fan Shuo, had such formidable strength in the field of alchemy. A thought suddenly struck him, and his expression became peculiar as he asked, "Brother Jin, Brother Zhang once said that if the Beauty-Retaining Pill is successfully refined, two individuals must use it. Could it be..."

He pointed towards the central tower of the city, the Tower of Heaven, his gaze flickering.

Jin Zhanyi coughed a few times, nodding in response without showing any emotion.

The two exchanged glances and stopped discussing the matter further. However, Zhou Yi already had a clear understanding. No wonder they were willing to pay such a great price to exchange for the prescription of the Beauty-Retaining Pill. It all made sense now!

Chapter 388

In the western corner of the inner city of Lingxiao
Treasure Hall, a sea of white birch trees stretches,
their trunks resembling silver-cast sculptures,
radiating a soft radiance regardless of the season.

Within a grove of white birch trees lies an area that
most consider off-limits. This is the alchemy section of

the Lingxiao Treasure Hall. Here, an almost warehouse-sized repository houses a treasure trove of rare spirit herbs, matured elixirs, and an abundance of herbal manuscripts.

Upon his first encounter with this haven, Zhou Yi was taken aback by the sheer number of individuals dedicated to the art of alchemy. What astonished him even more was the emphasis and cultivation that the Lingxiao Treasure Hall placed on alchemy.

To nurture a competent alchemist required an immense investment, far beyond the means of a small clan. Among the three major families of Taicang County in the past, only Zhou Wude possessed a foundation in alchemy. The other two families dared not venture into this forbidden territory. Even if they were to risk everything, it would be a daunting challenge to successfully train a genuine alchemist.

However, within this restricted area of the Lingxiao Treasure Hall, Zhou Yi witnessed a multitude of alchemists. Their distinctive robes revealed their identities. Although the majority were low-level alchemists, the sheer number of them left Zhou Yi utterly amazed.

The interior of the birch trees Forest was enclosed by a massive wall. In places where there were no walls between the inner and outer cities, walls had been reconstructed in certain crucial locations. Beyond the encompassing fence, a single gateway stands, and as Zhou Yi looked back, he observed a stream of youth entering and exiting – their faces a canvas of excitement or disappointment. Yet, amidst this ceaseless flux of emotions, an undeniable vitality and unity thrived.

Following Zhou Yi's gaze, Jin Zhanyi chuckled, "Zhou Brother, the majority of our sect's adept alchemists are here in this place. That's why the apothecaries here assess the fresh herbs sent from various regions, along with tattered herbal manuscripts and unknown origin elixirs." He subtly tilted his chin with an air of pride and continued, "These are disciples from various regions of Lingxiao Treasure Hall. When they travel outside and make herbal-related discoveries, they bring them here. If the elders in the alchemy district approve, they receive corresponding rewards."

Zhou Yi nodded slightly, profoundly envious. Along the journey to this place with Jin Zhanyi, he had begun to comprehend Lingxiao Treasure Hall's influence across the nation. The wealth amassed here from the countless treasures collected across the land every day was beyond imagination.

Turning back, he observed the alchemy district with its green-tiled roofs and green-bricked walls, finally understanding why there were so many alchemists here.

Suddenly, a wave of exclamations erupted, spreading like wildfire. Almost every person's face displayed an unusually excited expression. Zhou Yi's ears twitched slightly, and while he didn't understand the cause of their joy, he distinctly heard the words "Innate Golden Pill."

Jin Zhanyi chuckled wryly, "Someone has been incredibly lucky. I can't fathom who the fortunate soul is or what they found to earn the reward of an Innate Golden Pill."

Zhou Yi's steps froze, and he inhaled sharply, exclaiming, "Jin Brother, there's even the Innate Golden Pill as a reward here?"

Jin Zhanyi nodded slightly, "Indeed. If those disciples present something truly exceptional, they can indeed receive an Innate Golden Pill." He seemed to ponder for a moment before saying with uncertainty, "Since I joined Lingxiao Treasure Hall, there have been at least a hundred individuals who received this reward."

Zhou Yi swallowed hard, deeply struck by Lingxiao Treasure Hall's grand gestures. Jin Zhanyi wasn't even one hundred and fifty years old, yet over a hundred individuals had received this reward. Did that mean there was an opportunity like this almost every year?

This contrasted starkly with the various sects in the northwest. Even the main line of the Tianchi Sect, if they obtained an Innate Golden Pill, they had to ensure it was taken by the most outstanding disciples first. Ordinary disciples hardly even stood a chance.

However, gazing upon the expressions of those disciples of the Lingxiao Treasure Hall, Zhou Yi felt a distinct emotion. This sect had gradually replaced the splintered Five Elements factions over thousands of years, eventually becoming the foremost power in the East. truly had its reasons.

Although curious about what could possibly be worth an Innate Golden Pill, Zhou Yi knew this was Lingxiao

Treasure Hall's territory. Even if he were held in high regard, he couldn't easily gain access to such classified secrets.

Turning back, Zhou Yi said, "Brother Jin, let's head to the alchemy chambers."

Jin Zhanyi nodded slightly and turned without hesitation, making his way toward the courtyard within.Guided by Jin Zhanyi, they arrived at the alchemy area.

This was like a garden within a garden. As soon as Zhou Yi stepped through the gateway, he was met with a rush of intense heat. He glanced back in surprise; just a step away was an entirely different world. He studied the walls around him closely, a glimmer of realization dawning. The architecture here was undoubtedly peculiar, but he remained clueless about its true nature.

He sighed softly, reminded of the specialized peak at the Tianchi Summit designated for Venerables' cultivation. He vividly recalled how entering that region felt like stepping into another world.

Though not identical, there seemed to be some semblance between the two experiences.

Without a moment's hesitation, Jin Zhanyi strode forward and arrived at the central chamber in a matter of moments. Once Zhou Yi entered, he scanned the room, his eyes resting on a moderately sized alchemical furnace. The most striking feature of the furnace was the nine distinct reliefs on its surface.

All the reliefs depicted different forms of the same creature, a creature he had never heard of nor seen before.

His brows furrowed slightly as he suddenly recalled that this was the pattern of the divine dragon he had come across in ancient texts. However, these so-called divine beasts existed only in legends, so Zhou Yi had never taken such things to heart.

Jin ZhanYi laughed heartily and said, "Brother Zhou, this alchemy furnace is one of the treasured items guarding our Lingxiao Treasure Hall. The engravings on it depict a divine dragon."

Zhou Yi chuckled wryly. "Brother Jin, did you witness this with your own eyes?"

Jin Zhanyi let out a long sigh, his voice tinged with regret. "If only I were born thousands of years earlier..."

His words mirrored his personality – arrogant yet brimming with self-assuredness. Even in an era when mythical beasts still existed, the prospect of encountering one was a distant dream. Only those who had reached the divine path could harbor such certainty. Jin Zhanyi's confidence in his own abilities had reached remarkable heights; he firmly believed in his potential to advance to the realm of the divine path.

Zhou Yi took a deep breath, a similar fervor lighting up his face. "If you can, so can I..."

The soundless opening of a door within the room snapped them out of their thoughts. Zhou Yi's ears twitched, his heart racing as he caught a faint and elusive sound, only now realizing someone was approaching.

An elderly man slowly entered the room. He was an old man with white hair, and the most eye-catching feature on his face was undoubtedly his ruddy nose. But what was unimaginable was that this nose was situated on the old man's face. Far from making him appear unattractive, it instead added a kind of affable charm to him.

The old man entered the room, nodding slightly. His gaze fell upon Zhou Yi, and he smiled, saying, "You must be Zhou Yi, right? Those old folks from the northwest are truly fortunate. The Tianchi lineage has produced a genius like you – that's quite remarkable."

Zhou Yi respectfully bowed. "Honored Venerable, you flatter me." Though taken aback, he couldn't help but feel surprised. These venerables were reclusive and formidable experts, yet it seemed even they had heard of his name. This might not necessarily be a good thing.

Jin Zhanyi took a step forward, formally introducing, "Brother Zhou, this is Haodong Venerable, renowned as the foremost alchemist in Lingxiao Treasure Hall."

He turned his head, about to speak, but Haodong waved his sleeves, saying, "No need for introductions. The name, Zhou Yi, has been echoing in our ears for the past few days among us old immortals." He smiled and asked, "Zhou Yi, would you like to watch me refining pills?"

Zhou Yi replied with a serious tone, "During my time in the northwest, I learned a bit about alchemy. If there's a chance to observe, I wouldn't want to miss it."

A trace of surprise flickered in Haodong's eyes as he said, "You're actually skilled in alchemy?"

Chapter 389

Jin Zhanyi's brows lifted, mirroring his surprise as he turned around, fixing a gaze filled with astonishment upon Zhou Yi. While Jin Zhanyi might not have been well-versed in the art of alchemy, he understood well enough that achieving mastery in this path likely demanded as much dedication as the pursuit of martial arts.

Zhou Yi, not yet twenty, had already ascended remarkable heights in the realm of martial arts, a feat unparalleled in history. If he were to divert his attention to learning the intricacies of alchemy, one might question whether he'd remain human at all.

An awkward expression graced Zhou Yi's face as he responded, "Junior is merely intrigued by the subject, and thus dabbles in it. In the presence of someone as esteemed as you, I can by no means claim to be proficient."

Only then did Hao Dong's understanding seem to dawn. Yet, this was the logical course. If Zhou Yi were to excel in alchemy just as he did in martial arts, one would indeed wonder about his method of study.

After a moment of contemplation, Hao Dong posed several questions related to the art of alchemy. Zhou Yi answered a few smoothly, but some left him flabbergasted, with no answer forthcoming.

Nonetheless, even so, he had impressed Hao Dong.

The elder's eyes shimmered faintly as he spoke, "Zhou Yi, I've heard that you cultivate both the Five Elements. Are you skilled in the ways of wood and fire?"

Zhou Yi extended his hands. In the blink of an eye, one hand appeared as thin as a skeleton, while the other conjured an exaggerated small fireball. Though diminutive, the immense power of fire hidden within it was palpable to the two before it. This fireball had condensed from the essence of a Flame Flower.

Hao Dong nodded subtly, pondering certain matters. After a prolonged silence, he finally seemed to reach a decision and said, "Follow me."

Under the old man's guidance, they departed the alchemy area and entered another courtyard, brimming with an ancient, rustic charm.

Upon entering this place, Zhou Yi could already detect a fragrant aroma of herbs. He knew he had stepped into the pharmacy area.

As he entered one of the rooms, Zhou Yi's eyes widened ever so slightly. The room was brimming with rare herbs. If he wasn't mistaken, these herbs should be the precious ones recorded in the pill formula. The only difference was that the quantity here was several times greater.

Hao Dong smiled and said, "Zhou Yi, do you recognize these herbs?"

Zhou Yi nodded slightly. Under the influence of the Medicine Daoist, his knowledge of herbs was indeed impressive. Since obtaining the formula for the Beauty-Retaining Pill, he had delved deep into the study of the required herbs. Even for those without physical samples, he scoured ancient texts to memorize the colors and shapes of these rare ingredients.

Therefore, the moment he entered the room, he immediately identified the origins of these herbs and was deeply impressed by the grand investment of the Lingxiao Treasure Hall's undertaking.

Hao Dong continued with a cheerful grin, "Zhou Yi, although I have considerable skills in alchemy, I'm not particularly adept at selecting herbs. Could you help me pick out the ingredients for brewing the Beauty-Retaining Pill?"

Jin Zhanyi turned his head in astonishment, his mouth agape, struggling to find words.

Zhou Yi's expression turned somewhat peculiar as well. A master of alchemy, yet not skilled in herb selection? Wasn't this a contradiction? However, Zhou Yi vaguely felt that this old man might have some testing intentions, so he readily agreed and began to walk around the room.

All the herbs were placed on wooden shelves, organized into several tiers that nearly filled the room.

These herbs were exceedingly rare, but their preciousness wasn't evident in their arrangement here.

On each tier of the wooden shelves lay the same type of herb, which made it quite convenient for Zhou Yi. He reached out and gently brushed his fingers over one of the herbs. The power of the Wood element hovered in his palm, and he could distinctly sense the potent "life" energy contained within this particular herb.

This energy even reminded him of the colossal ancient tree in the Hengshan Medicinal Garden.

Although he was satisfied with the herb's medicinal properties, he hesitated briefly. Instead of immediately picking up the herb, he moved to the second herb of the same type.

His pace wasn't slow. Soon, he had touched all the herbs on that tier. Subsequently, without hesitation, he picked up the first one and placed it into a small basket at his side.

Hao Dong's eyes briefly flickered with surprise. He had personally selected these herbs over the past few days, and he was well acquainted with their characteristics and medicinal properties. Thus, when he saw the herb Zhou Yi had chosen, he instantly recognized that he had selected the best among its kind.

Still, there lingered a hint of doubt in his mind—did Zhou Yi select these based on his own skill or did he just luck out randomly?

However, that doubt was quickly resolved just moments later.

Zhou Yi's movements grew increasingly rapid. Sometimes, he would even touch a herb with both hands at the same time, immediately selecting the best ones.

Perhaps luck could explain it once or twice, but if it happened repeatedly, even a fool would realize he was skillfully confident.

Hao Dong nodded subtly, his heart filled with admiration. This young talent was not only skilled in both Fire and Wood elements, but his sensitivity to herbs was also unbelievably remarkable.

Using Zhou Yi's method to discern the quality of herbs was a rarity even across the entire Lingxiao Treasure

Hall. Even the One-line Heaven, which had already condensed the Wood Flower, had few who could sense the vitality within herbs.

Yet, Zhou Yi not only achieved this with ease but was also a martial prodigy.

To become a great alchemist, one needed not only extraordinary talent but also to tread a further path in martial arts. This was not just because martial arts greatly aided alchemy, but also because the stronger one's martial prowess, the longer one's life, and the deeper one's understanding of medicines.

Even if their alchemical abilities lagged slightly behind, time could make up for much.

Watching Zhou Yi adeptly select herbs, Hao Dong's heart wavered. Such a talent might never be encountered again if missed. However, the issue was that this person wasn't a disciple of Lingxiao Treasure Hall but hailed from the Northwestern Tianchi. If they were to impart alchemical knowledge, it might not be entirely beneficial for the sect.

Hesitating, Zhou Yi had already finished selecting all the herbs. He placed the basket before Hao Dong. The old man turned over the herbs with his hand a few times and sighed, "Your performance far surpasses my expectations."

Zhou Yi offered a slight smile. At this moment, it seemed inappropriate to say anything.

Hao Dong took the basket and returned to the alchemy room. Standing beside the alchemy furnace, he said softly, "Zhou Yi, stand here and assist me."

Zhou Yi's heart brimmed with joy, and he immediately positioned himself beside the furnace. Jin Zhanyi shook his head, stepping back a few paces. Alchemy held no interest for him.

Hao Dong began to process the herbs in the basket, not working alone but simultaneously explaining in detail.

Zhou Yi stood quietly on the side, listening attentively. Whenever he encountered something he didn't fully understand, he memorized it word by word. He knew that this old man might not be as proficient in alchemy as Fan Shuo, but he was certainly beyond the Medicine Daoist. He was the first person Zhou Yi had ever encountered with such knowledge.

Such opportunities to learn were rare, so he cherished them immensely.

An hour later, they had finished processing the herbs. Despite being top-tier experts, they were careful not to be careless.

Only when they completed the final step before alchemy did they both exhale in relief.

Gathering his focus, Hao Dong said, "Yi, let's begin the alchemy."

An hour of interaction had brought them closer. Hao Dong's address had become more casual.

Zhou Yi responded, his gaze sweeping beneath the furnace. However, a perplexed expression appeared on his face.

Underneath this furnace, there's nothing that can be burned, and there's no equipment resembling a Earth's fire. So, how do they control the temperature?

After hesitating, unable to suppress his curiosity, he asked, "Elder, there's no source of fire under this alchemy furnace. How are we going to brew the elixir?"

Jin Zhanyi, who had been silently watching the old man and the young man fiddle with herbs for quite some time, finally burst into laughter, "Brother Zhou, it seems you haven't witnessed the alchemical process of a venerable before."

A faint blush colored Zhou Yi's face.

Hao Dong chuckled quietly, not answering directly. He positioned himself in front of the furnace and, following a certain sequence, placed the first processed herb into the furnace.

Then, his expression turned serious. "Brewing the Beauty-Retaining Pill is a challenge even for me. I will give it my all. As for how much you can learn, it depends on your own destiny."

Zhou Yi promptly bowed in acknowledgment. Over the past hour, he had learned so much that he held deep respect for this old man.

Hao Dong nodded subtly, extending his hand flatly onto the furnace.

Then, in an instant, his hand turned crimson. Slowly, the temperature within the furnace began to rise. The nine different-shaped divine dragons surrounding the furnace also emitted faint red light, as if they were about to come to life.

Zhou Yi's eyes widened. He finally understood why there was no ignition source below.

Hao Dong, a Venerable, was using his intensely powerful fire elemental energy to refine the elixir in the furnace.

At that moment, Zhou Yi's expression changed. Though confident, he had never imagined someone could achieve this level.

He gained a new understanding of the formidable nature of this old man before him.

Chapter 390

Hao Dong's skin didn't undergo a widespread transformation into red; only the hand gripping the furnace had taken on a crimson hue. Judging by his appearance, it was evident he still had energy to spare. However, even so, Zhou Yi could sense the immense and astonishing fire energy possessed by the old man from the scorching aura that filled the air.

This was a true powerhouse, a super-strong individual who sent shivers down one's spine. Even though Hao Dong and others like Gao Weiliang were all Venerable Ones, Zhou Yi keenly sensed that even within the realm of Venerable Ones, there seemed to be some differences, akin to the distinction between the Innate realm and the One-line Heaven realm.

Under the circulation of the old man's true energy, the temperature within the furnace gradually increased.

"Whoosh... Whoosh..."

A series of heavy whistling sounds emanated from the furnace. These sounds were deep and forceful, almost resembling the breaths of some ancient ferocious beast, evoking a spine-chilling sensation.

Zhou Yi stared at the furnace with skepticism. He was certain that the sound originated from within it, yet he couldn't fathom why such a horrifying sound would be emitted.

Although most of Hao Dong's focus was on the alchemical process, he smiled and said, "Yi, the origin of this furnace is extraordinary. It was modeled after the ancient artifact known as the Nine Dragons Furnace. While its effects pale in comparison to the true Nine Dragons Furnace, among the top-tier furnaces of today, only a few can rival it."

Zhou Yi nodded slightly, his gaze fixed on this imitation Nine Dragons Furnace. Suddenly, he was struck by a thought and asked, "Elder, how does the Nine Dragons Furnace compare to the Five Elements Ring?"

before. After a brief pause, he replied, "Both of these items are legendary divine artifacts, far beyond the comparison of the weapons and treasures forged in today's world. Even their replicas possess immense power, so I don't know which one is more formidable."

Jin Zhanyi laughed heartily and said, "Brother Zhou, legendary divine artifacts are all tremendously powerful treasures. However, they disappeared from the world along with the departure of divine experts. Just like this Nine Dragons Furnace, known as the top divine weapon of the fire element in the world, it can transform into nine fire dragons, an unparalleled might."

He paused for a moment, seeming hesitant, before finally continuing, "Legend has it that the Eight Hundred Li Volcano was the result of a confrontation between a certain divine expert using the Nine Dragons Furnace and a divine beast, the Fire Qilin."

Zhou Yi was genuinely moved this time. He had been to the Eight Hundred Li Volcano before, where he condensed the Fire Flower. He hadn't delved deep into it. Yet, the impression left by that volcanic region was indeed profound. If such a massive Fire Mountain was truly the aftermath of a clash between a divine expert and a divine beast, then just how powerful and unimaginable were their abilities?

For a moment, Zhou Yi seemed to be lost in thought. Hao Dong's voice suddenly echoed in his ears, "Focus your mind and steady your breath, don't let your thoughts wander."

Zhou Yi's face reddened slightly, and he quickly responded, then refocused his attention and set aside thoughts of those legendary divine artifacts.

"Extend your hand, follow me," Hao Dong softly instructed as he gently touched another part of the furnace with his other hand.

Zhou Yi looked surprised and his heart began to race intensely.

In the process of alchemy, a alchemist must be completely focused and dedicated. Moreover, this unique method of alchemy requires precise control over one's True Qi, reaching the pinnacle of mastery. Although at the beginning, with Hao Dong's level of cultivation, he can afford some distractions, but as the alchemical process progresses to its final stages, even a slight deviation in the control of the alchemical forces within the furnace could lead to the failure of the entire process.

He didn't quite understand why the old man would want him to be fully involved in this.

Seeming to comprehend his hesitation, Hao Dong snorted coldly and said, "The likelihood of succeeding in refining the Beauty-Retaining Pill on the first attempt is extremely slim. You should experience this process as well, as it will be beneficial in the future."

Zhou Yi opened his mouth as if about to say something, looked deeply at the old man, then raised his hand and placed it where indicated. In a low voice, he uttered a "Thank you."

Neither Hao Dong nor Jin Zhanyi seemed to hear those two words, and the alchemy room fell into an eerie silence, except for the furious roars echoing as if from a giant beast within the furnace.

Zhou Yi realized the preciousness of this opportunity, Observing by the side of the furnace and personally experiencing the process were two entirely different concepts.

Hao Dong's actions clearly indicated that he was willing to let the first furnace turn into a failure if it meant passing on his alchemy techniques to Zhou Yi. No wonder he had emphasized it so seriously at the beginning. How much Zhou Yi could comprehend depended entirely on his own efforts.

A faint, almost imperceptible surge of fire energy entered the furnace. Though this strand of fire energy was weak, it branched into countless tendrils, forming a dense web-like structure within the furnace, monitoring every aspect of it.

During this process, Zhou Yi carefully avoided the immense fire energy descending from the top of the furnace. Compared to that overwhelming power, the tiny network of fire he had formed was like a spider web next to an elephant's leg, utterly insignificant.

However, the elephant seemed to pay no attention to the intrusion, or perhaps it was because the difference in strength between them was too vast for it to bother. Just as An elephant would regard another invading elephant with hostility, but it wouldn't even bother to glance at an ant in its vicinity.

Inside the furnace, powerful waves of heat surged, causing the herbs within to bob up and down in the torrent of heat, as if an invisible hand was tossing them around.

Zhou Yi observed for a while, and finally, he began to understand. The waves of heat inside were naturally created by Hao Dong, transforming formless energy into tangible fire. However, the control of this heat was precise. As the herbs were being roasted, every minuscule point received an entirely uniform level of heat, without the slightest deviation.

This level of precision would be impossible to achieve using conventional fuel or earthly fire as the heat source.

In a moment of enlightenment, Zhou Yi seemed to grasp why the top-tier alchemists needed to attain the realm of a Venerable. It was because only these powerhouses with boundless abilities could achieve the seemingly mythical alchemical methods he was witnessing.

Sighing deeply, Zhou Yi felt a strong urge to try it himself. However, he forcefully suppressed the impulse, knowing that if he attempted to release fire energy of the intensity that Hao Dong was currently employing, he wouldn't be able to sustain it for long. This was the gap, the most evident gap between himself and a Venerable.

Perhaps during the exchange of one or two moves, this disparity might not be so apparent, but in a prolonged battle, the difference would be magnified infinitely, turning into a fatal flaw.

Pushing aside all lofty aspirations, Zhou Yi focused on carefully sensing the techniques behind the surging fire energy. Gradually, in his mind, he formed a pair of hands composed entirely of flames. These hands evolved continuously, seeming to mold into a series of mysterious and profound fire-based hand seals.

Zhou Yi was certain that this was a unique method of manipulation. It was under the control of this technique that the fire energy could be perfectly harnessed to achieve such an extraordinary level of mastery.

His heart stirred, and he became completely absorbed in sensing this set of hand seal techniques.

Hao Dong glanced at Zhou Yi, his eyes brimming with undisguised admiration. His earlier words had been rather vague, but Zhou Yi quickly grasped the most crucial point.

This fire-based hand seal technique was also one of the top-notch fire-related techniques inherited from the era of the Divine Path . Furthermore, it was specifically designed for manipulating the Nine Dragons Furnace. It was said that the founder of their sect had paid an enormous price to obtain this technique after replicating the Nine Dragons Furnace.

However, it was precisely because of this technique that the maximum potential of this replicated Nine Dragons Furnace could be unleashed. While the direct combat effectiveness of this technique wasn't particularly great, when used to control a weapon, especially a remarkable treasure like the Nine Dragons Furnace, it was the best choice.

Of course, this technique wasn't solely for combat purposes. It could also be used to control everything within the alchemical furnace, allowing the herbs inside to be heated and agitated according to one's intentions, ensuring the smooth refinement of pills.

In the current Lingxiao Treasure Hall, only Hao Dong had mastered this technique. Other Revered Ones maintained a respectful distance from the art of alchemy and were even less likely to learn this technique.

Hao Dong occasionally worried that when his time came to an end, the centuries of experience he had immersed himself in regarding this technique would be lost forever. This concern was the reason he chose to transmit this technique in such an obscure way when he saw Zhou Yi's interest in alchemy.

Such subtle psychological changes were even unclear to him.

Naturally, Zhou Yi didn't understand all of this. He had focused all his mental energy on comprehending everything. His eyes were tightly shut, and his lips occasionally moved as if quietly reciting something. His face alternated between expressions of joy and deep contemplation, fully immersed in a world unique to him.

Beside them, Jin Zhanyi's brow furrowed slightly. In his heart, he didn't really agree with Zhou Yi's further pursuit of alchemy. Given Zhou Yi's exceptional talent in martial arts, not dedicating himself wholeheartedly to it would be a true waste. However, faced with the illustrious reputation of Hao Dong within the Lingxiao Treasure Hall, Jin Zhanyi kept his reservations to himself, not daring to voice his concerns.

As he watched Zhou Yi's increasingly joyful expression, his head shook with increasing frequency.

Chapter 391

Time passed by as usual, flowing like it always did. However, for different individuals, even though the same amount of time was passing, the perception of its passage could vary between quick and slow.

After a full hour had passed, Zhou Yi finally opened his eyes. Between his brows, a hint of fatigue lingered, but in his eyes, an overwhelming excitement gleamed.

This hour had been both agonizing and joyful for him. Hao Dong didn't hold back in repeatedly demonstrating the techniques of controlling fire element through hand Seal. In the process, he even risked the danger of ruining an entire batch of medicinal pills.

Truth be told, even Hao Dong himself had never imagined that at his age, with his self-discipline and composure, he could have such an irrational day. Although they hadn't exchanged a single word, the flow of true qi within the furnace allowed Zhou Yi to understand and master everything even more clearly.

This was how top-notch experts transmitted their knowledge—imparting not only fixed techniques but also the countless experiences Hao Dong had amassed over hundreds of years of immersion. This was even more significant than rigid hand Seals.

It was because Hao Dong had gone to such lengths to guide him in this unique way that Zhou Yi was able to truly grasp the technique within an hour. A satisfied smile curved on Hao Dong's lips as he finally felt at ease.

After dedicating a lifetime to mastering his unique techniques, he had finally found the perfect successor. The only regret was that this individual wasn't a disciple of the Lingxiao Treasure Hall. Moreover, since he wasn't, he wouldn't have access to the replicated Nine Dragons Furnace.

Using an ordinary alchemical furnace would significantly diminish the effectiveness of this technique. Nevertheless, regardless of the circumstances, he had given his all...

With a soft sigh, Hao Dong picked up the last herb and murmured, "Yi, be careful." Zhou Yi's expression brightened as he gazed at the herb in Hao Dong's hand. The joy on his face immediately subsided, replaced by a solemn nod. "I understand, Senior."

Hao Dong blew a gentle breath, and the top of the furnace automatically opened. With lightning speed, he placed the herb into the furnace, followed by gently closing the lid.

As the last herb entered the furnace, they had reached the critical moment. At this point, not even Hao Dong had room for distraction. He wholeheartedly poured his energy into the alchemical process.

Despite his previous implication that the first attempt might not be successful, he would not give up as long as there was a glimmer of possibility. He would put in 200% effort to turn that possibility into success.

Zhou Yi's expression was also extremely serious, in his perception, the inside of the furnace had already transformed into a world filled with flames. Especially those flames dancing like a pair of hands, which truly showcased the profoundness of this magical control technique.

If Hao Dong had maintained this pace from the start, Zhou Yi would have struggled to discern the patterns, let alone master this remarkable set of hand Seal techniques.

Feeling the increasingly vigorous surge of flames, Zhou Yi's heart overflowed with gratitude. He had already decided that if the opportunity arose, he would repay this favor twofold.

Though Hao Dong had pushed his own abilities to the limit, even in this situation, he didn't deliberately expel the fire essence belonging to Zhou Yi from the furnace. Their fire essences had developed a certain harmony during their earlier instruction, a kind of spiritual communication that held more power than any mere words.

The herbs within the furnace churned incessantly, their life forces beginning to coalesce. Once this power was fully and perfectly combined, it signified the success of the alchemical process. However, any deviation could lead to the dispersion of the life force instead of coalescence, resulting in the failure of the pill.

Both Zhou Yi and Hao Dong maintained expressionless faces, but their hearts were at their utmost limits, vigilant to the slightest deviation.

Suddenly, the stability of the life force within the herbs wavered. The coalescing life force seemed to shatter, dispersing in all directions. Zhou Yi's complexion changed drastically. While he had independently refined dozens of pills before, none of them were as precious as this batch. However, this sign was not unfamiliar to him.

He knew that this batch of pills might have truly failed.

Yet, just as this thought arose, he heard a faint hum from Hao Dong. In response to his hum, the nine fire dragons on the furnace's body instantly illuminated.

Inside the furnace, beyond the control of those large fiery hands, nine gigantic fire dragons suddenly emerged, circling ceaselessly. These fire dragons seemed to possess a certain sentience. Once they were trapped by the fire energy inside, the bursting life force within the herbs immediately ceased to overflow. Instead, it gradually converged towards the center.

Zhou Yi was utterly astonished as he sensed all of this. He finally understood why Hao Dong had praised this furnace so highly. The nine dragons actually had such miraculous utility. Had he not witnessed it with his own eyes, he would never have believed it.

Between the herbs, as influenced by the fire's energy, subtle changes occur in their life force. These various transformations, when combined, give rise to miraculous effects. This is the greatest function of a prescription . Without the guidance of a prescription, it's practically impossible to reverse-engineer the process of concocting pills.

However, meticulously following a prescription to successfully refine pills is by no means a simple task. Especially for advanced pills like the Beauty-Retaining Pill, the complexity is even more pronounced.

With the assistance of the nine fire dragons, Hao Dong stabilized the situation. However, even with their help, he had reached his limit. The herbs at the center continued to churn weakly, their life forces not dissipating but lacking any signs of coalescence.

Both Hao Dong and Zhou Yi knew that there must have been a flaw in the refining process, but they couldn't pinpoint the reason. Most people would likely have given up in such a situation, However, for Hao Dong to cultivate to his current level, his unyielding determination could be described as truly formidable. He hung on steadfastly, manipulating the nine fire dragons to experiment with various methods to refine the pill successfully.

Throughout the process, the thought of giving up never crossed his mind.

Zhou Yi silently sensed all of this, memories of the herbs and steps from the recipe flashing through his mind. He had obtained the recipe from the Medicine Daoist , who had studied it for over a hundred years, gaining an in-depth understanding of the herbs within it. When Zhou Yi received the recipe, he also acquired this knowledge.

At this moment, as he felt the refining process and then recalled the herbs and steps in the recipe, Zhou Yi had a faint sensation that he might have realized something significant.

Finally, his eyes lit up. In that moment, he had understood the reason behind it all. A powerful sense of joy surged within him, causing the dormant fire energy to erupt and rush towards Hao Dong's power.

If Zhou Yi's fire energy had just entered the furnace, it would have surely disturbed Hao Dong and triggered a ruthless counterattack. Not only would Zhou Yi have been injured, but the alchemical process would have failed completely.

However, Zhou Yi's fire energy had spent over an hour intertwined with Hao Dong's within the furnace. They had almost become one entity. Sensing Zhou Yi's eager fire energy, Hao Dong only hesitated briefly before relinquishing control of the Nine Dragons Furnace, leaving everything to Zhou Yi.

After all, he had tried countless methods and couldn't coalesce the life forces within the herbs. If Zhou Yi wanted to attempt it, he had nothing to lose. Yet, in the next moment, his heart began to race uncontrollably.

Zhou Yi's actions were far beyond what he had expected.

After taking control of the surging flames, Zhou Yi's true energy began to flow out like a tide. He suddenly realized the terrifying extent of energy consumption involved in alchemy using this method.

This was definitely not something that those below the rank of a Venerable could endure. He knew that he only had one chance. If he failed, he wouldn't have the opportunity to try again in a short span.

Focusing his mind and stabilizing his energy, Zhou Yi employed the newly learned hand seals to keep the waves of fire churning. However, simultaneously within the boundless fire energy, an abrupt addition of an earth element force emerged.

This particular force of earth element, not overly potent, circulated through the medicinal herbs. After completing a circuit, it transformed into a keen and sharp gold element force. Subsequently, it shifted into a water element force diametrically opposed to the fire energy, followed by transforming into the vigorous and lively wood element force.

However, as the cycle of the five elemental forces completed, a profound transformation occurred within the previously inert life force of the medicinal herbs.

They began to condense and gradually merge together. Hao Dong's expression was a mix of excitement and astonishment. As an observer, the contents of the alchemical recipe flashed in his mind, and a sense of relief finally appeared on his face. The steps and required herbs from the recipe, juxtaposed with Zhou Yi's actions, revealed the truth to him.

To his realization, the Beauty-Retaining Pill required the power of the Five Elements' cycle to be successfully concocted. At this moment, Hao Dong's admiration for Zhou Yi grew stronger. To think that Zhou Yi had grasped the intricacies even before he did, showcased his exceptional observational skills and innate talent in the path of alchemy.

Once again, he couldn't help but sigh inwardly. Why wasn't this youngster a disciple of the Lingxiao Treasure Hall?

Chapter 392

The surging flames at the center of the furnace suddenly churned a few times, almost on the brink of extinguishing. Both Zhou Yi and Hao Dong were almost drenched in cold sweat. They had reached the final step, and success seemed imminent. Failing at this critical juncture could be maddening enough to drive someone to despair.

The immense power of the fire element surged forth, almost immediately displacing Zhou Yi's fire energy. Yet, Zhou Yi withdrew his fire energy without resistance. Only when he personally executed the fire manipulation technique and attempted to control the nine dragons did he realize the enormity of the true energy consumption. Especially with the nine dragons swirling around him, they were like nine bottomless pits devouring his true energy. After the cycle of the five elemental forces, Zhou Yi even felt a sensation of being completely drained by them.

At the critical moment, he finally couldn't hold on any longer. Fortunately, Hao Dong had been closely monitoring the changes in the furnace. Their true energies had been in constant communication, which allowed Hao Dong to take over in the nick of time and stabilize the situation.

Taking a deep breath, Zhou Yi was surprised to find that he was drenched in sweat as if in a downpour. He shook his head, feeling a deep reverence for this replica artifact. It was even more challenging to control than the Five Elements Ring.

Despite his near exhaustion, he managed to maintain a trace of fire energy to observe the situation within the furnace. Through his perception, as soon as Hao Dong took control, he once again employed that unique fire manipulation technique. In this instance, even the nine dragons within the furnace began to stir with excitement.

It seemed like they understood that they had reached the final crucial moment, so there was no need to hold back anymore. The nine swirling dragons suddenly increased their rotation speed significantly. Gradually, the size of the nine dragons kept shrinking, while the life force within the medicinal herbs at the center of the furnace finally began to condense.

Countless flames danced wildly like birds in flight, and Zhou Yi deeply admired the unfathomable strength of

Hao Dong. Finally, the nine dragons burst open, forming a new furnace within the furnace, a transformation from the illusory to the tangible.

Inside this furnace within the furnace, the potent medicinal power had successfully merged. When Zhou Yi sensed this strange change, his face unconsciously showed an ecstatic expression. Drawing from his past experiences in alchemy, he immediately understood that the Beauty-Retaining Pill had been successfully concocted.

His heart finally relaxed, affording him a moment to slightly shift his focus to this extraordinary creation, the furnace within the furnace, born from the nine dragons. After closely observing for a while, Zhou Yi finally recognized that the appearance of this furnace was almost identical to the imitation Nine Dragons

Furnace. The only difference was the additional decoration of nine fire dragons on top of the imitation Nine Dragons Furnace. If those dragon decorations were removed, the internal and external structure of the two furnaces, aside from their sizes and tangibility, would be virtually indistinguishable.

However, he also understood that the decoration of the nine dragons was not placed on the furnace by chance. If one were to really remove the nine dragon decorations, this Nine Dragons Furnace would likely become nothing more than an empty name.

As the transformation within the furnace within the furnace stabilized, it gradually began to dissipate. Zhou Yi silently watched this process, and suddenly, a slight change crossed his face. A thought flashed through his mind, and his body couldn't help but tremble with excitement.

Even though he exerted a great deal of willpower and made a full effort to control his body, due to the sudden surge of emotions, it was difficult for him to achieve this

Hao Dong's gaze flicked in his direction, a slight hint of surprise in his eyes. He couldn't quite understand why Zhou Yi had suddenly become so emotional. It seemed as if Zhou Yi had transformed into an entirely different person from the composed and wise individual he had shown just moments ago.

Jin Zhanyi leaped forward a step and carefully asked, "Brother Zhou, what's the matter?" After months of interaction, their relationship had grown quite close.

Jin Zhanyi's concern was genuine, devoid of any ulterior motives.

Zhou Yi took a deep breath, his facial expression a mix of tears and laughter. He bit his lip, finally saying, "The Beauty-Retaining Pill, it's a success."

Hao Dong and Jin Zhanyi exchanged a glance and both rolled their eyes in unison. Jin Zhanyi could only laugh helplessly, "Brother Zhou, are you so moved by a few Beauty-Retaining Pills? Are they worth such emotion?"

Zhou Yi chuckled several times, managing to control his overwhelming excitement. He said, "Brother Jin, with this Beauty-Retaining Pill, I can preserve Li Xun's youthful appearance for a lifetime. Just thinking about it makes me unable to contain my emotions. Please forgive my outburst, Senior and Brother Jin."

Jin Zhanyi's mouth twitched slightly, and he finally couldn't hold back his words, "Brother Zhou, your love for each other is touching, and I can't say much about it. But considering your extraordinary talent in martial arts, it's truly regrettable if you can't focus solely on your cultivation."

Hao Dong cleared his throat and interjected, "Yi, your talent in martial arts is indeed unmatched, but your talent in alchemy is equally impressive. If you can spare some energy for alchemy, it won't hinder you much."

The muscles on Jin Zhanyi's face twitched slightly, but in the end, he still didn't have the courage to directly refute the senior.

Zhou Yi sighed inwardly, surprised to encounter someone like Medicine Master in the Lingxiao Treasure Hall. He composed his thoughts and nodded slightly, saying, "Thank you for your guidance, Senior. I will certainly delve into alchemy and will not give up."

Hao Dong's face revealed a relieved expression. He had put a great deal of effort into secretly imparting the technique of controlling fire to Zhou Yi. If Zhou Yi were to give up his development in alchemy, it would undoubtedly frustrate Hao Dong greatly.

Jin Zhanyi shook his head subtly, determined to change Zhou Yi's perspective when they were alone together.

Hao Dong nodded and said, "Yi, in fact, Jin's words hold some truth. For us martial practitioners, romantic attachments are not of great significance."

Hao Dong nodded and said, "Yi, actually what Jin said is not wrong. Love and emotions, for those of us who follow the path of martial arts, are not that important."

After pondering for a moment, Zhou Yi spoke, "Elder, Junior Brother Jin, if love and emotions are not that important, then why did you use so many Innate Golden Pills to exchange for the formula of the Beauty-Retaining Pill? And why did you prepare so many precious herbs? If my estimation is correct, it seems you are determined to succeed in refining the Beauty-Retaining Pill no matter what the cost."

Hao Dong and Jin Zhanyi exchanged glances and fell into a momentary silence. Finally, Jin Zhanyi forced a bitter smile and said, "Brother Zhou, all of this is the order of the Sect Master. No matter what, we have to abide by it."

Zhou Yi smiled faintly and asked, "Then, for whom did your Sect Master issue such orders?"

The elder and the young exchanged a glance, finally sighing and refraining from persuading further.

Hao Dong turned his head and gently tapped the pill furnace, causing its lid to slowly lift. The lid of the Nine Dragons Cauldron was somewhat different from a regular pill furnace. It was embedded in the top of the cauldron and couldn't be simply lifted; it had to be twisted open gradually.

As the lid of the furnace opened, a fragrant aroma immediately wafted out. In the next moment, the entire room was filled with this peculiar fragrance. The gazes of Zhou Yi and the others were simultaneously drawn to the inside of the pill furnace. Even though Hao Dong and Zhou Yi had already explored the interior using their fire manipulation abilities, their hearts were still quite stirred at this moment.

Being able to successfully refine the Beauty-Retaining Pill on the first attempt greatly exceeded their expectations. Even Hao Dong secretly felt fortunate that he had involved Zhou Yi in the process beforehand; otherwise, even if he had grasped the intricacies of the formula, he wouldn't have been able to accomplish the Five Elements conversion.

Glancing at the formula, he understood that to refine the Beauty-Retaining Pill successfully, several top alchemists would need to work together. Only through such a collective effort could they achieve the unique Five Elements transformation required. However, achieving such unity and synchronization was by no means an easy feat. The slightest disharmony among them would undoubtedly lead to the failure of all their prior efforts.

If it weren't for Zhou Yi, this genius who possesses the ability to cultivate all five elemental affinities, Hao Dong wouldn't have had much confidence in successfully refining the Pill.

Inside the cauldron lay eight pills emitting a faint five-colored glow. Although these glows were somewhat dim, the discerning eyes of the three could still perceive their extraordinary nature.

Hao Dong nodded slightly and said, "Eight Beauty-Retaining Pills, not bad. This harvest is quite good."

Zhou Yi's face was also filled with a smile, his gaze fixed on the pills, making it hard for him to contain his happiness.

At a glance, it seemed like his joy was solely due to the eight Beauty-Retaining Pills, However, only Zhou Yi himself understood that this smile merely concealed a kind of almost manic joy in his heart.

Of course, within this joy, there was also a hint of unease. Such intricate emotions were truly not something easily conveyed to others.

Hao Dong waved his hand, and two crystal-clear jade vials flew over from a cupboard on the wall of the alchemy room. Opening one of the vials, he placed the eight Beauty-Retaining Pills into the two vials – two pills in one vial and six in the other.

As he lifted the jade vial, Hao Dong hesitated briefly and eventually took one of the Beauty-Retaining Pills from the vial containing six pills, placing it into the vial with two pills.

Then, he tossed these three Beauty-Retaining Pills to Zhou Yi.

Zhou Yi was surprised and said, "Senior, according to our agreement, I only need two pills."

Hao Dong gestured with a slight wave of his hand and said, "In this alchemical process, if it weren't for your assistance, it would have undoubtedly failed. Three Beauty-Retaining Pills are rightfully yours."

Zhou Yi contemplated for a moment and finally bowed deeply to Hao Dong.

In this alchemical endeavor, he not only obtained three Beauty-Retaining Pills but also learned a set of fire manipulation techniques. However, what truly overwhelmed him with joy was the Nine Dragons Cauldron.

This replicated artifact had brought him an unimaginable surprise at the critical moment. In his mind, what lingered was the image of that furnace

within a furnace...

Chapter 393

After leaving the alchemy area, Zhou Yi looked up at the glaring sunlight above. While his facial expression had returned to normal, the surging tide of ecstasy in his heart continued to rise and fall like waves. Elder Hao Dong had taken the successfully refined Beauty-Retaining Pill into the tower, undoubtedly to report the good news to the sect master.

Achieving the success of refining the Beauty-Retaining Pill so quickly was beyond even Elder Hao

Dong's expectations. The joy on his face resonated with Zhou Yi and Jin Zhanzhan.

"Brother Zhou, are you really planning to delve into the path of alchemy?" Jin Zhanzhan asked in a low voice.

Zhou Yi pursed his lips and replied, "The path of alchemy is truly fascinating, and I do want to give it a try."

Jin Zhanzhan shook his head slightly. Having spent months with Zhou Yi, he knew that once this guy made up his mind, it was difficult to change it.

Yet, this trait was almost a commonality among successful individuals. Without such resolute determination, there would be no dazzling achievements to speak of.

Sighing softly, Jin Zhanzhan earnestly advised, "Brother Zhou, if you want to delve into the path of alchemy, I don't object. However, I have a suggestion that I hope you'll consider."

Zhou Yi replied solemnly, "Please go ahead, Brother Jin."

Jin Zhanzhan halted his steps and looked at Zhou Yi with seriousness he had never shown before. "My suggestion is that you wait until you've become a venerable before delving into alchemy. Prior to that, it's best to focus your energy on martial arts."

Feeling the genuine concern emanating from Jin Zhanzhan, Zhou Yi responded earnestly, "Rest assured, Brother Jin. I won't lose sight of the main goal. I won't be distracted until I become a venerable."

Only then did a relieved smile appear on Jin Zhanzhan's face as he said, "As long as you remember these words."

The two exchanged a smile and walked back side by side to their living quarters. As Zhou Yi paused in front of his room's door, he casually smiled and said, "Brother Jin, during the alchemy just now, I gained some insights and wish to seclude myself for contemplation."

Jin Zhanzhan's eyes flickered with a tinge of envy. He replied, "Brother Zhou, feel free to seclude yourself. I'll watch over for you."

After thanking Jin Zhanzhan, Zhou Yi entered his room. The moment he stepped inside, the smile on his face vanished, replaced by an indescribable excitement that he still struggled to suppress. Even at this moment, he had not fully recovered from his recent discovery. Nevertheless, he firmly believed that if anyone else had made the same revelation, they would likely be even more ecstatic than he was.

Touching the tracer given by Brerbo, which was hanging on his chest, Zhou Yi called out in a hushed tone, "Brerbo, I need your assistance, please come quickly."

Setting down the tracer, he sat down and took deep breaths, inhaling and exhaling. Each breath he took seemed to stretch on forever, and whether inhaling or exhaling, it was remarkably distinct, carrying a powerful true energy. Under the impact of this force, the entire room seemed to sway slightly.

In the room opposite him, Jin Zhanzhan frowned slightly. Although he hadn't deliberately eavesdropped on anything, the weighty sound of breathing was like thunder in the sky, impossible to ignore.

The first thought that flashed through his mind was that this technique was truly peculiar. Then, he skimmed through all the various techniques he had encountered in his decades of martial arts practice. Despite his extensive experience, he still couldn't discern the nature of this distinctive technique. After listening intently for a while, he finally had to admit to himself that he didn't understand it and couldn't make sense of it.

Shaking his head, he let out a sigh. This young triple-flower expert was like an enigma he couldn't decipher. However, no matter what, he had never imagined that the rhythmic breathing of Zhou Yi was merely a method to calm his own turbulent emotions.If he had known, he might not have been so perplexed, though it would certainly have been irritating.

Yet, no matter who it was, no one could have guessed that Zhou Yi, at his current level of cultivation, would resort to such a method to steady his state of mind.

It was unclear how much time had passed before Zhou Yi's emotions gradually settled. His breathing became more subdued, no longer having the exaggerated effect from before. Just at that moment, a water stain silently seeped in through the crack of the door. This stain gradually expanded, transforming into Brerbo without a sound.

Regarding Brerbo's unique method of appearing, Zhou Yi had developed an immunity. He smiled faintly, stood up, and lowered his voice as he said, "Brerbo, I need to go out for a while. Could you take over for me?"

Brerbo nodded silently. Ripples spread across his body, and in the blink of an eye, he transformed into another Zhou Yi. The transition was smooth and seamless, with no apparent flaws even to the genuine Zhou Yi.

"You'd better take Treasure Pig with you. It wasn't very happy just now," Brerbo calmly suggested.

Zhou Yi was taken aback. "Why wasn't it happy?"

"Because I'm leaving."

Zhou Yi shook his head helplessly. These two inhuman beings had an unusually close relationship. But if it weren't for that, Treasure Pig wouldn't have slipped out of Tianchi.

"Where is it?" Zhou Yi asked in a hushed tone.

Brerbo provided detailed directions to a location outside the city. Although Zhou Yi didn't understand why they had chosen that specific place, he had no objections.

After a few quiet instructions, Zhou Yi's body trembled slightly, enveloped in a layer of faint mist-like energy. He then silently delved into the earth.

Though his methods of entering and exiting the city were different from those of Brerbo, they were quite similar in terms of their concealment capabilities.

Despite the abundance of experts in the Lingxiao Treasure Hall, there were very few who could sense the underground environment.

Furthermore, with Zhou Yi's Cloud Mist power concealing him, it was practically impossible for anyone to detect his movements without prior knowledge.

Once away from the city, Zhou Yi emerged from the earth, determined his direction, and soon located the cave Brerbo had mentioned.

Before he even entered the cave, a streak of white light dashed toward him like a flying object. The speed of this white light was almost too rapid for Zhou Yi to react.

Subsequently, Treasure Pig landed on Zhou Yi's shoulder, grunting and squealing.

Zhou Yi slapped his forehead in frustration. "Treasure Pig, I'm not Brerbo. Come down first."

"Hum hum hum..."

Zhou Yi blinked his eyes. Who knew what this fellow was trying to convey. Shaking his head, he removed the creature's two front hooves from his shoulders. Ignoring its protests as it nudged him with its large snout, he grasped its neck and sped off into the distance.

The power of the wind unleashed its might without restraint. Zhou Yi had accelerated to an incredible speed, a pace he hadn't used for continuous travel since the night he fled for his life.

However, at this moment, it felt as if there was a fire burning within him, heating him up from head to toe. If he didn't release it soon, who knew if he might explode. Though Zhou Yi had nearly exhausted his entire body's true energy within the alchemy room, after resting for a while, he had recovered at least fifty percent.

During his frantic dash, one hand held onto Treasure Pig's neck, while the other grasped a white stone. The stone's power surged into him, offering him the best possible replenishment of his true energy.

※※※※

Finally, daylight faded, and the sun peacefully set below the horizon. Zhou Yi also came to a stop. He looked back, unable to determine how long he had been running, but one thing was certain – he had distanced himself far from the Lingxiao Treasure Hall.

Feeling the surging and abundant true energy within him, Zhou Yi felt extremely satisfied. To be able to maintain and even replenish his true energy during such a strenuous run was a feat that likely only a few individuals in the world, besides himself, could achieve.

Tucking the white stone away, Zhou Yi surveyed his surroundings. He found himself in a desolate and deserted mountain valley – an ideal spot for his purposes.

Suddenly, a series of faint "hum hum" sounds reached his ears from the side. Zhou Yi turned to see

Treasure Pig's eyes, small and twinkling, seemingly filled with a mischievous glint of intelligence.

During their recent sprint, the creature had sensed a different demeanor in Zhou Yi, unlike his usual self. This realization led Treasure Pig to stop resisting. It wasn't until this moment, as they both came to a stop, it softly grunted a few times.

Zhou Yi chuckled softly, letting Treasure Pig down and gently patting its head. He said, "Little guy, today I'll show you something special."

Seemingly understanding Zhou Yi's intent, Treasure Pig's small eyes sparkled with excitement. Zhou Yi inwardly sighed. It was no wonder the sect master of the Tlanchi held this little creature in such high regard. Such a spirit beast would likely be adored by anyone.

Except perhaps for the Medicine Daoist , who looked at Treasure Pig as if he were an innate core!

Unfastening his clothes, Zhou Yi took out the silver ring hanging around his chest. He held the ring in his hand, but at this moment, he hesitated for a brief moment.

The saying went, the greater the hope, the greater the disappointment. If what was inside this ring wasn't what he expected – if it was all for naught – he would undoubtedly feel a great sense of dejection.

"Heh heh heh..."

The Treasure Pig at his feet emitted a series of urging sounds. Zhou Yi took a deep breath and finally infused his true energy into the ring.

As the potent true energy entered the silver ring, a dark space suddenly appeared before them. Treasure Pig seemed to understand the preciousness of this item. It obediently lay down on the ground, its small eyes never blinking as it fixed its gaze on the dark space.

Zhou Yi reached out and slowly retrieved something from within.

Treasure Pig's eyes immediately brightened. With a swift movement, it pounced, its two front hooves firmly pressing down on the item, as if declaring its ownership.

Chapter 394

Zhou Yi shook his head slightly, feeling extremely helpless about the behavior of the Treasure Pig. However, upon further thought, if not for the innate nature of the Treasure Pig, this item wouldn't have ended up in his possession in the first place.

The object he had taken from the spatial storage was the small furnace they had found in the tea shop on their way to the east. Zhou Yi examined the furnace closely, and it did indeed resemble the furnace-within-a-furnace he had seen before.

If it were merely due to the similarity in appearance, Zhou Yi wouldn't be so excited. But considering the Treasure Pig's preference for this item, its value was undoubtedly greater than the replicated Five

Elements Ring. Even the replicated divine artifact paled in comparison to the allure of this furnace in the eyes of the Treasure Pig.

Following the creature's usual habits, the value of this item was likely greater than that of the replicated Five Elements Ring, and anything surpassing the replicated divine artifact would likely be an actual divine artifact.

Thus, after realizing this, Zhou Yi's excitement was completely justified. He turned the furnace over in his hands, and his expression subtly changed. The Treasure Pig continued to grasp it with all four hooves, refusing to let go in a peculiar manner, clearly unwilling to relinquish it.

"Come down, Treasure Pig," Zhou Yi said with a friendly tone, trying to coax the creature.

However, the Treasure Pig resolutely shook its head, showing no intention of yielding to Zhou Yi's request. Its refusal to heed Zhou Yi's words was unsurprising, given its temperament from their extended time together.

Zhou Yi furrowed his brows as he realized the Treasure Pig's stubbornness. He had come to understand the creature's character quite well. If the Treasure Pig was set on something, it was practically impossible to change its mind.

With a cold snort, Zhou Yi placed the furnace on the ground and his expression darkened. A sense of chilly unease seemed to emanate from the surroundings, causing the Treasure Pig to shiver involuntarily. It glanced at Zhou Yi, its small eyes studying him carefully, seemingly assessing whether he was genuinely angry.

In the end, the Treasure Pig released its four limbs and stood upright on its hind hooves. It then lifted the furnace high with its front hooves, toddling step by step towards Zhou Yi. It rubbed the furnace against Zhou Yi's leg in a playful manner.

Zhou Yi couldn't help but find it both amusing and exasperating. He took the furnace back from the Treasure Pig, and the Treasure Pig let out a few snorts before sitting down on the ground. Its short tail swayed listlessly behind it, Its expression seemed to carry an indescribable sense of grievance.

With a resigned sigh, Zhou Yi realized that this creature was not only incredibly intelligent but also adept at sensing human emotions. Coupled with its adorable appearance and pristine white fur as smooth as silk, it was no wonder the Treasure Pig easily won people's hearts.

He lifted the sulking Treasure Pig and immediately, it turned its head away, seemingly disdainful. However, one of its small eyes glanced sideways, surreptitiously observing Zhou Yi's actions.

Shaking his head, Zhou Yi said, "Little one, this item might be a divine artifact. Would you like to see its power?"

The Treasure Pig's face, previously turned away, immediately swiveled back. Its small eyes sparkled with excitement. Its slightly elongated nose stretched forward, nuzzling affectionately against Zhou Yi's face. This was the creature's way of showing affection.

Chuckling, Zhou Yi gently set the creature down behind him. Then, he half-closed his eyes and attempted to infuse True Qi into the furnace. The Treasure Pig seemed to sense the aura of seriousness from Zhou Yi and obediently nestled by his feet, its eyes fixed on the furnace, anticipating its transformation.

A surge of vast True Qi flowed from within Zhou Yi into the furnace. The immense and unparalleled True Qi surged like tidal waves crashing down. However, despite Zhou Yi's True Qi surging wildly, the furnace remained unmoved, akin to a bottomless pit, completely unresponsive to the forceful impact of the True Qi.

Zhou Yi let out a long exhale, ceasing the futile attempt to surge his True Qi. Beside him, he heard the discontented grunting of the Treasure Pig. He turned to face the Treasure Pig's skeptical gaze and slightly embarrassedly said, "Just a moment, it will be ready soon."

The Treasure Pig tilted its head, seemingly unsure whether to believe him or not.

Seeing Treasure Pig's doubtful expression, Zhou Yi shot it a somewhat exasperated glance.

He then turned his attention back to the furnace in his hand. After the previous attempts, he was certain that he couldn't destroy the item using his current abilities, unless he resorted to using the Great Guandao. Given this, he felt more at ease to experiment further without worrying about damaging the furnace.

Placing the furnace on the ground, Zhou Yi crouched down, and his aura suddenly expanded wildly. It surged even more intensely than before, surpassing its previous intensity.

The Treasure Pig's eyes brimmed with hope. After witnessing such a surge of power, it gained a newfound confidence.

In a matter of breaths, Zhou Yi's hands formed a mysterious hand seal. Within the seal, faintly, there seemed to be a small wisp of ethereal fire, carrying an inconceivably enormous might.

With solemn expression, Zhou Yi pushed this ball of fire into the furnace.

His heart was tense. This was his final attempt. If he couldn't ignite the furnace with this newly acquired fire manipulation technique, then he would be out of options.

At that point, whether the furnace was the legendary artifact Nine-Dragon Furnace or not would be inconsequential to him.

An unusable and uncontrollable furnace, no matter how many secrets it might hold, was still just a furnace. As a wisp of ethereal fire entered the furnace, Zhou Yi's expression shifted subtly, his heart filling with joy.

Under the influence of his controlled fire manipulation, this wisp of ethereal fire seemed to genuinely trigger some sort of mutation within. He could clearly sense that a certain power within the furnace was somewhat stirred by this strand of fire, on the brink of awakening.

Though he hadn't fully harnessed this power yet, Zhou Yi could already feel its surging and immense presence. In the face of this power, the only feeling he had was one of insignificance.

Even though he was already a powerhouse at the Three Flowers realm, a figure noteworthy even in the entire world, Zhou Yi found himself utterly powerless against the concealed force within the artifact. He couldn't muster even the slightest hint of resistance in the face of this hidden power.

The mere touch of this distant mental connection instantly sent shockwaves through Zhou Yi's determination, nearly overwhelming him.

This sensation was akin to a towering mountain descending from the sky, making him feel as though he could perish at any moment. A loud roar erupted from Zhou Yi's mouth as if he was discarding a burning hot object, and he flung the artifact away from his hands.

The Treasure Pig was startled by his roar and scurried away, However, it swiftly returned, carrying the fire furnace and placing it in front of Zhou Yi.

After a moment's hesitation, Zhou Yi picked up the furnace again. He gently patted the understanding creature's large head, allowing his shaken emotions to settle.

When everything calmed down, a mixture of astonishment and delight coursed through his heart.

The scene just now had made it clear to him that the furnace was indeed extraordinary. Even if it wasn't the legendary Nine Dragon Furnace, it was undoubtedly a valuable treasure. However, the problem was that the power contained within it was overwhelmingly potent. With his current level of strength, trying to control the power within was akin to an ant trying to shake a tree—it was an impossible task.

Just like a moment ago, that attempting to control this power could be disastrous. Fortunately, he had acted quickly and tossed the furnace away. Had he delayed even for a moment, the mental pressure alone might have crushed him.

Letting out a soft sigh, he felt a frustrating sense of being near a treasure yet unable to grasp it. Quietly contemplating for a while, an idea emerged in Zhou Yi's mind.

Since direct control seemed impossible, perhaps he could try guiding the power instead. He focused his mind once more, expelling the frightening images that had haunted him moments ago. Keeping such images in one's mind wasn't advisable for a cultivator.

Gathering his vast inner energy, he executed a series of intricate hand movements above the furnace. A faint ethereal fire reappeared, but this time the power contained within it seemed somewhat diminished.

He no longer dared to directly oppose the power within the furnace. Slowly, he channeled his inner energy, using a special technique that was akin to using a feather to push a massive weight. He wanted to guide the power within the furnace to see what extent of power it could manifest.

Gently, he infused the faint ethereal fire back into the furnace.

In that instant, he once again sensed that terrifying and nearly despair-inducing power. Unexpectedly, however, this power didn't respond as he had anticipated—it didn't erupt out of the furnace. In fact, there was no reaction at all.

The faint ethereal fire he had infused into the furnace seemed to vanish into an endless sea of flames, disappearing without causing any ripples or disturbances. At this point, Zhou Yi was at a loss. He turned his head to look at the puzzled-looking Treasure Pig, but he couldn't come up with any feasible solutions.

He let out a deep sigh, his heart filled with bitter amusement. The power within this fire furnace was truly too proud... Yes, that's the feeling it gave him—proud.

It was as if the power within the furnace had gained a hint of consciousness. When he couldn't touch it, it didn't bother with him at all. Once he grasped a method to interact with it and tried to control it, it would retaliate fiercely. And when he attempted to draw its attention, it was like a proud ancient behemoth, completely ignoring the summons of an insignificant ant below.

Holding the furnace high above his head, Zhou Yi felt an infinite sense of emotion. It truly lived up to its reputation as a divine artifact. Yet, the question remained: was having this thing by his side a blessing or a curse?

Suddenly, there was a movement within Zhou Yi's chaotic Dantian, and an equally powerful force began to stir...

Chapter 395

Zhou Yi's expression changed slightly, as he was familiar with this kind of power.

This power, he absorbed it during the decisive battle against the Qilian Twin Devils, drawing a strand of mystical energy from the seventh level of the Tower of Heaven. How this strand of power was attracted into his body, only the heavens know.

Regardless, this power has settled within his Dantian as if it rightfully belongs there.

He has made numerous attempts to understand this power. Eventually, he discovered that the only way to utilize it is by first employing the Raising Heaven Seal, and when the seal reaches its peak, immediately unleashing the Overturning Heaven Seal.

Only through this method could he unleash the extraordinary and massive power held within the Tower of Heaven-reaching Treasure.

Apart from this, there was no other method to manipulate this power. Not even the Earth Seal, a defensive technique, could control it.

However, at this moment...

When Zhou Yi raised the fire furnace above his head and inadvertently assumed the posture of the Raising Heaven Seal, the mysterious power surged along his meridians, traveling from his arm.

In an instant, this power was almost at the fire furnace.

Zhou Yi was alarmed, and without thinking, his hands began to move. Although he held the fire furnace aloft, his ten fingers moved like a blur, leaving behind a series of afterimages in the air.

The power of the fire element swiftly coalesced within his hands, the gestures of manipulating fire energy unfolding in the shortest span of time. In the shortest time possible, he released the control over the power.

His palms felt a faint heat, and countless threads of energy burst forth, weaving together to wrap around the mystical power that was about to dissipate from his hands.

Perhaps this power was incomparably formidable, perhaps it had an astounding origin, or maybe it was beyond his current level of control. However, at this moment, Zhou Yi intercepted this power with determination.

After all, this power originated from within his Dantian. Since the last time he had unleashed the Fantian Seal, this power had fused with him.

Of course, Zhou Yi was acutely aware that if he didn't possess a unique constitution—one that could accept all things like chaos—this power could never belong to him. For an ordinary person to forcibly absorb such power would only lead to their body exploding.

However, since he possessed this unique constitution, he also had boundless possibilities. Just like the current Zhou Yi, he carefully entwined this power within his palms.

A flicker of hesitation briefly appeared in his eyes, but it quickly gave way to determination. In the path of martial cultivation, every step was like treading on thorns. How could one advance without taking any risks?

Finally, the power in his hands surged forward like an arrow released from a bowstring, rushing into the fire furnace brimming with boundless mystical energy without hesitation.

Of course, based on the lessons he had learned before, Zhou Yi continued to employ the power of guidance. However, this time, it wasn't just his own power contained within the guidance. It also encompassed the mysterious power originating from the Tower of Heaven within his body.

A flicker of ethereal fire enveloped a strand of wondrous power, and once again, they made contact with the immense energy within the fire furnace.

This was the utmost limit that Zhou Yi could achieve. He couldn't imagine what would happen if these two forces collided without his control. Therefore, in that split second of lightning and fire, he made the wisest decision.

He used the strand of mystical power within him as a guide, leading the immense power within the fire furnace.

In an instant, two forces from different systems but of equal strength collided. The intense explosion that Zhou Yi had been worried about did not occur. When these two forces truly clashed, his spirit was suddenly invigorated.

As if through some kind of spiritual connection, he saw a grand and tumultuous scene unfold before his eyes. Within the fire furnace, there existed an endless, raging sea of fire—a world of flames. In this fiery realm, only the boundless flames existed, leaving no room for anything else.

Within this endless sea of fire, massive and unimaginable beasts roiled, seemingly composed entirely of the flames. They frolicked in this sea of fire, playing without restraint.

In a trance, Zhou Yi sensed that the nearest colossal beast turned its head. It was a fire dragon, its body seemingly boundless in length.

A pair of eyes as massive as peaks glanced in his direction. In that momentary gaze, Zhou Yi inexplicably felt as if he was seen through, as if the dragon had penetrated his very being.

A profuse cold sweat erupted from Zhou Yi's body, saturating his clothes within moments. However, he remained utterly unaware. His entire consciousness had been captivated by the fire dragon's gaze. It was as if there was an indescribable power within that gaze, tempting him to throw himself headlong into it.

Though Zhou Yi's rationality screamed at him not to immerse himself completely, his willpower was gradually being eroded away.

The dragon's eyes held no emotion, yet from that emotionless gaze, Zhou Yi interpreted a message. The dragon hadn't truly regarded him; before the dragon, he was as insignificant as an ant. To the dragon, he was merely noticed in passing, akin to how a human might glance at a crawling ant on the ground—nothing more.

Suddenly, a surge of anger erupted from Zhou Yi's heart. His eyes widened, and every muscle and drop of blood in his body seemed to boil in this moment. If there was something more painful in this world than being looked down upon, it was being utterly disregarded. Being looked down upon indicated that at least someone had noticed you. But being ignored, that blatant feeling of being overlooked, that was what truly left an indelible mark on a person.

Even though he was well aware of the insurmountable gap in strength between them, in this moment, Zhou Yi seemed to have lost his rationality, resembling a madman. He parted his lips and let out a roar that could have even startled himself.

Then, he raised his hand above his head, and the Five Elements energy within his body began to swirl wildly: from water to wood, from wood to fire, from fire to earth, and from earth to metal. The powerful eruption of the "Thirty-Six Forms of Mountain-Crushing," the twenty-fourth form, burst forth with all his might.

The immense power of metal broke through the sea of fire before him and surged toward the distant dragon. With his life on the line, he unleashed a formidable strike. But after tearing through the sea of fire and finally connecting with the dragon, a flash of sparks was all that occurred. Everything reverted to normal, as if nothing had transpired.

Zhou Yi's all-out attack had only managed to rupture the sea of fire and reach the dragon's body, but he lacked the strength to go any further.

His entire strength was nothing before the dragon—a feeble attempt. A snorting sound came from beside him, and Zhou Yi looked in surprise. The Treasure Pig had somehow entered this space, looking around with apparent curiosity.

Finally, the dragon turned its head, but it wasn't drawn by Zhou Yi. It was captivated by the Treasure Pig in Zhou Yi's hands. For some reason, Zhou Yi felt as if he were going mad. In the dragon's calm gaze, he seemed to discern a trace of affection. Of course, this trace of affection wasn't directed at him but at the Treasure Pig in his hands.

This little creature confronted the colossal and disproportionately large dragon from his embrace, displaying not a hint of fear.

A strange power surged from within Zhou Yi's body. His heart skipped a beat; he sensed it. This was the power of his Dantian, that chaotic Dantian capable of absorbing all forms of elemental energy.

In the next moment, his body seemed to transform into an endless black hole, sucking everything around him into it. The weakness he had felt after unleashing his all-out strike had vanished entirely. Boundless fire-element energy filled his Dantian, granting Zhou Yi an overflowing sense of bliss.

The dragon's gaze finally showed a flicker of change. Its eyes no longer held that dismissive indifference when it looked at Zhou Yi; instead, they brimmed with astonishment. It seemed to have discovered some unforeseen astonishment.

The scene before him began to collapse. Without reason, Zhou Yi understood that the wondrous power from the tower had been depleted. The connection between himself and this mystical realm was fading.

However, in that very moment, the dragon opened its colossal maw.A surge of raging flames rushed into the crumbling space, engulfing Zhou Yi and the Treasure Pig entirely.

Zhou Yi closed his eyes. He knew all too well that resisting such immense fire-elemental power was futile. At this moment, a faint regret crept into his heart. He knew the power within the furnace was overwhelmingly potent. Why did he recklessly provoke it?

Yet, his body shivered slightly, and the next moment, he found himself back in his original form.

Zhou Yi was surprised to realize he had safely returned to this desolate mountainous region. His eyes were filled with delight, and even the desolate scenery around him seemed to have transformed into a captivating beauty in his gaze.

However, in the next instant, his expression abruptly changed. He distinctly sensed that within the furnace, an immense power far beyond his imagination was held captive. Yet, this power remained confined within the furnace, as though a fierce beast imprisoned in a cage, unable to break free.

In an instant, Zhou Yi recollected the dragon's final action. As if struck by inspiration, he grasped many things in a heartbeat. Without hesitation, he adjusted the furnace's orientation, aligning its mouth with the desolate mountain ahead.

Then, he twisted the furnace's lid forcefully. The not-so-large lid immediately started spinning, and a tremendous, inhuman surge of overwhelming momentum, a thick red torrent of boundless flames, erupted almost the instant the furnace's mouth opened. The immense fire-elemental power surged forth, so swift that even Zhou Yi holding the furnace couldn't react in time.

In a split second, it seemed as though the entire world had turned into a sea of flames.

Chapter 396

Red...

Heat...

His surroundings were enveloped in an immense crimson hue, and for a moment, Zhou Yi could perceive no other colors. The fervent heat surrounding him caused a tingling discomfort on his skin, and in an instant, his clothes were reduced to ash. Had he not been wearing the Red Wolf King's leather armor against his skin, he would have been left stark naked.

Even so, the Red Wolf King's leather armor seemed to possess a sensation of melting.

Squinting his eyes, Zhou Yi slowly opened them after a moment. Muscles twitched faintly on his face, and his gaze carried an inexplicable daze. He raised his head to glance at the furnace in his hand, then lowered it to survey his own body and the Treasure Pig at his feet.

Once again, man and pig exchanged a bewildered look.

Before them lay a scorched wasteland; everything had turned to nothingness. The trees that once adorned the land hadn't charred but vanished, obliterated by an unimaginable force of fire.

The charred ground spread in a fan shape from Zhou Yi's position, extending outward. Within a range of about thirty yards, there was naught but scorched earth. Beyond those thirty yards, while the ground was still scorched, scattered remnants of burned items appeared. However, these remnants had merged with the scorched earth, making it impossible for Zhou Yi to identify their origins. This pattern continued until about Hundred yards out, where things gradually returned to normal.

From this, it was clear that the most potent zone of the fire's influence stretched about thirty yards ahead of Zhou Yi. Once that range was surpassed, its power diminished gradually. It wasn't until around Hundred yards out that this force slowly waned.

Zhou Yi took a deep breath, expecting a breath of fresh, cold air, but instead, he inhaled an intense scent of burning.

Fortunately, his abundant True Qi prevented him from being choked to death by that breath.

With lingering fear, Zhou Yi looked ahead and was certain that he couldn't withstand such a violent force of fire. If he were to stand directly in front of the flames, even if he had comprehended the essence of the Wind element, mastered the Earth-Tunnelling Technique or even conjured the Fire Flower, he would still be vaporized.

Although condensing the Fire Flower allows one to harness the fire's energy from the heavens and earth, there is a limit to how much the human body can handle. Once this limit is exceeded, the Fire Flower, instead of aiding in resistance against the fire's power, can trigger an explosion of the fire's energy. This turns it into a lethal aid for self-destruction.

In a moment of absentmindedness, a thought flickered across Zhou Yi's mind: if facing this fire's power, would a Venerable survive in the sea of flames? However, this thought passed as quickly as it came, and he didn't entertain any delusions of finding a Venerable individual to test it out.

He vividly remembered that the dragon had casually breathed out a flame, and yet, that seemingly minor flame had caused such immense destruction. If all nine dragons were to be unleashed, at full strength...

A chill swept over Zhou Yi's heart, and he couldn't help but feel a sense of unease. He had begun to believe somewhat in the origins of the legendary Eight Hundred Li Volcano. Perhaps it truly resulted from the clash between a divine expert wielding the Nine Dragons Furnace and a divine beast.

He lowered his head and gently tugged at the Treasure Pig's hide, as if speaking to himself, "Is this... my doing?"

The Treasure Pig seemed to want to intensify Zhou Yi's sense of guilt and nodded its head forcefully.

However, Zhou Yi's gaze didn't turn toward the Treasure Pig at all. Instead, he closed his eyes and began to contemplate quietly. He recalled everything that had happened just like a dream.

Most surprisingly, he found himself having the audacity to unleash a full-force strike in front of the dragon. This action left him deeply astonished, questioning where he had found such courage.

Shaking his head, even a fool could realize that the furnace in his hand was undoubtedly the legendary artifact, the Nine Dragons Furnace. Yet, while it possessed immense power, it was also a double-edged sword. He was certain that if even a whisper about it leaked, countless individuals would relentlessly pursue him, whether he fled to the ends of the earth. They would either snatch the artifact from his grasp or eliminate him entirely.

At this moment, he had made up his mind. Regardless of the circumstances, he couldn't allow anyone to know that he possessed such a potent artifact. Perhaps, when his strength was enough to stand proudly above all, he could reveal it without fear. But that was definitely not now.

A sudden thought crossed his mind, causing Zhou Yi to turn his head and look at the Treasure Pig by his feet. He asked in surprise, "Treasure Pig, how did you get in here just now?"

During the mysterious connection with the Nine Dragons Furnace, the Treasure Pig had somehow sneaked in as well. Moreover, the enormous fire dragon had treated the Treasure Pig with a markedly better attitude than himself, which left him feeling doubtful and uncertain.

The Treasure Pig tilted its head, appearing to be pondering as well, its small eyes squinting in apparent discomfort.

Zhou Yi gave a wry smile, rubbed the Treasure Pig's head, and said, "Forget it, no need to think about it."

The Treasure Pig immediately seemed relieved, lifting its head once more.

Even though he hadn't discovered the reason, Zhou Yi understood that the Treasure Pig's origins were far from simple. As he placed the Nine Dragons Furnace back against his chest, he hesitated.

For some unknown reason, after the recent ordeal, Zhou Yi couldn't shake the feeling that a mysterious connection had formed between him and the Nine Dragons Furnace. This connection wasn't through his true qi, but rather on a pure spiritual level. It resembled the connection with the Divine Path Scripture, where the events in a fixed and special space had left an indelible mark on his memory. Once recognized by that world, he could use true qi as a guide and enter at will.

Holding the Nine Dragons Furnace, Zhou Yi contemplated for a moment before finally deciding to give it another try. He raised the Nine Dragons Furnace above his head and began to move his hands rapidly.

On his fingertips, an invisible force seemed to emerge. With its support, the Nine Dragons Furnace rested on his fingers, allowing Zhou Yi to condense the hand-seal technique for manipulating the power of fire and infuse it into the Furnace.

Zhou Yi's eyes lit up suddenly. This time, he could sense a significant difference from before. The immense power within the Nine Dragons Furnace was no longer as unattainable as before; instead, he felt a slight connection with it.

His hand seals continued to dance, and as his movements progressed, the power within the cauldron began to loosen. Slowly but surely, a trace of power emerged from the Nine Dragons Furnace. It was like a tiny spark, rapidly growing in strength.

Zhou Yi's nostrils started to bead with sweat, something he hadn't anticipated. He hadn't realized that controlling the power within the Nine Dragons Furnace would consume so much true qi and time.

His fingers felt as heavy as a thousand pounds as he moved them painstakingly. This moment was completely different from when he hadn't been in control of the Nine Dragons Furnace and its power.

Zhou Yi's true qi surged out. When he finally managed to complete the final hand seal and infused the guiding power into the Nine Dragons Furnace, there was barely any true qi left in his body.

Releasing a long exhale, Zhou Yi's eyes sparkled with an excitement that had reached its peak. He had actually succeeded—using his own strength, he had drawn out the power from the Nine Dragons Furnace. Although the power he had drawn out was far from comparable to the total amount contained within, it was still much better than the awkward situation he had faced initially.

Sensing the changes within the Nine Dragons Furnace, the familiar and surging colossal power made Zhou Yi acutely aware of how potent the fire power within truly was. He changed his direction and gently opened the lid.

Once again, a tremendous energy surged out in an instant, and his vision was engulfed in that sea of red light...

This time, the might of the fire power was no less formidable than the flame the dragon had unleashed. Perhaps, this was the most potent force that Zhou Yi's current strength could harness.

After a while, Zhou Yi burst into hearty laughter. His laughter was brimming with joy. Anyone who stumbled upon such a treasure by chance and then figured out how to use it would be filled with immense happiness.

With his head held high, Zhou Yi was in high spirits. His chest was filled with passion, and he wanted to let out a long howl to vent his feelings. However, before he could even speak, his eyes suddenly narrowed.

Within his line of sight, two streaks of light appeared out of nowhere. These streaks of light were coming from the sky, and their destination was none other than his direction.

Unexplainably, a sense of ominous foreboding arose in Zhou Yi's heart. Without hesitation, he held the Nine Dragons Furnace and the treasure pig in his arms, then a surge of cloud mist energy lifted him off the ground and enveloped the pig completely.

Almost in the same instant the cloud mist energy enveloped them, Zhou Yi descended into the earth. The entire process was as fast as lightning— from the moment he spotted the streaks of light to the moment he burrowed underground, it happened in the blink of an eye.

Moreover, the ground had turned into a scorched earth around Zhou Yi, even affecting the area under his feet due to the residual impact. As a result, it was impossible to tell from the surface that someone had used Earth-Tunnelling Technique here.

Two beams of light in the sky didn't rush over at full speed; they maintained a certain pace as they flew closer.

This wasn't a top-tier power of the Wind element, but true flight in the sky, akin to the freedom of birds, almost unbelievable.

However, their speed didn't seem much faster than that of a venerable person's maximum speed, suggesting a strong caution for this area.

No matter how deliberately they delayed, this journey quickly passed. When the beams of light arrived above the scorched earth, they circled around twice before plummeting down like shooting stars.

Chapter 397

The meteor's descent was incredibly swift, but in an instant, it had firmly halted on the ground. Subsequently, the dazzling light dissipated, revealing two figures.

If Zhou Yi were still there, he would surely notice that one of these figures was very familiar. It was none other than Elder Hao Dong, the renowned top alchemist of the Lingxiao Treasure Hall. At this moment, his gaze was sharp as he scanned his surroundings. There was no trace of the warm smile he usually carried, replaced by a deeply serious expression. Especially after carefully examining the ground around, his brows slightly furrowed.

"Elder Hao, can you tell who might be responsible?" the other elder asked. This elder appeared slightly younger than Hao Dong, with a handsome face that far outshone his companion.

Hao Dong shook his head slightly and replied, "Junior Brother Xu, I can't discern it. Can you?"

After a moment of contemplation, Junior Brother Xu also shook his head and said, "Even among our peers, those who can condense fire energy to this extent are few. However, I can't fathom why they would come here and put on such a display."

Hao Dong raised his head once again, his gaze scanning around for a moment before he spoke, "Perhaps it's not provocation."

Junior Brother Xu was puzzled. "Elder Hao, in your opinion, what could be the purpose of this?"

Hao Dong paced slowly, seemingly unhurried. After a short while, he had traversed the entire scorched area. When he finally stopped, he was precisely standing where Zhou Yi had released the power of the Nine Dragons Furnace the second time.

"Junior Brother Xu, if I'm not mistaken, this person has consecutively released immense fire power twice in this spot," Hao Dong said with a grave expression. "Without moving from this position and without leveraging the power of heaven and earth, solely relying on their own strength, they were able to unleash such terrifying destructive power. It's truly astonishing."

Junior Brother Xu's expression changed slightly. He remained silent for a while before finally saying, "Indeed, Elder, your insight is accurate. This person's manipulation of fire energy is indeed from within rather than compressing and detonating the fire energy absorbed from heaven and earth."

Hao Dong chuckled and replied, "Junior Brother Xu, it's because I myself cultivate fire energy that I was able to discern this."

Junior Brother Xu nodded, saying, "Since this person hasn't intentionally drawn in the power of heaven and earth and is solely relying on their own strength to release fire energy... I understand now. They must be studying martial techniques."

Hao Dong nodded in agreement. "Exactly, that seems to be the only explanation. I can be certain that this person must have mastered a brand-new martial technique. Perhaps when they arrived here, they suddenly entered an enlightened state. Once they understood it, they couldn't help but consecutively release such powerful fire-based combat techniques twice."

If Zhou Yi were here and heard these comments, he would surely be amazed at the wisdom and experience of these old men. Although Hao Dong hadn't witnessed the events firsthand, his deductions were quite close to the truth. However, regardless of his strategic thinking, he couldn't possibly fathom that the person releasing such powerful fire energy was not a fellow high-level expert, but merely Zhou Yi someone who hadn't even reached the level of a Venerable.

A hint of envy flickered across Junior Brother Xu's face. Regardless of the individual, their reactions were almost always the same upon hearing the term "enlightenment."

After a moment, Junior Brother Xu inquired, "Elder Hao, how do you plan to handle this matter? Should we report it to the Sect Master for a decision?"

Hao Dong hesitated for a moment before saying, "Although the Sect Master gave instructions before entering seclusion that if a major event occurs, we can ask for his emergence, in my opinion, this person is likely just a passerby and not intentionally provoking us."

A hint of agreement appeared on Junior Brother Xu's face as he said, "This person had already left on their own before we arrived, clearly avoiding a confrontation with us. If they intended to provoke us, they wouldn't have retreated so readily."

Suddenly, they both seemed to have noticed something and turned their gazes toward the direction of the Lingxiao Treasure Hall.

In just a moment, figures flashed, and the two duty-bound Venerables of the Lingxiao Treasure Hall, Gao Weiliang and Du Wenbin, rushed over in haste. The immense power of fire energy released by the Nine Dragon Furnace was truly massive. Though these Venerables were a hundred miles away, they still sensed the immense fluctuations of true energy at this location. Even the two top-tier figures at the peak of the tower were alerted and personally investigated the matter, so the two duty Venerables couldn't afford any negligence.

However, compared to flying through the sky, running on the ground was still slower. Despite the deep apprehension that Hao Dong and Master Xu felt towards the enigmatic expert who wielded the power of fire, they had reservations during their flight. Nevertheless, their arrival at this location was still ahead of the two duty-bound Venerables."

Gao Weiliang and Du Wenbin both bowed, saying, "Greetings, Elder Brothers."

While they addressed them as elder brothers, their gestures were overly respectful, almost to the point of showing full deference.

Hao Dong nodded slightly and said, Junior Brothers, you need not concern yourselves with this matter." After a moment of contemplation, he continued, "However, pass on the order for disciples within a thousand miles to be vigilant. We need to see if similar incidents occur within this range."

Gao Weiliang and Du Wenbin immediately acknowledged without hesitation.

Hao Dong looked up at the sky, a cold smile playing on his lips. He said, "If this person truly is just passing through, then this unintentional mishap can be forgiven. But if they release their power again within a thousand miles, it would be a deliberate provocation. At that time, I will personally take action to see whether this person's control of fire is powerful or if my mastery of fire is superior."

As he spoke, his tone was brimming with unwavering self-confidence. Even in the face of the scorched earth below, his confidence remained unshaken.

Junior Brother Xu burst into laughter and said, "Elder Brother, your majesty remains undiminished from the past. If you really get a chance to encounter this person, let me witness it by your side."

They exchanged a smile and simultaneously emitted a radiant light. This light enveloped them, transforming them into two streaks of meteors shooting towards the sky, heading for the Lingxiao Treasure Hall's Tower of Heaven .

Gao Weiliang and Du Wenbin exchanged a wry smile. These two had the same temper as before.

Then, they surveyed their surroundings. Gradually, their expressions turned grim.

Hao Dong could afford to overlook the extent of the destruction here, but that didn't mean the other dignitaries could do the same.

After a long while, Gao Weiliang took a deep breath and said with a deep voice, "Du Junior Brother, what do you think of this person?"

"Powerful," Du Wenbin replied without hesitation. "Although this person's fire energy might not match up to Elder Brother Hao's, the difference is negligible. It's far beyond what any of us can handle."

Gao Weiliang nodded slowly and suddenly asked, "If you were to face this person head-on, Du Junior Brother, how confident are you in escaping?"

His question wasn't about winning; it was about escaping. This showed that in his mind, they had already accepted that they were not on the same level as this person. If they were to encounter this person, their only choice wouldn't be to fight to the death, but rather to turn and flee. Whether they could actually escape was uncertain.

Du Wenbin frowned this time. After a moment, he sighed lightly and said, "In this environment, my chances of escaping are slim. However, if the circumstances change, it's hard to say."

Gao Weiliang smiled wryly and said, "Who could wield such immense fire energy? I wonder who this person could be."

Du Wenbin's gaze swept around. Although he knew that Elder Brother Hao and the others must have searched thoroughly earlier and found nothing, he still lowered his voice and said, "Elder Brother, could it be someone from the Southern Region?"

Gao Weiliang's expression immediately turned somewhat peculiar. He cleared his throat and said, "Junior Brother, let's follow Elder Brother Hao's advice. The matters here are not within our scope."

Du Wenbin's eyes widened in realization, and he nodded quickly, saying, "You're right, Elder Brother. It's best if we don't get involved."

They exchanged a glance of mutual understanding and immediately turned to leave.

Over the next month, the Lingxiao Treasure Hall served as the center of attention. All disciples within a thousand miles, whether they were inner or outer sect disciples, even members of the royal family of the Da Shen Empire, received invitations or commands.

Countless people had come to see the scorched earth a hundred miles away from the Lingxiao Treasure Hall. Subsequently, within this thousand-mile area, numerous individuals were vigilant, trying to find another piece of scorched earth, and especially trying to locate the mysterious figure behind the creation of this scorched land.

Although everyone knew that encountering that mysterious individual would likely mean losing their lives, the temptation of the reward offered by the

Lingxiao Treasure Hall still led countless people to join the search without hesitation.

However, the final outcome left all the devoted searchers disappointed. After several months of searching, not a single clue was found. The person responsible for the scorched earth seemed to have vanished into thin air. If it weren't for the vast expanse of charred land and the longstanding prestige of the Lingxiao Treasure Hall, many would have doubted whether this was an elaborate prank.

Yet, no one knew that upon discovering that there was no second scorched earth nearby, both Hao Dong and Junior Brother Xu breathed a sigh of relief. While the Lingxiao Treasure Hall wasn't afraid of trouble, they didn't want to stir up conflicts during the period their Grandmaster was in seclusion.

However, none of them had ever considered that the perpetrator of the scorched earth wasn't any of the formidable individuals they imagined, but rather a newcomer who had concealed themselves within the Lingxiao Treasure Hall.

While all the peripheral disciples were diligently searching, none of their attention was directed towards the enormous city itself.

This was an outcome of arrogance and overconfidence, which ultimately led their focus astray...

Chapter 398

The silent courtyard was shrouded in darkness,

illuminated only by the moonlight that cast a radiant

white glow upon the ground. Jin Zhanyi stood in the

courtyard, his gaze fixed on the two streaks of

meteors in the sky, his expression constantly changing.

As a direct disciple of the Lingxiao Treasure Hall, he certainly knew what those two streaks of meteors represented. However, he couldn't fathom what kind of event had stirred the two elderly . After all, the status of these two elderly was extremely prestigious, and they rarely involved themselves in worldly affairs. Even during the previous upheaval in the Martial Repository, they had turned a blind eye, refusing to intervene.

If it hadn't been for the personal orders of the Sect Master this time, Elder Hao Dong wouldn't have taken action to refine the Youth-Restoring Elixir. Thus, whatever event had alarmed these two elderly must have been of significant importance, possibly even concerning the rise and fall of the entire sect.

In comparison, the departure of the two duty-bound elders wasn't as significant.

For ordinary matters, Jin Zhanyi might have been tempted to join the crowd out of curiosity. However, this time, he dared not act recklessly.

Before long, two streaks of light once again streaked across the sky, as the two elderly masters returned to the Tower of Heaven.

In this night, everyone in the Lingxiao Treasure Hall who knew the identity of those who had arrived with the streaks of light found it difficult to sleep. It wasn't until the next day, when Gao Weiliang issued the order to search for the scorched earth, that people began to grasp a rough understanding of the situation.

While suspicion and unease gripped the Lingxiao Treasure Hall, Zhou Yi had quietly returned to his room from the underground. He had also brought the Treasure Pig with him. Within his room, several sets of clothes were prepared for changing. Zhou Yi effortlessly swapped into a new set, effectively taking Brerbo's place.

This enigmatic bodyguard transformed into a watery form without any complaints, departing from the Lingxiao Treasure Hall in his unique manner. Zhou Yi never worried about whether he would be discovered.

The Treasure Pig displayed clear hesitation. It seemed to want to follow but was reluctant to leave

Zhou Yi's side. After all, beside Zhou Yi, there was an incredibly powerful artifact that held no less allure for the Treasure Pig than Brerbo did.

Zhou Yi rearranged a few tables and chairs in the room, constructing a crude nest for the Treasure Pig. He then placed the Nine Dragons Furnace in the nest and grasped the pig's large ears, whispering softly, "Little fellow, do you know what this thing is?"

The Treasure Pig nodded and made humming sounds.

Zhou Yi's expression grew extremely serious as he continued, "You should be well aware of how valuable this thing is. If someone else sees it, they'll definitely try to take it away from you."

The Treasure Pig seemed taken aback for a moment before immediately pouncing on the furnace. It clung to it with its hooves, its small eyes blinking rapidly, as if to say, "Whoever dares to take it, I'll fight them."

Zhou Yi nodded in satisfaction and said, "You stay here and guard it. Don't go out."

The Treasure Pig hummed a few more times, and anyone could easily understand its intent from its actions.

Zhou Yi chuckled, finally revealing a foxy smile, and added, "Of course, if you get bored, you can give me the item."

The Treasure Pig's small eyes immediately grew cautious, and they glittered as they stared at Zhou Yi.

Zhou Yi playfully flicked its head with his finger and said, "You little rascal, you can't possibly take this thing to find Brerbo, right? If you want to be with him, you must leave this thing behind."

The pig's head tilted to the side, seemingly grappling with the dilemma of whether to stay or go.

Zhou Yi shook his head and stood up, no longer paying attention to the little guy.

While the artifact was currently in his possession, it was this lucky little fellow who had truly discovered it. Moreover, the most crucial point was that the fire dragon within the Nine Dragons Furnace was undeniably friendly towards the small creature, and its gaze even held a hint of doting.

Zhou Yi had a vague feeling that his ability to harness some of the Nine Dragons Furnace's power might be related to this little fellow.

With that in mind, letting this little guy stay with the Nine Dragons Furnace might bring about some unexpected benefits.

Zhou Yi didn't dare to underestimate this seemingly spiritual artifact. However, he was confident that apart from Brerbo, the Treasure Pig seemed to lose interest in its other "treasures" after three days at most. Even a divine artifact like the Nine Dragons Furnace would likely be abandoned without a second thought, and the Treasure Pig would then go looking for Brerbo. At that point, the artifact would naturally return to Zhou Yi's possession.

With the Treasure Pig taken care of, Zhou Yi tidied up a bit. It was already the early morning of the next day.

He stepped out of his room, deeply inhaling the fresh air in the courtyard. The sensation was quite wonderful, especially when he thought back to the noxious smell from the previous night. It made the moment even more precious.

"Brother Zhou, how's your enlightenment going?" Jin Zhanyi's voice came from a distance, and then the courtyard door opened as Jin Zhanyi walked in.

Zhou Yi gave a slight smile and said, "I've gained a bit of insight. I can only say I've gained a little."

Jin Zhanyi gave him a once-over and laughed, "brother Zhou, with that delighted expression on your face, what you've comprehended this time must be quite remarkable."

Zhou Yi didn't deny it, and he nodded with a smile.

In reality, he hadn't really comprehended much last night. However, receiving even a slight acknowledgment from the Nine-Dragon Furnace and being able to harness a bit of its power was still an enormous source of joy.

Jin Zhanyi's expression suddenly became serious. He said, "Brother Zhou, Senior Hao just sent a message, hoping that we can focus on cultivating in the Lingxiao Treasure Hall. Especially the two of us. In three months, we will be heading to the Central Great Plains, and we can't afford to be careless."

Zhou Yi's heart warmed, and he replied, "Brother Jin, please thank Senior Hao on my behalf."

Jin Zhanyi chuckled and said, "You have an easy rapport with Senior Hao. Fortunately, you're not a disciple of the Lingxiao Treasure Hall but rather from the Northwestern Tianchi Mountain. Otherwise, I'd really worry that Senior Hao might forcibly take you in as a disciple and impart his alchemy skills to you."

Zhou Yi smiled wryly, shaking his head. In Jin Zhanyi's heart, there was nothing but martial arts. However, in this world, there were many fascinating things. Moreover, Zhou Yi had vaguely noticed that there was a faint connection between the path of alchemy and martial arts.

If one could manage it well, it wouldn't hinder martial arts progress but might even be of assistance.

Yet, very few people truly saw this connection, and even fewer could successfully grasp it—a rare and precious insight.

Jin Zhanyi glanced at Zhou Yi and said solemnly, "Brother Zhou, I understand your intention. You're planning to use the Five Elements Flowers as the foundation for achieving the Three Flowers Gathering at the Apex. Now that you've condensed three Five Elements Flowers, you can start attempting to lay down the foundation."

Zhou Yi's face reddened slightly, and he muttered, "Brother Jin, how should I go about it?"

Jin Zhanyi was momentarily taken aback and then asked in response, "What did you say?"

Zhou Yi's lips curled in determination, and he plainly stated, "I'm asking how to proceed and lay down the foundation for achieving the Three Flowers Gathering at the Apex"

Jin Zhanyi widened his eyes and said, "Brother Zhou, didn't your elders teach you?"

Zhou Yi felt annoyed inwardly. He came from the Hengshan Lineage, where the highest cultivation belonged to Yu Jinglei. However, Yu Jinglei had only condensed two flowers, so he had no knowledge about how to reach a Three Flowers Gathering at the Apex.

Although there seemed to be relevant records in the secret chamber behind the ancestral hall, Zhou Yi had abided by the ancestral teachings and hadn't read them before reaching the Three Flowers realm. Now, even if he wanted to read them, it was impossible. He certainly wouldn't travel all the way back to the Hengshan Lineage again.

With a light cough, Zhou Yi said, "Brother Jin, I'm a descendant of the Tianchi branch of the Hengshan Lineage, so..."

His eyes sparkled with a hint of flattery.

Jin Zhanyi chuckled wryly and said, "Fine, take a look then."

He lightly patted his waist, and a shadow shot out like a flying arrow. Then, in the blink of an eye, it elongated in the wind, transforming into a nearly three-meter-long dragon spear.

Although the length of the dragon spear was far from that of a Guandao, it still emitted a sharp aura after being infused with true qi. Especially on the tip of the spear, a chilling radiance flickered, making even the hairs on Zhou Yi's body stand on end.

"Brother Zhou, feel the difference in my dragon spear," Jin Zhanyi said solemnly.

Zhou Yi hesitated for a moment, then reached out and touched the dragon spear. However, his expression changed immediately.

The moment his palm touched the dragon spear, a tremendous force surged forth. This force was very familiar—it was Jin Zhanyi's true qi.

Zhou Yi initially thought Jin Zhanyi was attempting to catch him off guard with a strike, but he soon realized that it wasn't Jin Zhanyi's doing; it was the reaction of the dragon spear itself.

A large amount of true qi gathered on his palm, and the two forces were in a slight standoff. Eventually,

Zhou Yi managed to suppress the true qi within the dragon spear.

A hint of astonishment flickered in Zhou Yi's eyes, and he said, "Your true qi..."

Jin Zhanyi nodded slowly and said, "During 'Three Flowers Gathering at the Apex,' you vaporize and absorb the spiritual weapon into your body. From then on, you can use it as a bridge to connect with the power of heaven and earth, truly mastering the forces between heaven and earth. However, vaporizing and absorbing the spiritual weapon is far from easy. That's why 'foundation' comes into play before that."

He paused here, his wrist trembling slightly. The dragon spear emitted a clear dragon chant: "Before vaporizing the spiritual weapon, you need to infuse your true qi into the chosen spiritual weapon. Only by filling this weapon with the power of your Three Flowers and fully integrating all your strength with the weapon can you find the optimal three points of support."

He gazed deeply at Zhou Yi and continued, "Three points form the most stable structure in the world, and they are the source of all power of confinement.If you manage to identify your own three points of power, then you can consider yourself to have laid a strong foundation for achieving the Three Flowers Gathering at the Apex."

Zhou Yi's brows furrowed slightly. He seemed to grasp something, yet also seemed to be in the dark.

At some point, Jin Zhanyi had quietly departed. He had revealed everything he understood; whether Zhou Yi could comprehend it depended on him alone.

Chapter 399

In the same room, the Treasure Pig was snoozing on the side. Even in deep sleep, it still curled its four hooves, tightly hugging the Nine Dragons Furnace. Although its name contained the character "pig" and its hooves resembled those of a pig, its hooves could bend freely as if boneless. Without this feature, it wouldn't have been able to securely hold the Nine Dragons Furnace.

Moreover, with its willingness, it could create a slight suction force on its hooves. Although this force wasn't significant, it was enough to suspend its small body over something it liked. For instance, at this moment, when Zhou Yi lifted the Nine Dragons Furnace, the slumbering Treasure Pig seemed to open its eyes briefly. Once it realized it was Zhou Yi, it immediately continued to ignore him and sleep. Nevertheless, its body still remained suspended above the Nine Dragon Furnace, showing no sign of slipping off.

Shaking his head, Zhou Yi placed the little creature and the Nine Dragons Furnace on the bed, covered it with a new thin blanket.

Subsequently, he fetched a chair and sat quietly by the bedside. While Jin Zhanyi's words were simple, they were more comprehensible because of their simplicity. With Zhou Yi's current cultivation level, he could clearly understand the underlying principles.

However, the issue lies in the difficulty of putting theory into practice. If it were genuinely that simple, the experts at the Three Flowers realm in this world would have achieved the Three Flowers Gathering at the Apex long ago, and there wouldn't have been decades of stagnation.

His hands caressed the Five Elements Ring slowly, feeling the unique nature of this artifact weapon. The perpetual flow of the five elements within it was undoubtedly one-of-a-kind. Even the combined efforts of Qilian Twin Devils wouldn't have achieved such a harmonious unity.

After a moment of hesitation, Zhou Yi opened his mouth, and three distinct colored tangible flowers sprouted forth. The Fire Flower, the Earth Flower, and the Metal Flower. These three Five Elements flowers spun in the air, releasing the vast forces of their respective elements within the confined space.

However, under Zhou Yi's deliberate control, the power of these three Five Elements flowers didn't expand without restraint. Instead, he carefully transferred their power into the Five Elements Ring. Since entering the Lingxiao Treasure Hall, Zhou Yi hadn't used this imitation artifact again. Especially after his encounter with the Qilian Twin Devils, he heeded Jin Zhanyi's advice and didn't even bring it onto the battlefield.

Now, as Zhou Yi infused the true qi from the three Five Elements flowers into the ring, he immediately sensed the immense power within the Five Elements Ring gradually transforming. He couldn't help but sigh inwardly, reminiscing about the sensation he felt while interacting with the Nine Dragons Furnace last night. The difference between the imitation artifact and a genuine one was indeed like heaven and earth, with no comparison possible.

However, now that he was attempting to lay the foundation for the Three Flowers Gathering at the Apex, he could only use the imitation artifact, the Five Elements Ring.

Even though he possessed a genuine divine weapon in his hands, he didn't have the courage to use the Nine Dragons Furnace as the spiritual weapon for

Three Flowers Gathering at the Apex.The only outcome of trying to use something beyond his capacity was self-destruction; there was absolutely no other possibility.

Zhou Yi was well aware of this fact. Gradually pushing aside his distractions, he focused his concentration. Through the connection of his true qi, he seemed to transform into the three Five Elements flowers that danced in the air.

The three types of energy seemed to transform into his three streams of consciousness, entering the Five Elements Ring in this manner. At that moment, Zhou Yi suddenly felt as though his understanding of the Five Elements Ring had reached a new level. With the three different elemental forces swirling within the ring, Zhou Yi gained a fresh understanding of this spiritual weapon.

He seemed to enter a new space, where flickering flames, solid earth, boundless seas, dense forests, and the indomitable sharpness of the metallic forces shimmered before his eyes. Of course, this spatial experience was far from comparable to last night's scene.

If the space within the Nine Dragons Furnace was a true space, then the space within the Five Elements Ring was an illusion – a very unreal one at that.

However, reaching this point already left Zhou Yi feeling immensely astonished.

This Five Elements Ring wasn't intended for use by experts in the Divine Path; it was merely an imitation of a divine artifact. However, as is commonly known, the manipulation of spatial power is a skill exclusive to experts in the Divine Path. Since the Five Elements Ring wasn't created by a Divine Path expert, the existence of an space world within it is unlikely.

But in reality, when Zhou Yi's three different elemental forces entered the Five Elements Ring, he could faintly sense the embryonic form of a space world.

His brows furrowed deeply. Could the master who forged the Five Elements Ring truly possess boundless power, even capable of creating spatial forces?

Zhou Yi's facial expression shifted unpredictably. After a moment, his consciousness completely submerged into the world of the Five Elements Ring. He wanted to genuinely experience the full potential of this imitation artifact.

In a trance, he entered a world of perpetual cycles – the world within the Five Elements Ring. Inside, the forces of the Five Elements spun like revolving wheels. Each rotation generated new power; the Five Elements nourished and influenced each other, an endless cycle.

However, within the Five Elements, apart from the cycle of nurturing, there also existed the forces of mutual restraint. After each cycle, when new power was generated, an equal amount of old power would dissipate and fade away. In this process, the Five Elements Ring had formed an intricate cycle, perfectly balanced in every aspect. It wouldn't change unless external forces intervened.

A faint realization emerged in Zhou Yi's heart. Perhaps even the creator of this artifact had never thought such changes would occur. There was indeed a unique space within the Five Elements Ring, but the power of this space wasn't bestowed by its creator; it naturally arose due to the circulation of the Five Elements.

The world Zhou Yi was experiencing was built upon the foundation of the Five Elements' power. While countless other forces existed in this world, such as wind, lightning, ice, mist, and more, the power of the Five Elements was unquestionably the most fundamental. As long as the five forms coexisted, this world could persist and continuously evolve.

Within the Five Elements Ring, a minuscule space of Five Elements' circulation had undoubtedly been formed. The basis of this space was the Five Elements Ring itself. As long as the circulation of the Five Elements' power continued, this space would never disappear.

Zhou Yi's expression gradually changed as he suddenly thought of a very likely scenario. Once he successfully achieves the Three Flowers Gathering at the Apex using the Five Elements Ring and replenished the water and wood forces, would the space within the Five Elements Ring become usable for him? Could he control a space exclusively his through the Five Elements Ring?

With this thought, even Zhou Yi couldn't help but feel a surge of excitement and amazement. A space that belongs solely to oneself, that's the true highest-level divine ability only found in legends among Divine Path experts. Although Zhou Yi already possesses a silver ring, a space accessible to anyone, how could it compare to a space that is exclusively his own?

He let out a soft sigh and suppressed this wild idea. While the notion was appealing, achieving it was far from easy.

Not only does he need to achieve the Three Flowers Gathering at the Apex, but he also needs to condense the water and wood Flowers, which is not something that can be accomplished in a short period of time. Since this is the case, excessive contemplation is futile.

He refocused his attention. The three different attributes of the Five Elements' forces roamed within the Five Elements Ring, as he tried to follow Jin

Zhanyi's guidance and locate the three fundamental points.

However, after a while, Zhou Yi was astonished to find that the three forces he had infused into the Five Elements Ring were being assimilated by the inherent Five Elements' power within.

Initially, the forces of fire, earth, and metal surged and overwhelmed the forces of water and wood. But in a matter of moments, the world within the Five Elements Ring began its adjustments.

All the forces were transforming rapidly. The fire, earth, and metal forces weakened slightly with each cycle, while the water and wood forces gradually grew stronger. As Zhou Yi awakened from his mental exploration of the Five Elements' space, he abruptly realized that a perfect balance had been achieved within the Five Elements' power.

At this point, Zhou Yi could only smile wryly. He reluctantly withdrew from the world within the Five Elements Ring. Opening his eyes, he held the Five Elements Ring in his hand, feeling a sense of speechlessness.

Trying to find three stable points within the Five Elements Array using the power of the three elemental attributes seems like an almost impossible task.

As long as the cycle of the Five Elements continued, his three elemental forces would only disperse with each cycle, redistributing and re-forming a perfect cycle.

Tapping the Five Elements Ring twice gently, a clear and melodious sound resonated, like the sound of an alarm bell, ringing in Zhou Yi's mind. He snapped back to awareness. If the cycle of the Five Elements within the ring were to stop, would the ring still be the imitation divine artifact it originally was?

In that case, this imitation artifact might lose a significant portion of its power, reducing it to an ordinary weapon. The embryonic space forming within the ring would likely collapse, and even attempting to reconstruct such a space afterward might become nearly impossible after this disturbance.

As Zhou Yi considered these potential drawbacks, he quickly dismissed the idea of halting the cycle of the Five Elements within the ring. He realized the consequences could be disastrous.

However, his initial hope of merging his true qi with the Five Elements Ring seemed increasingly difficult to achieve. How could he form three stable points within the Five Elements' true qi with his three different types of true qi?

This was indeed a complex issue...

Chapter 400

A gentle cold breeze swept in, carrying a faint hint of warmth. The harsh winter was on the verge of passing, and in the days ahead, the most significant season of the year, spring, would arrive.

However, at this moment, Zhou Yi had been staying within the Lingxiao Treasure Hall for a full three months. Even the upcoming Spring Festival, a holiday of utmost importance, would find him within the confines of the Lingxiao Treasure Hall.

The customs here were much like those in the northwest. The Spring Festival was considered the most important holiday, and during that period, the entire city would be filled with laughter and joy. Even Zhou Yi's homesickness was alleviated to some extent.

Nevertheless, this was Zhou Yi's first time spending the Spring Festival away from the northwest, causing a tinge of melancholy in his heart. Yet, he understood that as his strength continued to grow, the days of venturing outside would become inevitable. The desire to return home every year for the New Year was already an impossible luxury.

The further one progresses in the cultivation of martial arts, the more things they have to give up. Zhou Yi had a deep understanding of this point.

However, since he had already made this choice, he would proceed resolutely and without hesitation. This path was, in reality, one of no return...

Stepping outside and gazing into the distance, Zhou Yi's eyes seemed to traverse infinite space, envisioning the greatly missed Zhou Family Village.

"Zhou brother, homesick?" The familiar voice of Jin Zhanyi came from afar.

Zhou Yi retracted his gaze and admitted, "Yes, I'm feeling a bit homesick."

Jin Zhanyi approached, lightly patting his shoulder and saying, "You'll get used to it."

Zhou Yi forced a bitter smile and shook his head. Deep down, he knew that one day he would indeed become accustomed to it. However, he wondered if the future version of himself would still be the same as he is now.

Jin Zhanyi, being an experienced individual, understood that such matters couldn't be forced. One had to come to terms with it on their own in order to untangle this emotional knot. Perhaps after a hundred years or so, when most of his loved ones had passed away, Zhou Yi would follow the path of other Innate experts and wholeheartedly seek breakthroughs in martial arts.

"Zhou brother, have you made any breakthroughs during this month of seclusion?" Jin Zhanyi shifted the topic and inquired.

Zhou Yi had encountered significant troubles while trying to reach the Three Flowers Gathering at the Apex. Jin Zhanyi was naturally aware of this matter. To resolve the issue, Zhou Yi had announced his seclusion a month ago. Now that he had come out of seclusion, his appearance indicated that he hadn't solved the problem.

Indeed, a trace of helplessness appeared on Zhou Yi's face as he replied, "Brother Jin, I've tried every method I could think of, but I still can't find the corresponding three fixed points within the Five Elements Ring." He sighed lightly and continued, "Unless the Five Elements' cyclic flow comes to a halt, how can we find fixed points on this circular space? But if the Five Elements stagnate, can it still be called the Five Elements Ring?"

Jin Zhanyi hesitated, not daring to casually evaluate the situation.

Zhou Yi's talent was unique; possessing the ability to cultivate all five elements simultaneously was unheard of in the entire Da Shen Empire. But while there had been a few experts with such talents throughout history, the most famous was the founding patriarch of the Five Elements Sect in the past. He ascended to the Divine Path and, armed with the divine artifact Five Elements Ring, was invincible far and wide, rarely meeting an opponent.

However, that was all history now. In the present, Zhou Yi, who cultivates all five elements, is currently exerting great effort to achieve the Three Flowers Gathering at the Apex.

After a moment of contemplation, Jin Zhanyi expressed regret, "Zhou brother, if you weren't cultivating all five elements, you could easily solve this issue."

Zhou Yi was slightly puzzled. "Why is that?"

Jin Zhanyi pointed towards the tower. It was currently early morning, and the eastern sunlight cast its rays upon the tower. A large shadow enveloped the courtyard where Zhou Yi and others resided.

"If you were only cultivating three elements, you could directly enter the martial library and choose a suitable weapon to infuse. With your aptitude and talent, achieving that would undoubtedly be a breeze."

Zhou Yi also looked up at the tower and chuckled, "Jin brother, it seems you've misunderstood. I am not a disciple of the Lingxiao Treasure Hall."

Jin Zhanyi waved his hand and said, "I know, but both Lingxiao Treasure Hall and the Northwestern Tianchi are longstanding sects. If you choose a weapon here, the Tianchi will naturally compensate us with one. Or, when you become a Venerable, the elder of our sect will invite you to be a guest Venerable. If you accept, the Lingxiao Treasure Hall will definitely not be stingy with a weapon."

Zhou Yi sighed helplessly. In fact, over the past three months, Jin Zhanyi had intentionally or unintentionally brought up the topic of being a guest Venerable several times.

Even if Zhou Yi were dull, he understood Jin Zhanyi's meaning. However, he had complex feelings towards the Lingxiao Treasure Hall. If he hadn't possessed the Nine Dragons Furnace and hadn't been discovered invading the arsenal by the Venerable Zhuo Shengfeng that night, he might have agreed.

But now, he had concerns. If his relationship with the Lingxiao Treasure Hall became too close and he accidentally revealed something, not only might he not become a guest Venerable, but he might also face relentless pursuit and attempts on his life from all corners of the world.

Seeing Zhou Yi's brow furrow, Jin Zhanyi finally couldn't hold back and said, "Zhou brother, it seems you have some... misunderstanding about our sect. In fact, our sect has maintained a good relationship with the Northwestern Tianchi for thousands of years. The Venerables have private connections, and there's a history of being guest Venerables for each other throughout the generations." He hesitated for a moment, lowered his voice, and continued, "To be honest, our sect's Master once accepted the Tianchi's request to become a guest Venerable when he was young."

Zhou Yi suddenly looked up, disbelief evident in his eyes.

Jin Zhanyi cleared his throat and said, "Of course, that's not the case anymore. Since the sect master has taken over the Lingxiao Treasure Hall, he naturally can't continue as a guest Venerable for another sect. But if even he can become a guest Venerable, do you still have any concerns?"

Zhou Yi's smile turned increasingly bitter as he did indeed have concerns, but these concerns couldn't be expressed straightforwardly.

Jin Zhanyi has been talking for a while, but Zhou Yi seems like a dull gourd, feeling quite uninterested. If it weren't for the months they had spent together and their close friendship, Gold Battle would have waved his sleeve and left long ago.

With a sigh of resignation, Jin Zhanyi glared at him fiercely and said, "Zhou brother, let me ask you one thing. Since you came here, we've practically been serving you like a master. What exactly are you dissatisfied with regarding the Lingxiao Treasure Hall?"

Zhou Yi felt deeply ashamed, for Jin Zhanyi's words were far from an exaggeration. Since his arrival, not only had Jin Zhanyi been a constant companion, but he had also granted him access to the martial library. Though Zhou Yi had yet to find a solution to the Three Flowers Gathering at the Apex, the Lingxiao Treasure Hall had truly done everything it could to accommodate him.

He lowered his head and gazed at the Five Elements Ring. Suddenly, an idea formed in his mind. He looked up with a determined expression and said, "Jin brother, I know you mean well. But I can't give you an answer right now."

Jin Zhanyi's heart brimmed with joy. It was the first time Zhou Yi had loosened his stance in three months, and to Jin Zhanyi, it was indeed good news.

"Zhou brother, do you need time to consider? That's okay. How long do you plan to take?"

"Twenty years."

"Twenty..." Jin Zhanyi's eyes nearly popped out. Did he really need twenty years to think about it? Suddenly, he realized something and had an epiphany. He said, "You plan to make your decision after you visit the Totem Clan, don't you?"

Zhou Yi nodded slightly, but deep down, he thought, You're pushing me to this point...

Raising both eyebrows, Jin Zhanyi's voice rang out, "Brother Zhou, the Lingxiao Treasure Hall is not one to shy away from challenges. Once you become a guest Venerable, we certainly won't stand idly by in this matter."

Zhou Yi slowly waved his hand and said, "Jin brother, as you know, this is a personal grudge between me and the Totem Clan. I don't want to involve the sect in this matter."

Seeing that Jin Zhanyi still seemed intent on persuading him, Zhou Yi decisively waved his sleeve and said, "Jin brother, my mind is made up. There's no need to say more."

His words were filled with righteousness, and even he himself was moved by them. At this moment, he felt grateful to Bear Wuji for that twenty-year agreement. Without it, he might not have passed through this easily.

Jin Zhanyi gave him a deep look and finally nodded heavily. He said, "Alright, since you've made up your mind, I won't persuade you anymore. However, twenty years from now, I will definitely accompany you. Even if the Deep Mountain Totem is a dangerous place, I'll subdue any dragons and tigers, making them submit and yield."

Zhou Yi was greatly surprised, looking at Jin Zhanyi in disbelief. He said, "Jin brother, this matter has nothing to do with you and nothing to do with the Lingxiao Treasure Hall."

Jin Zhanyi burst into hearty laughter and said, "Certainly, this matter has nothing to do with the Lingxiao Treasure Hall, but it does concern Jin Zhanyi." His eyes sharpened, and he continued, "Rest assured, within twenty years, I, Jin Zhanyi, will definitely advance to become a Venerable. I won't hold you back

Zhou Yi was stirred with excitement. This was the second person who had expressed a willingness to venture with him to the Deep Mountain Totem. Moreover, Jin Zhanyi was making this pledge before he even advanced to a Venerable. This friendship was enough to leave an indelible mark on Zhou Yi's heart.

His expression was ever-changing. Jin Zhanyi was indeed treating him with utmost sincerity; how could he not sense it?

However, he had too many hidden secrets. Until he had absolute self-preservation strength, he didn't dare to get involved in too many matters.

Jin Zhanyi slapped his forehead and said, "Zhou brother, Venerable Gao said that three months have passed, and we can now set off for the Central Great Plains." His eyes gleamed, and he continued, "This is a fantastic opportunity, a chance for a breakthrough. It's the same for both you and me."

Zhou Yi was momentarily taken aback and said, "Jin brother, I'm afraid my issues can't be resolved by sparring with others."

Jin Zhanyi chuckled and said, "Zhou Brother, I wasn't expecting you to attain enlightenment through that means either. However, from what I know, among the experts in the Central Great Plains this time, there might be someone who can provide some insight for you."

Zhou Yi's eyes lit up slightly as he asked, "Who?"

"Yu Wuchang of the Da Shen Royal Family."

Printed in Great Britain
by Amazon

38627443R00367